About the Author

Bill Sheehy is a storyteller, only for most of his working life, it was called journalism. Now living in a cottage near the beaches of Australia, he experimented with fiction. In the past few years, he has produced a handful of novels. Writing fiction is more fun and more difficult than writing for newspapers. The magic of creating interesting people and placing them in interesting places with interesting problems to solve is very entertaining. The experience of living on a sailboat and now in Queensland, along with a bit of WWII history, is the basis of *Saltwater Diamonds*.

Saltwater Diamonds

Bill Sheehy

Saltwater Diamonds

Pegasus

PEGASUS PAPERBACK

A CIP catalogue record for this title is available from the British Library

ISBN-978-1-80468-081-0

*Pegasus is an imprint of
Pegasus Elliot MacKenzie Publishers Ltd.*
www.pegasuspublishers.com

First Published in 2025

**Pegasus
Sheraton House Castle Park
Cambridge CB3 0AX England**

Printed & Bound in Great Britain

Prologue
3 March 1942

On 3 March 1942, three Mitsubishi Zeros, led by Lt Nakamura Miyano of the Japanese Navy, had flown out of their base at Rabaul, Papua New Guinea and bombed Broome, Australia.

Broome, a small pearling port on the northwest upper corner of the country, had become a refuelling point for aircraft on the route between the East Indies and major Australian cities. As a result, Broome was central in the movement of people fleeing the Japanese invasion of Java. Broome had also become a significant Allied military base.

Lt Nakamura and his two other pilots were overjoyed with their day's effort. Broome had not been expecting an attack, and there was literally no defence. The destruction the three Japanese planes caused was massive; at least two dozen aircraft were left burning and it was impossible to know how many people were killed. Lt Nakamura was all smiles as he led his flight eastward, back to the base at Kupang.

Normally, he would not allow his pilots to chatter, but this was a day to celebrate. Settling back, Lt Nakamura let his gaze drop down, taking in the rugged shoreline as it flowed nearly 30,000 feet beneath his

Zero-sen. He was proud of his airplane; it had proven itself to be fast and very manoeuvrable, faster and more manoeuvrable than any of the enemy's planes.

Following the shoreline, the route back crossed over the Gulf of Carpentaria, up over the tip of Cape York and then it was a straight shot across the Coral Sea to PNG. Relaxed, he was thinking about what kind of country he was seeing below when he noticed a silver arrow-shape, far below and headed in the opposite direction.

'Attention,' he cut into the idle chatter, 'I have spotted an aircraft flying in a westerly direction at about four o'clock below. It appears to be a twin-engine passenger plane. We will dive in formation, and if it is, as I believe, an enemy craft, we will destroy it.'

'Sir,' a weaker voice cut in, 'our fuel doesn't allow for more bombing runs.'

Lt Nakamura knew the men in his flight. It had to be Sub-Lt Kaigun Chui, always worrying and too cautious. His other pilot rarely spoke and could always be counted on to follow orders.

Nakamura's eyes never left the silver arrow passing below. 'Remember the words of our Emperor,' he barked harshly, making his words brittle. '"The fruits of victory are tumbling into our mouths." Follow me. We will make one pass, strafing with your remaining armament.'

The screaming of the big 950-hp radial engine sounded like an angry hornet as the plane dove at a very steep angle down towards the target. Flipping the covers on the triggers of both the 20mm cannons and the smaller

7.7mm machine guns, Nakamura's smile had lost any sign of humour.

Levelling out, he touched the triggers as he flashed by the larger airplane. Pulling back on the yoke, his plane streaked up, gaining elevation, finally levelling off at about 20,000 feet.

'Report,' he barked.

Sub-Lieutenant Kaigun Chui, his voice fluttery as if he'd just ran a kilometre, responded, 'I recognise the plane as a Dutch Indies Airline passenger plane. Your strafing run struck amidships. The pilot manoeuvred away, and my bullets did little damage.'

Looking down and back, Nakamura spotted the airliner, flying lower but still in the air.

'We will make one more pass,' he ordered.

'Sir,' Sub-Lt Chui again. 'I have no more ordinance and little fuel.'

Nakamura slammed his fist against the yoke. Quickly checking his armament, his frown deepened.

'Right. I have enough for one run. You two continue on towards base. I will catch up.'

Not hearing if either of his two pilots bothered to respond, Lt Nakamura peeled off in a steep turn, heading back towards the airliner. That plane was low, flying just metres above the ocean. There would be time for only one pass. Nakamura's humourless smile had returned as he once again flicked the covers off his cannon's triggers.

***

Alexander Baranoff hadn't liked the trip from the beginning, and things hadn't improved halfway to Broome.

It certainly wasn't the first time Baranoff had flown the old twin-engine passenger aircraft between Bandung, Dutch East Indies and Broome, Australia, and it likely wouldn't be the last. There were still a lot of people in Bandung wanting to escape the invading army. That was what made this trip unusual. Instead of the thirty seats filled to overflowing with passengers, there were only nine men sitting back there. Baranoff wasn't comfortable with that, but orders were orders.

Ever since the Imperial Japanese had invaded Indonesia, Baranoff and a couple of other passenger planes operated by the Royal Netherlands Indies Airways (KNILM) had been ferrying people to safety in Australia. Making the 2,620-kilometre flight took just over six hours and now, three and a half hours into the trip, he still was feeling uneasy.

'You must learn to relax.' Eddy Jung laughed.

A young Brit expat, Jung had been flying the co-pilot's right seat for the last three or four trips. When the two men met, the youngster made it clear he wanted to be known as Eddy Young. 'My family name is German, and with the war going on in Europe, well, I'd feel better if I wasn't carrying a German name.' Alex Baranoff had flown with the Russian air force during the Great War and, while having little tolerance for anything German, chose to tease his co-pilot about the name change.

Eddy hadn't seen anything out of line about making the trip with only a handful of men on board. As far as he was concerned, anything happening outside the cockpit didn't count. Eddy just wanted to fly.

Baranoff had asked the KNILM official about taking off with the light load, but had been told simply that these were important men and it was vital they reach Australia. Watching them come aboard, it was obvious they weren't typical refugees. From the style of their suits and the way they wore their clothes, he thought they were probably US military officers.

'Don't bother with that,' the airlines official curtly ordered. 'Just get them to Broome as quickly as possible. And put this somewhere too,' he said, handing the pilot a canvas-covered package. 'There will be a man meet you when you arrive and ask for it. Put it somewhere safe.'

Taking the package, Baranoff felt a hard box inside the canvas material. From the size and weight, he thought it was a cigar box. The idea of carrying only a handful of men and being asked to transport a box of cigars for some high mucky-muck irritated the pilot. This certainly wasn't the way to win a war.

The KNILM plane had passed over the long land mass of Cape York Peninsula and was once again over water. Eddy was at the controls, keeping the plane on heading at about two thousand feet. Baranoff was relaxed, looking down at the white line of the surf breaking against the shore. Maybe the younger man was right, he thought. Maybe his unease was just a matter of too much imagination.

That thought barely ended when Eddy yelled and jerked the yoke hard to port, turning the plane on its side. Before Baranoff could react, he heard the thudding of bullets striking the aircraft. They were under attack.

'It's a couple of Zero's,' Eddy screamed, pushing the nose of the passenger plane down and keeping the yoke hard over. 'Oh, damn.' He coughed and slumped over the controls.

Baranoff's training took over and pushing his co-pilot back, he took control. The big plane didn't respond as quickly as the Laped Type XII he'd flown in the Great War, but he used the same tactics, sharply losing altitude and turning, first away from the attacking planes and then back under their screaming pass.

When the Zero's pulled away and didn't continue their attack, Baranoff brought his aircraft back to level flight. Reaching over, he felt Eddy's neck for a pulse but felt nothing. His fingers were wet with blood when he regripped the yoke.

A shuddering of the plane warned him that things were not good. Glancing at the instrument panel, he saw red lights. Oil pressure was falling. And the altimeter indicator was spiralling down. The plane was falling out of the sky.

The cabin door thrown open.

'We've got a lot of wounded back here,' one of the military men hollered.

'That is not the problem right now,' Baranoff barked, 'get everyone buckled in as tight as possible. We are losing airspeed. We're going in.'

Keeping as calm as he could, Baranoff took a deep breath and leaned forward, trying to find a place to land. The shoreline, coming closer as the plane was losing altitude, gave him no room to put down. There was only a thin stretch of beach.

Coming in at tree-top height, the shore disappeared off to the right as a small bay opened up. What looked to be a wide tidal flat gave him hope. If he could line the plane up and hold it as level as possible, maybe he could slide it on its belly.

His hand automatically reached for the lever to lower the landing gear, but he stopped it. Catching the wheels on the sand flats would cause the plane to flip over in a conventional, wheels-down landing on soft beach sand. Holding the nose of the plane up while lowering the wing flaps to slow the aircraft, he almost succeeded.

The force of hitting the packed sand bounced the plane, slamming the fuselage hard, causing the right wingtip to catch, spinning the heavy body halfway around before coming to a dead stop.

For a long moment, everything was silent. He hadn't been aware of how much noise there had been, not since the first gunfire had sprayed the plane.

The passengers. Unbuckling his safety harness, Baranoff tore open the cabin door.

Already, one man was pushing against the outer door, forcing it open. Others were helping remove seatbelts. For once, Baranoff was glad he hadn't been carrying a full load. As the men helped each other off,

Baranoff turned back to the cockpit. The radio still worked.

Flipping switches and dialling to the open frequency, he intoned the emergency call. 'Mayday, mayday, mayday. This is KNILM transportation flight 74, calling mayday, mayday, mayday. We have been strafed by Japanese military aircraft and crash-landed. We are approximately west of Cape York Peninsula, on mud flats of the Gulf. Mayday, mayday, mayday. Anybody receiving? Over.'

Flipping the switch, Baranoff listened. Nothing but static. He had landed the plane and made the mayday call. What else could he do? Fire. Quickly, he started turning off all the plane's equipment, except for the radio.

The static suddenly stopped. 'Aircraft making the mayday call, can you read me? Over.'

'Roger that. This is KNILM transportation flight 74. We have been shot out of the air and flopped onto a large tidal flat. We have wounded passengers. We are sitting on tidal flats west side of Cape York Peninsula, at the bottom of the Gulf. Over.'

'This is Darwin Airport. Have been advised a military PBY flying boat will be enroute to your location as soon as possible. How badly injured are your passengers? Over.'

'Darwin Airport. All passengers have been evacuated to shore. I have no report on their condition. The tide is coming in and the aircraft will soon be under water. Will remain on board as long as possible. We are carrying little survival gear. Over.'

'Acknowledge your situation. It is unlikely the tide will cover your aircraft. Protect yourselves as much as possible. ETA of the flying boat is about five hours. Over.'

'Darwin, I copy. Arrival of rescue plane about five hours. That is well after dark. Would expect rescue effort more likely in the morning. Over.'

The radio was silent for a long moment. For some time, Baranoff had been hearing water lapping somewhere against the plane's body.

'This is Darwin. Have been advised the flying boat will depart Darwin at first light.'

***

None of the men huddled on the shore that night got much sleep. Of the nine passengers, four had been wounded, two fatally. Emergency equipment from the plane had not included tents or tarps. Thin wool blankets and small pillows from the passenger compartment were the best they had. A fire had been built and coffee and tea, along with a meagre supply of dry crackers, made up dinner. There was little grumbling from the men as they sat around the fire, huddling under the thin blankets. At least, Baranoff thought, it wasn't raining.

Awake, he watched as the blackness of the night sky slowly faded as the sun rose in the morning. Shivering, he turned to look out over the sand flats where he'd landed the shot-up airplane. The flat was empty. The plane had disappeared with the tide.

That's when he remembered the little canvas-covered cigar box. It had gone with the plane.

Chapter One (Recently)

Sailing into the dock in Maui, they had been met with tropical flowery leis. That didn't happen at the dock in Brisbane. Instead, the boat was met by big, serious-looking men. Men flashing shiny silver badges and high-tech guns, sternly yelling for everyone to remain calm and don't move. Sure.

The day had started out as perfect a day as anyone could dream about. Sailing under warm, steady winds, the boat moved gracefully along in the smooth sapphire blue of the Coral Sea. Since picking up the luxurious fourteen-metre motor-sailing catamaran in Suva, JC McCoin had thought he was in heaven. A lovely boat, calm steady winds, two of the four-member crew attractive women and all the time getting paid the daily rate – what more could anyone want? Plus, no one was pushing to make port. Pure bliss.

Life for McCoin had been going along pretty good for quite some time. That is if you're a boat bum with no desire to grow up. But now, with a dozen or so big, burly, no-bullshit cops staring him down, he was starting to sweat.

'What the hell,' JC croaked, trying to live up to his title of skipper. 'Our papers are in order and I notified

Customs three days ago, just like we're supposed to. What's going on that earns this kind of welcome?'

'Shut up,' the biggest, meanest looking of the group growled. Nodding to no one in particular, he frowned. 'Get 'em cuffed and off this tub.'

Quickly the five newcomers found themselves sitting on the floating dock, their hands secured behind their backs by plastic handcuffs – the most colourful handcuffs JC had ever seen. Not that he'd ever seen any, except on TV. This wasn't a television show.

Of the five, JC and the four other members of the crew, the only one who seemed relaxed was the fifth man. Not a part of the crew. The boat's owner – or at any rate, the representative of the owner. After leaving Fiji, Webster stayed out of the way, keeping pretty much to himself. That was all right with everybody. After all, that was what he'd hired them for – to sail the vessel from Suva, Fiji to Brisbane, Australia.

JC had never been in the South Pacific before and when the opportunity came his way, he raised his hand high and fast.

'It's a bit under 1800 nautical miles,' Ralph Lewis, his boss back in San Diego, had said when he called about the job. 'From what I can figure, it'll take you about two, maybe three weeks, this time of year. How about it? It's out of your usual waters, but you do have your passport, don't you?'

Yes, JC nodded into the phone. Never leave home without it. 'But what about visas,' he asked, 'and, I don't know, any inoculations I'd need for that part of the world?'

He'd worked with Ralph for a couple years, delivering boats of all kinds out of San Diego Harbour. Normally, they moved boats for people who didn't want to make the long slog but wanted their floating playpen ready when they flew in. This typically meant travelling south to Capo San Lucas, Baja Mexico. They weren't all south though, there had been runs north too, up the coast as far as Portland and once into Seattle. JC's dream delivery job was to take a boat up the inside passage into Southeast Alaska. If you loved being out on the water as much as he did, then, for sure, you understand. His continuous smile was evidence of enjoying the good life.

Crossing to Maui had been his first trip into the Pacific Ocean. A big damn body of water. Twenty-three days of enjoyment, though, part of a delivery crew bringing a boat across that part of the big ocean. The forty-two-foot ketch they'd sailed to Hawaii was a dream. It was the benefit of having the mizzen mast aft of the wheel that made it easy; simply set the course, adjust the sails and the boat would hold a direct line. The crew making up the delivery team had little to do but watch the sails and work on suntans. For JC, sailing was habit-forming. After only four days of Hawaiian beer and sandy beaches, JC caught himself looking out to sea. Lady Luck was on his side when Ralph called.

'Hey, there, JC,' his voice boomed from the beige phone in the hotel room. 'You getting tired of life there in paradise?'

When he'd first gone to work for Ralph, it'd been the boss who'd made all the deliveries, usually hiring as temporary any crew as he needed. About a year ago, the man had decided to get serious. 'I figure it this way, JC. I'll pay you twice what you normally get. I'll sit on my duff and answer the phone. Someone wants a boat delivered; you hire the crews you need and make the trip. I think there's enough business in the San Diego area to keep us both working full-time. What do ya say?'

Why not? JC had the necessary certificates and licenses that allowed him to handle any vessel up to twenty-four metre on any ocean, coastal or inland waterway. For a boat bum, it seemed too good to be true. And, until they tied up at the dock there on the Brisbane River, it had been. Now, stretching his back and trying to get comfortable with his hands tied up, he was beginning to wonder.

From the beginning of that trip, he'd felt life was as good as it could get. Little did he know.

Chapter Two

The *Sea Cloud* was listed as being fourteen metre long, or for those Yanks on board, forty-five feet from stern to bow. She was a smooth sailing catamaran, complete with queen-sized berths aft in both hulls. Two other queen berths were forward on each side.

When Ralph had called, he'd said the man to talk to was named Webster and he'd meet him in the Mala Ocean Tavern in Lahaina. Howard Webster didn't look like a sailor. JC was wearing the new pair of tan khaki shorts he'd bought that morning. New shorts, a brand new Hard Rock Café T-shirt and well-worn, and comfortable rubber-soled boat shoes. Webster, on the other hand, wore a three-piece suit, complete with a vest and tie.

Identifying himself, JC took the man's hand, studying him. Not an outdoorsman, this Webster. Too soft. But then, too often, those were the kinds of men who liked to own yachts. Men who'd spent more time making their fortune while men like JC were out sailing.

'Let's take our drinks over to a booth and get to know each other,' said Webster, shaking JC's hand.

'The man I spoke to in San Diego,' Webster said once they'd gotten comfortable in a booth, 'assured me you could sail my boat as far as I wanted to go. How many people will we need for the cruise and how will we find them?'

'Ralph said your boat is a forty-five-foot cat and you want it to sail from Fiji south to Australia?' Webster nodded.

'I checked a cruising website. That's about 1500 nautical miles. This time of year is good for that part of the southern ocean, the Coral Sea. It should be pretty smooth sailing. I figure it'll take three weeks unless you want to motor part of the way. That'll cut it down a bit. For that long, I'd like enough crew, so we stand four-on, eight-off watches. Six people, counting myself. Five, if you want to be part of the watch.'

Webster smiled and shook his head. 'I'm not a sailor. So where will we find five more people?'

'In San D' it'd be no problem. There are always sailors, usually young, people who love to sail. Here in Maui, I'd visit the harbours and put out the word. I don't know about Fiji, what we'd find down there.'

'Let's find your crew here. Then we can fly down and pick up the boat.'

Ralph had thought it'd probably be easy to find enough crew. It didn't take JC long to discover differently. He could have had all kinds of people if they were sailing from Maui. Not too many were interested once it was explained we'd be flying to Suva, Fiji, and then sailing the vessel to Brisbane. Where? Brisbane, Australia? Oh, uh, no, I don't know about that. Can't you find enough people in Fiji?

What was wrong with Brisbane? JC had never heard anything bad about it. Fact is, he'd never heard much about any part of Australia. But he was game to travel and as it turned out, it didn't take long until they finally almost had enough people. Carl Tipton, two women and himself. As it turned out, another man, Harry Bridges, was picked up in Suva. Not as many bodies as JC would have liked, but Webster said they were short of time. It'd have to do.

The flight south took about six hours, but JC thought they were a long six hours. He'd never liked flying, and by the time their plane landed, he was tired.

As it turned out, JC didn't get to see much of Fiji. He, Webster and the crew flew into the international airport and were met by a guy carrying a sign. Apparently, Webster was used to planning ahead. From the moment they piled into the taxi, it was clear he wasn't going to waste time sightseeing. Webster did buy them a nice lunch before heading down to the harbour, though. The fifth member of the sailboat's crew was waiting on the dock. Webster said he'd mentioned to someone about needing another body or two and Bridges was it.

The interview with Harry Bridges went quickly. While Webster and JC talked with the newcomer, the others were stowing away their gear.

Tipton and the women, Sandy and Lucy, had some blue-water experience, Harry Bridges didn't. Actually, JC wasn't too pleased with Bridges.

The reason was probably dumb, but JC was uncomfortable because he was a little shorter than

Bridges. A couple inches under the other man's six feet. Now a "couple" inches, say two or three, isn't much, but to look Harry Bridges in the eye JC found himself looking up and when interviewing for a place on his crew, JC wanted to go eyeball-to-eyeball. Being what he called height-deficient had bothered him at one point in his life, but not so much any more. Not really.

Once, about when he had reached his teens, JC was positive that he'd been adopted. His mom and dad laughed when he asked them. 'No,' they assured him, he was their child. 'Although, there are times...' his dad said, but not finished the statement.

'What makes you think we adopted you?' his mother asked after shushing her husband.

JC wasn't sure he wanted to tell them. He didn't want to hurt anyone's feelings. But, well, when some friend of his mum's had asked how tall she was, he'd heard his mum say she was five and a half... five feet and a half inch. And laugh. Well, his dad was five and a half, five feet and six inches. JC had seen that on his dad's driver's license. The problem was, JC himself was taller. He remembered when he'd discovered he was as tall as his mother. They had laughed about it. Now, a year or so later, he was a bit taller than his dad. How could that be? He was sure he'd been adopted.

Not really believing them, he didn't say anything else about it. But he knew. Then one morning while shaving he discovered the truth. He didn't often shave. After finding a few hairs, thin and not very black, growing out of his chin, he decided to grow a beard.

That'd be cool. Keeping a close watch on his chin, he waited, but no more hairs showed up. Maybe if he shaved them off, it'd start things going. So, one morning, after brushing his teeth, he shaved.

Again, he waited and watched. After a week, or maybe two, those same few straggly hairs grew back. Not enough to be a beard, just enough to look stupid. So he got in the habit, every so often, to shave them off.

That morning, though, while looking in the mirror, giving his chin a close inspection, he happened to look up and saw his father's face looking back at him. His dad's little dimple in the middle of his chin, the same slightly crooked nose and the same watered-out grey eyes staring at him. For certain, he was his father's son. He hadn't been adopted. He just happened to grow a little taller than his parents. Not much, but a couple inches.

At about five feet and ten inches, he wasn't able to look this Bridges guy eyeball-to-eyeball. But as Webster pointed out, there hadn't been that many others beating down the door.

'And,' he said, his smile not reaching his eyes, 'not to put too fine a point on it, please remember who's paying the bill.'

JC didn't like it but who could argue with that?

'Don't worry yourself,' Harry Bridges said, a big Howdy Doody smile lifting his cheeks when he talked. The smile, JC came to learn, was always shining. And was pretty empty. At first, he thought it was because Bridges was older but taking a closer look he decided they were about the same age, in their mid-thirties. The difference was, Bridges had obviously had a rougher time of it than JC ever did. And less hair to show for it.

He'd come aboard, wearing faded board shorts and a red collared T-shirt. And a worn, faded 49ers cap. At one point, he'd pulled the cap off and used a hand to wipe the bare skin that had been hidden. The fringe of hair above his ears was muddy-water brown, growing long enough in back to allow for a four-inch ponytail. The other thing JC noticed and didn't like much were the tattoos covering his right arm. He'd never been a fan of tattoos and doesn't really understand why anyone would have them. Especially the kind Mr Bridges was happy with, running the length of his arm. The kind that's known by the tattooed public as a full-sleeve tat. But JC didn't say anything about it. Webster was sure to laugh at him and call him old-fashioned.

Webster did most of the talking during that interview. JC was too busy studying the man. And thinking about the tattoos. Every time he saw someone with a lot of tattoos, it made him think of his granddad. The old man only had one, a little blob of faded blue on his right arm up near the shoulder. JC tried to imagine his granddad with a tattoo like this one. On a young guy, when the ink was still fresh, such art can be bright and colourful. Bridges' tats were. But what will it look like in forty or fifty years? All faded and dim. It really bothered him when it was a good-looking young woman wearing such ink stains.

'Sea sick?' Harry Bridges chuckled when asked about his lack of blue-water experience. 'I spent two years on an oil rig out in the Gulf of Mexico. That beast didn't move, but when the weather hit, it was damn hard not to believe it wasn't the rig that was dancing around. Naw, I don't get sick. And I can learn quickly. So I don't know the sails. How hard can it be to keep the boat on a heading?'

Nothing more was said, and with enough bodies on board, JC decided not to bother. After all, it was just a cruise to deliver a boat, something he'd done many times before. Daylight the next day saw them underway, heading southwest for Brisbane.

JC had some concerns about sailing as skipper with the owner on board. One thing he didn't want was to have someone try to tell him how to run the boat. Or the crew. He needn't have worried. Webster made it clear from the get-go.

'I'll take the bed there in front of the little kitchen,' he said when the boat was underway. 'You and your crew know what you're doing. I don't. So I'll stay out of your way. Fact is, it'll be best if I stay out of your way and your people; you know, just leave me to fend for myself.'

Bed in front of the kitchen. JC didn't frown. Obviously, Mr Webster wasn't a sailor. 'Uh, I don't want to be out of line,' he hesitated to ask, 'but we'll be out on blue water. And that will likely mean some rough sailing. How are you about seasickness?'

Webster laughed. 'Don't worry yourself about that. My job will be to get the boat ready once we reach Brisbane. The boat is corporate-owned and there are a number of executives coming to spend time on it down there. I'll be all right, you'll see.'

Spend some time on it. Not her, but it. Definitely, not a sailor.

Chapter Three

From the very beginning, the two women made it clear they were not going to do all the cooking. As it turned out, Tipton was the best of all things – a good sailor, even-tempered and a wonderful cook.

Both women appeared to be in their mid-twenties. Sandy Johnson and Lucy Dollarhide. Sandy was slender and stood as tall as she could. JC judged her to be about five feet. His mother, being on the short side, JC was pretty quick to notice such things in other women. Lucy, on the other hand, was as tall as him, they looked eyeball-to-eyeball when introduced. Her body, though, without a definitive waist showing under a faded Hawaiian shirt, gave the appearance of being stocky. Bulky even. Her hair was cut short, almost in what once was called a butch. JC didn't find out until a lot later she was.

So there he was, thirty-five years old, standing a few inches under six feet in his socks when he wore them, weighing the same as he did in high school, about 180 lbs. Not a native Californian, although his grey eyes, and sun-bleached blond hair, which needed cutting, fit the common image of a surfer dude from that area. He'd never learned to surf. Never learned to swim either. Well, not the smooth, clean way a lot of people did.

But even spending most of his time on boats, delivering them up and down the west coast, it didn't matter. His grandfather had lived into his late 80s, so JC felt there were a lot of years left before he was called to find what he wanted to do when he grew up.

***

Sailing blue water sounds exciting, but to be honest, it's actually boring. They stood regular watches, making sure the boat stayed on the correct heading and keeping an eye on the weather. That could be a factor in the southern reaches of the Pacific, but it was the middle of June, the so-called dry season. According to the weather forecasts he'd checked, the time to stay in some safe moorage was November through April, the cyclone season. They had little trouble. Webster, true to his word, stayed pretty much out of sight.

Over all, the trip was pretty uneventful. To think people actually paid big bucks for a cruise like this. Reaching the river mouth at Brisbane wasn't hard. Long before land had been sighted they had watched passenger jets coming in to land somewhere in that same direction. Following suggestions on the charts, JC had the sails stowed and they motored the six miles up the wide, muddy brown river.

JC had been careful to adhere to directions about coming into Brisbane. The rules meant calling Australian Customs a minimum of 96 hours before arriving. He'd done so and expected to find a Customs official on the dock when they pulled in, not half a dozen cops.

Coming out of the blue water of the ocean and into the slow moving river was almost depressing. Feeling the push of the river current, he was happy to have the engine running. On the plus side, the channel was well marked and even with what traffic there was, it wasn't difficult. Until they pulled up to the dock at the Rivergate Marina. Anywhere in the world, a marina is a marina, but even before he saw the uniforms, it hit him, this was a foreign country. Not as foreign as with Canada or Mexico, but really foreign. Australia.

Typical tourist, JC was gaping at the container dock on one side and the huge airport on the other. Just lazing along as they were, it was coming on late afternoon by the time the *Sea Cloud* reached the Customs and quarantine dock at the Marina. Just in time to be greeted by a bevy of gun-toting lawmen.

Now, sitting on his butt on the dock, listening to the others complain, the only thing he could think of was drugs. The whole world was up in arms, fighting the war on drugs. That had to be it.

Chapter Four

'Okay,' the tall, well-dressed, unfriendly-looking officer barked, 'according to the log, you're the leader of this boat on this trip. That right?'

They had been sitting there on the dock, the five of them close together with Webster a little off to one side, for what seemed like hours. At least for the growing ache in JC's lower back, it seemed like hours. Long enough for Harry, Carl and the girls to stop talking about it. All the time, he noticed, Webster had sat quietly, expressionless, staring off at something unseen. *Stoic*, he thought. Even acquiescent. The mental exercise of describing the boat owner's representative kept his mind busy. Kept him from worrying.

There were lots to worry about. Think about it. There they were, five Americans sitting handcuffed on a dock in Brisbane, Australia. A helluva long way from home. Did anyone know where they were? Well, Ralph knew where they were going, but what did that mean? Nothing.

The endless train of depressing thoughts was interrupted when one of the big cops came out from below. From the angry frown, JC knew he wasn't bringing good news. 'Hey, you.' He pointed a long finger at him. 'The boss wants to talk to you.' Motioning to the uniformed officer who'd been keeping an eye on them, he actually snarled. 'Get him in here. The captain of this freaking tub.'

The uniform helped JC up, holding his arm when he climbed over the railing. The big, angry one motioned him into the cockpit.

'You can take the cuffs off, Lou,' the man who was obviously the head cop said. Nodding to one side of the padded bench that curved around the huge table, he went on. 'Sit yourself down and let's talk a bit.'

The table had been the one place on the vessel they had all used for everything from meals to board games to bullshit sessions. Now, with papers spread out and the head man leaning forward on his elbows, it had become his desk. It felt good to JC to be able to use a free hand to massage a wrist.

For a long moment, the head cop simply sat, studying the younger man. 'You're a Sepo, you know?' he finally asked, letting his lips move up a bit in what could have been a smile or even a sneer. 'Got any idea what that means?' JC shook his head.

'Yeah. Well, you're a Yank. Get it? Cockney rhyming. Yank to septic tank, shortened up to septic, to Sepo. Get it now?' His chuckle didn't carry much humour. 'Yeah. Well, I've been looking at this book, *The Ship's Log*. You came on board this boat in Fiji, that right?'

'That's right,' JC said, wanting to get this over with. 'Hired to bring the vessel south to Brisbane. So, why did we get the welcoming committee? Is that the usual Australian way of doing things?'

'Nope. But then you're a special case, aren't ya.' It wasn't a question. 'Okay, let's do this the legal way. First off, I'm Inspector Colin Lambert, Australian Federal Police, head of the Serious and Organised Crime Unit, out of the Brisbane office. You, according to the log, which I found in that drawer under all the radios and other electronic stuff, are JC McCoin, the temporary skipper of the sailing vessel *Sea Cloud*. Now, from other sources, I know you are a thirty-five-year-old American, unmarried, no criminal record, travelling on an American passport with a 90-day Australian visa. You came on board late in the afternoon of 14 June. Early on the next morning, 15 June, you and your crew sailed this vessel out of Suva, Fiji, heading south, arriving this morning, the first day of August. That much is clear. So, Yank, tell me about the 180 kilograms of cocaine we found down below.'

Cocaine? As far as JC was concerned there hadn't even been a joint on board.

Chapter Five

Dumbfounded JC McCoin simply sat there, trying to make sense of his words. Cocaine: 180 kilograms of cocaine.

The AFP inspector didn't give him enough time to figure out what that meant in pounds. 'That's about 400 pounds in your world,' Lambert explained, glancing down at a little bound notebook, 'with a street value, I'd say, of about $90 million, give or take. Australian dollars, that is. Quite a haul, wouldn't you say?'

Ninety million dollars? Holy crap. 'And it was on board?' The American's voice sounded thin, probably because his throat had tightened up. He felt like he could hardly breathe.

'Yes, on this boat, under your command from Fiji to here. I haven't informed the Fijian government yet, but it's quite likely they'll want to talk to you. When we finish talking, that is.'

JC shook his head. 'Man, this is news to me. That we were carrying 400 pounds? Where in hell could there be that much hidden out of sight?' The questions came rushing out. JC's mind was in panic mode and out of control. 'I mean, we lived on this vessel for more'n two weeks. How could that be?'

JC was numb; he didn't know how to react. Millions of dollars' worth of cocaine? They had sailed calmly into port carrying millions of dollars' worth of cocaine? He just couldn't get his head around it. How could that be?

Lambert must have read my mind. 'That's one of the questions we're asking; how could you not know? Let's start at the beginning, if that is acceptable with you?' JC shook his head, thinking it wasn't as if he had a choice. 'When did you take on the job of sailing this boat to Australia?'

'Well, I got the offer when we reached Maui. Maui, Hawaii.'

'Yeah, I know where Maui is. What were you doing in Hawaii?'

'Making a delivery. I was part of a crew delivering another sailboat to her new owners. Sailed over from San Diego. That's where I work out of, San Diego. We deliver boats up and down the coast. The US coast.'

'And how did you learn about this boat?' The AFP officer made notes in the little booklet as McCoin answered.

'Ralph, uh, Ralph Lewis, my boss back in San D.' When I called from Maui to let him know we'd arrived, he suggested I take a few days off, enjoy the sunshine and Hawaiian beaches. Then, after about a week, he called and asked if I wanted to take on a delivery cruise from Fiji to Australia. At the usual pay and no real tight schedule. I jumped at it.'

'The usual pay, what is that?'

'Oh, I get paid a standard $200 a week. American dollars. For this job, I had to find enough crew to make the trip. They are paid less than that. Hey,' he just remembered, 'we're supposed to get paid as soon as we're tied up. Who's going to deal with that?'

Lambert's smile grew a little warmer but only by a tiny bit. 'I wouldn't think that was your main worry. Let's get back to your coming on board in Fiji. Apparently, you had found your crew. How was that done?'

'Well, it wasn't easy. Usually, finding crew for a delivery isn't difficult. There's always people, usually young people, hanging around the harbour, willing to take a few days or a week to go sailing. But nobody in Maui was interested in flying to Fiji for a sail to Australia. Even with the round-trip airfare, I had a helluva time finding enough people.'

'But you did. Tell me about them.'

'Ah, hell. These guys – they're your typical boat-bums. Well, all except Harry. Tipton, he's a bluewater sailor, been crewing for some big-shot yacht owner in Maui. A surfer. I think he'd rather be on his board than having sex. He came along thinking he'd get a chance to surf some beaches down here. The girls, they'd had bluewater experience too. Sandy and Lucy. Two more surfers. They had come across from San Diego on a big power boat and liked the Hawaiian lifestyle. Did some kind of tourist guiding with a charter dive boat. They came onboard wanting to see more of the South Pacific.'

'That leaves one,' he said, checking his notebook again, 'a Mr Harry Bridges. What about him?'

'Harry's background, at least what little he told us about, had been on oil rigs. We picked him up in Fiji. I don't know what he was doing there. He had some first-aid and safety certificates. His experience wasn't on boats, but he proved to be a quick learner and a steady hand. Truth is, if I'd had any other one come forward, I'd have left Harry in Fiji. But he did his job and didn't cause too much trouble.'

'Tell me about Mr Webster. He wasn't part of your crew, was he?'

JC, forgetting for a moment the trouble he might be in, almost laughed, but then, remembering he was being questioned about a load of cocaine, sobered up. 'No. He said his job was to get the *Sea Cloud* to Brisbane and then make her ready for the arrival of vacationing company execs. And no, I don't know what company owns the boat. I didn't ask and he never said.'

'Did Mr Webster help out? I suppose there were watches to stand and someone had to cook the meals, clean up and duties such as that. Was he helpful?'

Once again, JC could only shake his head. 'Nope, none of the above. From the get-go, he made it clear he wouldn't be part of getting the boat to Australia. Fact is, he rarely left his stateroom. He'd come up for meals but didn't hang around after. We didn't see much of him. Made me wonder, I mean, there we were sailing through some of the best sailing water in the world under, for the most part, clear blue skies and he didn't even come up on deck to work on his suntan. But he was paying the bill, so we didn't bother with him at all.'

Lambert nodded, making notes as JC tried to explain. 'You say he stayed in his stateroom. That makes me wonder, where did everyone sleep?'

'Well, there are four staterooms, one aft and one forward in either hull. Webster took the one ahead of the galley on the port hull and the two girls had the one aft. I shouldn't be calling them "girls", but, well, after all that time living close like we were, they stopped being women and became, I don't know, more like sisters. Anyway, that left the starboard hull for the three of us men. Each stateroom has a queen-sized berth, so the sleeping situation is comfortable. With the watch schedule I set up, there was always one of the men up, so we never had to share a bed. Plus, with the weather as fine as it's been, a lot of nights most of us spent up on the forward deck, sleeping under the stars.'

'So let me get this right: Webster took the stateroom on that side.' He pointed to the port side. 'In front of the kitchen area, and the two women had the rear stateroom. Did that give the women enough privacy?'

'Oh, yeah. You've seen the layout. There's a full head in both hulls. Small and a bit cramped, of course, but this is a boat built for comfort. Each head has both fresh and saltwater showers and she carries enough fresh water for our use. But that begs the question: where in hell could 400 pounds of cocaine be hidden that one or the other of us wasn't tripping over it?'

JC didn't really expect the lawman to tell him, but the interrogation had almost become a friendly discussion. The police inspector fooled the American by actually smiling as he answered.

'Easy. It was all packaged in individual kilogram packs. Almost two hundred of them, all laid out in nice order, filling the space normally taken up by a queen-sized mattress. Your Mr Webster was sleeping on a bed of pure cocaine.'

Chapter Six

'Which,' he continued, 'brings us up to now. And the question is, what to do with you and your mates. We've had our eye on your Mr Webster for some time. It was when he changed the members on the boat that we got worried.'

There was something JC didn't understand. 'You were aware the *Sea Cloud* was carrying drugs? Why wait until we reached harbour to make the arrest?'

'Two very good reasons. First, our laws about the importation of drugs are a lot different than that of the other countries the boat travelled through. Secondly, we were hoping to net more of the drug runners. Those behind all of this. That, I'm sorry to say, didn't happen. It appears that Mr Webster will end up bearing all the weight of this crime.'

'Other countries, you say. How long has this boat been watched?'

'My sources started telling me about this shipment some time ago. Probably even before the drugs were loaded on board.' He was actually smiling now. 'According to information received, I made a few calls to associates who were able to keep an eye on the boat as it set sail for the crossing. Most of the cocaine run into Australia comes from South America. Other kinds of drugs come from other parts of the world, but cocaine is mostly produced in Colombia and Bolivia, although West Africa is quickly becoming a major producer. So, yes, we watched and waited. That's how I knew when the load arrived and then left Fiji. Originally, we thought the boat would head for Sydney and were a little surprised when it came in here. But then, when you called Customs, we made sure we were on hand.'

Just doing the job, JC asked himself, and making the correct call to Customs and what do I get? Arrested as a drug runner. What the hell was he going to do? That was the question trying to work its way through his muddy thinking. He needn't have bothered. The next thing Lambert said wiped all thoughts from his mind.

'The question I have to ask myself now, though, is what to do about you and your four mates sitting out there on the dock? How big a part did you play in this little escapade? How come, if what you claim is true, did someone decide to hire you to bring the load on south? Was this the bright idea of someone higher up the food chain, using you as camouflage? If so, it sure as hell didn't work. And where was that genius, in Maui? Or clear back in San Diego? Or is it one of the big-time drug runners here in Brisbane? That's the question, the real question.' He stopped, looking pensively at the Yank. 'Didn't you say your boss back in California turned this job over to you? See what I mean? With you, we got nothing but questions.' Lambert stopped again, shaking his head slowly. 'Doesn't look good for you, does it? I mean, here you five are, foreigners in a foreign land, having brought 180 kilograms of illegal drugs into the country. That is something I have to think about.'

The mental image of spending the rest of his life in prison flashed through JC's mind.

Chapter Seven

There was no sign of the excitement we'd all felt when coming into the harbour with any of my crew when JC was escorted back onto the dock. On the bright side, Lambert hadn't handcuffed him again, simply directing him to join the small group before walking over to talk to the uniformed watchdog.

'Okay,' he said, after a few minutes and stepping back to face the group, 'here's the way I see it. There is a slight chance you Yanks were just being used. I'm not totally convinced, but maybe. So here is what I've decided. I'll keep your passports for a while. You go on doing whatever it is you were planning on doing in our fair city. Check in with me, oh, let's say every other day or so. Meanwhile, I'll have a little talk with Mr Webster here. And we'll be making some long-distance phone calls, checking your background, things like that. Go on.' He motioned to the uniformed officer to remove the cuffs from the others. 'But keep this in mind; we'll be watching. Think of it as being let out on a long lead. Don't be doing anything that'll upset me.'

Getting away from this fiasco was all they wanted, but there was one thing bothering Tipton. 'Wait a minute,' he said, squaring his shoulders and glancing first at JC, then at the AFP Inspector, 'you're saying stay in touch. Okay, but I was given a round-trip plane ticket and promised a couple hundred dollars to bring the boat down here. I got the ticket but no passport and no pay check. What about that? Who do I complain to about that?'

Lambert's smile grew just a little as he shook his head and nodded in JC's direction. 'Not my concern. Talk to your skipper.' Taking Webster's arm, he turned and walked the man back aboard the *Sea Cloud.*

'Okay, Skipper, what now?' Tipton wasn't smiling.

All the former "skipper" could do was throw up his hands. 'Hey, I'm in the same boat. I don't know. Let me call Ralph, my boss, and see what he can do. Right now, all I want to do is get a long way away from here. Some place I won't have to worry about having a cop glaring at me. This is all new to me. Any of you have any ideas about where to go?'

Naturally, in keeping with everything going bad, nobody had anything to suggest. To simplify things, they decided to find a taxi and get taken to somewhere a few phone calls could be made.

The marina, it turned out, was a couple miles out of the main business district of the city itself. Piled into the taxi, JC asked for the centre of town. No body complained, probably because everybody wanted to get as far away from the sailboat and the drug cops as they could. The driver didn't say much, which gave JC time to think. After crossing the river, the freeway followed the waterway, curving through all manner of residential and commercial areas. He'd asked for a shopping centre and that was where they ended up. Holding the last of the cash money he had, JC went looking for a phone booth.

Waking Ralph up to ask for money was probably not the best thing he could do, and to make it worse, he'd forgotten about the time difference.

'What the hell…' man on the other end grumped.

It didn't make him sound any friendlier when JC explained about the 400 pounds of cocaine on the boat he'd been hired to deliver. The news that it was likely someone from the Australian police would be contacting him didn't make the older man sound any happier.

'They'll want to know about who you talked to about running that boat down from Fiji,' JC explained. 'That's a lot of drugs and the inspector who interviewed me is treating it seriously. But right now, we got other problems. I've got a crew without passports or money. Hell, I even had to call you collect.'

'Ah, crap, yeah. Give me a minute to wake up. Let me think. Boy, there isn't going to be much I can tell your cops about the delivery job. I took the deal over the phone. The deposit came in and I called you. Say, I could send that deposit money down to you so you could pay off those people you hired. How about I do that?'

For the first time since coming ashore, JC felt the tension in his stomach thin out. Well, a little, at any rate. Quickly arraigning for the cash transfer, he went out to reassure the crew.

'That drug cop,' Harry asked, quickly counting the money when JC gave it to him. 'He say anything to you about when we get our passports?'

'Yeah,' piped up Sandy Johnson, the most demanding of the two women, 'Lucy and me, we didn't count on being stranded down here. Getting back to California is high on our list. What do you think is going to happen?'

JC could only shake his head. He'd been in new ports all along the west coast, but never with the cloud of hundreds of pounds of illegal drugs hanging over his head.

Chapter Eight

The day had started out so good for Inspector Lambert; he should have known it couldn't last. For the first time since being shunted out to the bush, Colin Lambert was sure he could see his way back to the city – back to Sydney. Being raised in the big city, anything smaller was, in his opinion, out in the country. Too close to the so-called outback for him. It couldn't get any worse than that. But it could get worse. He found that out when called by the district superintendent for a meeting. Suddenly, all the good feel of the day was gone.

Riding up in the elevator, Lambert thought about the process he'd followed in making the drug bust. It was hard to see where he had gone wrong and the amount of drugs taken off the street had to make him look even better. Thinking back over it, he nodded and almost relaxed. The information was right on the money. He and his mob had dealt with the situation as per the accepted AFP procedure. The interviews with the Americans from the sailboat had been video recorded, tape recorded and, for the most part, had followed the script. The Deputy Public Prosecutor would not, could not, find one thing to complain about. He had handed the DPP a clean case. So why had he been called to the AFP's regional office?

He'd only been to the District Super's office once before when the big man had welcomed him to Brisbane. Waxman's big smile, as fake as any snake oil salesman's, didn't dull the sharpness of the demotion knife. Lambert was a Sydney copper, dammit, and he had no business being up here in this over-grown country town. The welcome speech had lasted two minutes, from hand-shake to hand-shake and with a quick pat on the back, the newcomer had been escorted out. He hadn't been back; no reason to do so. Until now.

As expected, after checking in with the Super's secretary, a cold-faced grandmotherly type sitting behind a chest-high bench, he was made to wait.

'Detective Inspector Colin Lambert to see District Superintendent Waxman,' he stated, speaking clearly, his words clipped and lacking any nonsense.

'Yes.' The grandmother nodded, looking up and taking her time to inspect what she could see of him. 'Have a seat' – she glanced to one side – 'I'll inform the superintendent.'

Lambert watched as she picked up one of the three phones on her desk, punched a couple buttons and spoke quietly. Putting the phone down, she didn't pay any further attention to the visitor.

Lambert sneaked a peek at his wristwatch. Ten minutes, he judged, Waxman would make him wait ten minutes. As anyone in the ranks would tell you, the length of time they made you wait was a sure indication of why you were there. The longer you sat, waiting, the deeper in the shit you were.

This was a ploy he was used to. He had been attached to the Sydney Regional Office since graduating from AFP College down in Canberra. Working his way up the ranks, he never doubted he'd spend his entire career in the New South Wales capital, until, out of the blue, he was shipped off to Brisbane. It was SOP for the Sydney Superintendent to make an officer wait, and the half-dozen times he'd been called on the big man's carpet down there, the time factor had proven true. The problem this time was he didn't have a clue why he'd been notified to come to the regional office. Not knowing what this demand on his time was about, Lambert figured a minimum of ten minutes. So sure of it, he made a bet with himself, anything over ten minutes was a loss and the loser had to buy the drinks.

'Inspector?' the grandmother called before he could get comfortable in the chair. 'Superintendent Waxman will see you now. Down the hall, first door on your right.'

Not even a full minute. What was this all about? No matter about the bet he had with himself, it was sure he'd need more than one drink when it was over.

***

'Come in, Inspector,' Waxman called as Lambert went through the door, gently closing it behind him. Looking around, he saw another man sitting in front of the desk.

Not bothering with introductions, Waxman pointed a finger at an empty chair.

'Okay,' said Waxman, no preliminaries, just getting right to it, 'let's see if we can get to the bottom of this. Inspector Lambert, your raid on the *Sea Cloud* this morning resulted in the arrest of one man, confiscation of 180 kilograms of cocaine and the seizure of the sailing vessel.'

Lambert could only nod. So far, the superintendent was on the nose. That quickly ended. 'Other than that,' Waxman said harshly, 'it was a true cock-up.'

'What?' Lambert was stunned. 'We followed procedure, sir. I made sure the paperwork we handed to the Director of Public Prosecutions office was clean and concise. How was that a cock-up, sir?'

'Because, dammit,' Waxman said, his voice raising in anger, 'you had no business making the raid.' Lambert was staggered.

'Inspector, what led you to the *Sea Cloud*?' the other man asked softly.

Still looking at Waxman, Lambert could only shake his head. 'Because I felt it was my job as an officer of the Australian Federal Police.'

'I didn't ask why' – the man's voice sounded full of smiles – 'I asked what led you to that vessel.' Glancing at the man, Lambert saw the visitor's pass hanging on a lanyard around his neck. Dwayne Edwards. Just a name; no title or indication of status.

'You're right, as far as it goes,' Edwards said. 'The arrest of the man, Webster, will hold and he'll more than likely face a number of years in prison. But the question remains: how did you learn the shipment was to arrive on that boat, on this day?'

Lambert didn't know how to respond. 'I'm sorry. I don't know who you are.'

The man's smile barely lifted his lips. 'Again, you're right. We haven't been introduced. I'm from the Deputy Commissioner's office in Sydney. We are part of the AFP's Serious and Organised Crime Unit. My department's focus is on the importation of illegal drugs into the country. That's why it is important for us to learn how you found out about the *Sea Cloud*.'

The explanation sounded reasonable to Lambert. His anger slowly faded. 'From a snitch,' he said after a moment. 'An arrest we made a while back, a street dealer. Rather than bring him in, we made a trade. By dobbing in his contact, we let him walk free.'

Glancing at Waxman and seeing that man's lips tighten into a hard line, Lambert quickly went on. 'Oh, we'll get him again. No doubt about that. The drug world hasn't gotten so big up here, not as it is in Sydney or Melbourne. And,' nodding slightly towards Waxman, he hurriedly went on, 'by making the trade, we got a couple more names. People we could watch in hopes of being led ever upwards. I'm sure you are familiar with how it works.'

The quiet man nodded. 'And this snitch of yours, he told you about the shipment coming in?'

'Well, he's been telling me a lot of things. A few days ago, he called to tell me about a rumour he'd heard.

He didn't quite say where he heard it, but he assured me his source was good. He was positive about that. I doubt he wanted anything to get back to whoever had been doing the talking. All I got was that a big yacht was due to arrive at the Rivergate Marina. According to what he'd heard, a big shipment had left a South American port, stopped in Fiji and would be coming west to Brisbane. The *Sea Cloud* was the only cruiser that we had reports of that fitted. When the skipper of the *Sea Cloud* called to set up Customs, I was notified and scheduled my mob to meet it.'

Nobody said anything for a moment. 'Well, bloody hell,' the quiet one said softly. 'If that isn't the short end of the stick. We work our butts off, watching, waiting, planning and scheming and what happens? Some bloke off the street up here in Brisbane knows more'n we do. It certainly isn't fair dinkum.'

Lambert almost smiled but held his poker face. 'I gather this shipment was part of an on-going operation?'

Waxman finally found his voice. 'That's not something you need to know about, Lambert,' he said abruptly.

Chapter Nine

'Oh, Superintendent,' Edward said gently, 'I think our good inspector has earned the right.' Turning to face Lambert directly, he explained. 'As it happens, Inspector, we've known about this shipment since it came out of the jungle. Thanks to the cooperation between the various countries, we've been able to follow it all along the way. All was good, running smoothly as predicted until the *Sea Cloud* reached the harbour in Suva. That's when unexpected changes were made. The crew that brought the boat across from South America was put on a plane and sent back. A new crew was hired. Then, instead of sailing into Sydney, which we had been told was the drop-off point, the *Sea Cloud* comes into Brisbane. That really left us sucking wind.'

'That new crew were Yanks out of Hawaii,' said Lambert.

Edwards nodded.

Waxman slammed a pencil down on his desk. 'Is all this necessary, Mr Edwards? Making our mistakes public?'

Edwards smiled. 'Oh, I doubt it's making anything public. Things might have gone right if the inspector here had been made aware of the operation. As it was, he did what any good AFP officer should be expected to do: he arrested the bad guys making the run. Or at least one of them.'

Lambert frowned. 'One of them? Are you saying one of the Americans in that crew was part of the drug runners?'

'We had a list of all the players, from the bloke driving the truck bringing the coke out to the seaport to the sailors making the next leg. Sad to say, we couldn't get photos of those people, but we knew how many and something about each of them. When the boat reached Fiji, for some reason, the crew boarded a plane back to South America. Only one of them stayed behind. We have a name, no description.'

Lambert frowned. 'One of the men sailing on the boat coming across from South America stayed when it reached Fiji? And you think he joined the next crew for the trip to Brisbane? Well,' he said slowly, thinking it out, 'obviously, whoever it was, he was a sailor. They picked up Bridges in Fiji. But he wasn't a sailor. That description fits only one man on board when the *Sea Cloud* came up the river. JC McCoin.'

Chapter Ten

With money in their pockets, the small group of Americans all went their own way. After a hug from the two women, a handshake from the men, JC decided to set out to enjoy the foreignness of being in Brisbane, Australia. His first thought was for dinner. It had been a long time since the snack they'd had coming in. Walking out of the shopping area, he spotted a bus stop. This might be a foreign country, but a bus stop was a bus stop. This one came complete with a map outlining the routes of buses stopping there.

The river, shown on the metal map, was a blue snake-track through the centre of the map, swooping in huge bends through the city. The names stopped him. Something called Indooroopilly, whatever that was, and Kangaroo Point. If nothing else, it proved he was a stranger in a strange land. The map's middle, with the blue river flowing in a broad curve around it, was clearly labelled CBD. King George Square was right in the centre. As good as any, he supposed, and caught the next bus going that way.

King George Square, sounding very British, was the place to start. Other than Baja California, he had never been to a foreign country, so his idea was to take some time and play tourist. At least until his passport was handed back.

On the bus and reading the business signs on building fronts as they passed by and listening to the talk around him, he came to the conclusion that Australians were a lot like Americans, only different. The language didn't pose a problem, although he had to guess over a few things he heard. Had to be slang, he figured. Somewhere, he'd read that Aussies loved their slang. He wondered about their food. Australian food. Maybe with kangaroo instead of beef? Didn't they eat a lot of lamb in Australia? Seems he'd read something about that too. Or was it New Zealand?

The restaurant he found wasn't very big, not like any Denny's or Appleby's. Being a foreigner in a foreign country, even one where you could understand what the people were saying was pretty cool.

'G'day, mate,' the maître d said as JC walked up, 'it's good timing. Things'll get busy as Larry in another hour but now I can seat you anywhere you'd like.'

JC pointed to a small table set for two over next to a window.

G'day. And mate. Pure Australian. Back in California, when you heard either of those phrases you knew it was a repeat of Crocodile Dundee on TV. He'd never really believed people talked like that, but apparently they do. At least here in Brisbane. Brisbane, Australia. Then the thought crossed his mind that they could, hearing his American accent, be putting it on for him. He'd never thought about having an accent. Back in

San Diego, you could tell from what they said that someone was from Texas or Louisiana. Or from New Jersey or up in the far northeast part of the country. But not him. Not a Californian.

Thinking about people calling each other "mate" reminded him that damn drug cop hadn't called him mate. Inspector what's-his-name. Have to remember to call him in the morning. Wonder what the chances were of getting his passport? He wasn't ready to fly back to San D', not yet anyway; still a lot of being a tourist to experience. *Hey, mate.* JC laughed quietly to himself.

Chapter Eleven

Over the next few days, he heard a lot of 'G'day, mate,' and 'how ya going, mate?' or even, 'how they hangin'?' He was sure a lot of it was thrown his way because of his being a Yank, but it was all done with a smile and a laugh. It didn't take him long to conclude two things: the people were good, and the Australian beer was great.

It couldn't last forever, though. His money wouldn't last for one thing. While he was enjoying himself, he knew sooner or later he'd have to get back to San Diego and work. Still, without the passport, he thought he'd just relax and enjoy life. That worked for a few days. Then, after an afternoon spent walking the docks down at the harbour, he realised the fun of being a tourist was fading.

Walking the docks anywhere was about the same. No matter if they talked funny, the people there were boat people, and boats were the same everywhere. At first, those working on fish nets or sanding some pieces of woodwork, watched suspiciously. He wasn't sure whether it was his accent or the interest he showed, but it didn't take long before his presence was accepted. He wasn't there to steal anything or cause trouble; he was just another boatie.

The first thing he did was walk down the dock where the *Sea Cloud* was moored. Knowing he was being watched, he stopped, stood a few feet away from the sailboat and simply looked. Boats, unlike houses, couldn't be left empty long. Being in the water, boats needed almost constant attention. Shaking his head, he took his time, seeing the early signs of neglect behind the yellow and black police tape.

'It's a cryin' shame, it is,' someone said.

JC looked around to see who was speaking. He half expected to find a uniformed police officer but smiled to see it was a man working his nets on the fishing boat on the other side of the dock. 'Something isn't done with that damn tape; she'll be starting to look like hell. Bloody coppers don't know much about anything 'cept causing honest people trouble.'

The net man wasn't looking at JC as he spoke, keeping his attention on the strands of netting as he weaved a shuttle, repairing a torn hole. 'I was watching when the plods made her welcome. You came off that boat, didn't ya?' Still not looking up, he nodded.

'Yah, I recognise ya.'

JC smiled. Wasn't much of anything the people living and working in a harbour missed. 'Uh huh. I and a handful of others brought her in. We didn't expect the kind of welcome we got, though.'

The fisherman chuckled and, tying off a strand, dropped the shuttle and, after spitting a stream of tobacco juice over the side, sat down on his boat's railing. 'You a Canadian? Or a Yank?'

JC laughed. 'What's that all about? People hear my accent and right away ask if I'm Canadian or American.

And there's a big difference in accents. But it's never American or Canadian. I don't get it.'

The fisherman finally looking up, smiled. 'Ah, it's just people trying to be nice. Look, if you're Canadian and I asked if you were American, it might hurt your feelings, to be mistaken like that. But asking the other way around – well, everyone knows, you can't hurt a Yank's feelings. That's all. Just people trying to be nice.'

JC had to laugh. Boy, first he's a septic tank and then a guy without feelings. These Aussies have a thing about Americans.

'Tell me, scuttlebutt has it, there was a ton of drugs on board. That true?'

'No. Not a ton. More like a few hundred pounds, or kilograms. Cocaine, I was told. Never saw any of it myself, but the drug cops would recognise it better than I would.'

'So there was a major drug bust and here you are, walking around free and easy. How come you ain't locked up in the watch-house?'

'Didn't have anything to do with the drugs. All me and the crew were hired to do was bring the boat in.'

The fisherman nodded. "Well, what'll happen to the boat, I wonder. Sure hate to see her be ignored. Hasn't been anyone around to check her bilges or anything." ''Course we keep an eye on things. But be good if someone was aboard now and again, just to air her out, if nothing else.'

JC had to agree. 'More'n likely, the police will lose interest in her once they make their case. I don't know how things work down here, but what'd happen back in the States, once the officials get what they want, they'd put the boat up for auction and sell her. She's a good sailer. Real comfortable. Probably be worth half a million or so.'

'Won't be, if she's left to rot.'

JC spent most of the afternoon walking the docks, looking at boats and talking to the people he saw about boats. It was one of the best days he'd had since coming up the river. Catching a bus back into the business district, he thought it was time to get back to real life. Time to push that drug cop about his passport.

The question of what to do next was solved that very evening.

Chapter Twelve

Inspector Lambert had almost forgotten about his run-in with the superintendent and meeting the guy from the deputy commissioner's office. Brisbane might be nothing more than an overgrown country town, but there was enough crime to keep the law busy.

Not the big, headline-making stuff – the kind that he'd need if he was ever going to earn a return to the big city. But for all of that, there was enough to keep him and his unit active. A lot of it was, in his view, busy work. Things like running DUI stings and investigating ram-raids or other break-ins, he could leave for his senior sergeants and the uniforms. His schedule involved too much community liaison work, explaining to people why their neighbourhood watch program wasn't working. Too damn much soft talk. What he needed and wanted was more cases of fraud, drug trafficking, money laundering or even people smuggling. Crimes that would get his name in the daily newspapers or on telly. That was the only way he'd ever get transferred back to Sydney.

His surprise when he was told someone named Edwards on the line was total.

'Mr Edwards,' he said, then slowing down. Sounding desperate or like a suckup wouldn't do. 'How can I help folks at the upper end?'

'Ah, Inspector, you didn't think I'd forgotten about you, did you? Not a chance. You're my link to the leaders of that big cocaine bust. If you've got a few minutes, I'd be proud to shout you for a cuppa.'

Coffee with someone from the Sydney office? 'Of course. You call it and I'll be there.'

Starbucks on Queen Street was close to Lambert's office and only a few blocks from Spring Hill. It was quite likely Edwards had been working out of the superintendent's offices in that neighbourhood.

Lambert didn't like Starbucks and rarely went to any of the outlets for his coffee. Too many choices, few of which he knew anything about. A simple, flat white would do for him. The menu didn't seem to faze Edwards; smiling at the young barista, he placed his order, an espresso macchiato. When it was delivered to their table, Lambert thought it looked just like a flat black. He wondered if the fancy name made it taste different. Making a mental note to try it sometime in the future, he poured sugar into his coffee and waited for the assistant director to speak.

Putting down the cup, Edwards nodded. 'A shot of caffeine. I can feel it hitting already. Are you still in touch with that crew of Americans?' he asked, changing the topic without warning.

'Uh, yeah. They call in almost every day. Bridges missed a couple days, but he's been spotted doing the nightclub rounds over in Fortitude Valley. Lot of trouble comes from some of those clubs, but his name hasn't shown up from there.'

'How about the others, uh, McCoin and Tipton?'

'Well, Tipton is the complainer. Every day he calls in and wants to speak to me and when told I'm not available, he makes it clear he wants his passport. Reportedly, his language gets quite, uh, colourful. Those Yanks do have some interesting curse words.'

'Yes, I imagine. All right. You can release Tipton's passport. Turns out, he's just what he claimed – a surfer dude. He's been spending a lot of time catching waves out at Snapper Rocks and Rainbow Bay. And McCoin?'

'He's made his calls. Doesn't turn up anywhere else. Oh, he did spend an afternoon back at Rivergate Marina. Mostly talking to people at the shipyard or walking the docks. I'd say he's tired of being ashore. Also has pushed for the return of his passport.'

'Okay, let's hang on to those, McCoin's and Bridges. I'm pretty sure the one I want is Bridges, but, well, let's not make life easy for either of them.'

'Yeah, but if they got themselves a solicitor, we'd probably have to prove up a case or give back their passports.'

It was Edwards' turn to frown into his cup. 'If push comes to shove, I guess we'll have to do something. But until then, let's wait it out. I'm not sure Bridges likes hanging around. I'm betting he'll do something and then I've got him. But until that happens, I'd like to keep a short lead on him.'

Lambert slowly nodded. 'Well, he's apparently getting on with the bunch over in Fortitude Valley. Our nightclub district. We know there's a lot of drugs going through there, but haven't been able to knock the trade down. Trouble is, we can't get close enough. Put our best undercover people in and isn't long before they're outed.'

'Hmm.' Edwards pursed his lips. 'That is too bad. It would be lovely to tie either of them, especially Mr Bridges, up with some of your druggies.'

'Might be good to get out of that environment,' Lambert said thoughtfully. 'Somewhere less crowded with the bad element but still in a situation where tabs could be kept on both men's activities. Somewhere, they'd stand out a bit while still having the potential for doing something stupid.'

Edwards studied the inspector for a moment. 'You have something in mind?'

Lambert nodded again and smiled. 'Uh huh. I have a plan.'

Chapter Thirteen

After he'd made his arrangements, it didn't take Inspector Lambert long to set up the meeting with McCoin. The idea was to make that meeting appear to be accidental. That was done by putting one of his better officers onto the Yank right after the man had made his check-in phone call. When the officer reported McCoin's frequent visits to a certain restaurant, all Lambert had to do was wait. Easy peasy.

McCoin was enjoying being a tourist. When he got a bit bored, he'd gone back down to the marina. Being around boats and boat people helped. Making friends at the shipyard was easy, everyone liked talking to someone with an honest interest in what they do. Always, the question of where he was from came up, and nearly always, once he said California, the Aussie would recount the holiday they'd spent there. Australians, he decided, were the friendliest people he'd ever met.

Along with the people, getting high marks was the Australian beer. And next on the list was the freshness and availability of seafood. He'd delivered a power boat to Ketchikan, Alaska once and wanted to go back. Up in the far north, the prize crab had been the huge King or ubiquitous Dungeness, but down here, the locally caught mud-crab had a flavour all its own.

His first dining experience had been in a little restaurant near King George Square that offered freshly caught seafood. That, he decided, would be the place to have a meal and decide what to do next. A good meal of mud-crab for strength, before going to deal with the drug cop boss about getting his passport back.

The restaurant wasn't very large; only a handful of tables, and by American standards was pretty pricey, but that was the fun of being a tourist. He hadn't been paying any attention to anyone and was surprised when someone called his name.

'Well, look who's here. JC McCoin, the drug-running Yank.'

McCoin frowned. As directed, he'd called the number they'd been given every other day, but all he had to do was tell the person who answered where he was. Not once had he spoken to Inspector Lambert, not once since leaving the *Sea Cloud*. Until that moment in the restaurant, he had almost forgotten the drug cop's warning that he'd be watched.

'You're not going to believe me, McCoin,' Inspector Lambert said, all smiles, 'but I was just thinking about you.'

No, McCoin thought, still trying to make sense of it; he didn't believe him. The big, friendly smile made it even more difficult. This was another side of the man, first Chief Lawman Lambert and now Friendly Lambert.

'C'mon over and meet a friend of mine,' Lambert said, waving his hand towards the table.

'Ya know,' Lambert said, quickly taking McCoin's hand in his as if they were long-lost buddies. 'You just might be the man we've been looking for. Shake hands with Noel Clarkson. Noel, JC McCoin. He helped bring the *Sea Cloud* down from Fiji. Remember, I was telling you about that? The biggest drug bust I've made yet. And old JC here, well, he was part of it.' That didn't make JC feel any better. 'Sit down, sit down.' Lambert motioned, pushing a chair out. 'You know,' he went on, not letting anyone get a word in. 'I never did learn what the JC stood for. Isn't Jesus Christ, is it?'

McCoin hesitated and then thinking about his passport, shook his head and took a place at the table. He knew his smile was weak, but it was the best he could give it. 'No,' he said. 'Afraid I can't walk on water or any of that. You still have my passport. Didn't you look at it?' He went on before the inspector could answer. 'And what did you mean? You'd been looking for me. I've called your office just like you told me to.'

'Ah, well, yes, I know. And it wasn't you exactly that we were thinking of. But Noel here has a sailboat moored out in the river, and he was asking if I knew anyone he could get to sail it up to Cairns. And about that time, you walk in. Now I ask you, is that fate or what?'

Noel Clarkson and Lambert had been friends since joining the federal police force. They had met on the first day at the AFP Academy and remained close long after, even when one was stationed in Sydney and the other in Brisbane. While Clarkson was still one step lower on the career ladder than his friend, they remained friends.

Curious, he had wondered what had happened to have Lambert transferred up to his town, but didn't ask. When the inspector laid out his idea, Clarkson quickly saw how he would benefit.

'You know that sailboat you've got? The one that doesn't get used much?' asked Lambert after inviting his mate for a drink.

'Yeah. It's still moored out in the river. Why? What have you got up your sleeve?'

'Ever think about sailing north? Up to the Great Barrier Reef? I understand there's world-class sailing up there.'

'My wife and I have thought about having our boat somewhere up there. We've dreamed about sailing around the Whitsundays for a long time,' said Clarkson, nodding. 'We've just never been able to take the time to sail her up there. Now, why would you be wanting to ask me that? Once again, I'll ask you, what've you got going on in that devious mind of yours?'

'Well, old mate, I've got a plan. One that could help me out in a couple ways and at the same time, make your dream of sailing up there come true. First off, I've got two Yanks I want to keep an eye on. Don't ask why, it's part of an ongoing investigation by the Serious and Organised Crime Unit by the New South Wales Commissioner's office.'

'Ah, didn't I hear some gobble about a big drug bust that originated out of Sydney office? A bust that, according to rumour, didn't go as was planned?'

'Yes. The bust was good, but… well, there are loose ends hanging out. These two American sailors are just that. Now, if they were to take your boat up to Cairns, I'd know where they were for the next few weeks. Plus, and keep this under your hat, I've got word from my best snitch that there are two heavy dealers up there. If it happened that my two Yanks got chummy with these drug baddies, well, it would solve one of my problems. Tie up one of the loose ends, if you see what I mean.'

Clarkson smiled, and thinking about holidaying up north, he was quick to agree. Now all Lambert had to do was get McCoin and Bridges to come across.

'Where is this Cans?' JC asked after hearing the inspector's proposal, 'and what kind of sailboat are we talking about?' Not, he thought to himself that it mattered. While he couldn't believe there was anything accidental about this idea, there was still the matter of the passport to consider. He couldn't simply tell the drug cop to piss up a rope. Anyway, delivering sailboats was what he did. He'd make more money working for Ralph back in San Diego but when would he ever get a chance to sail in Australian waters again?

'First off, Cairns is about the northern most city in Queensland.' Lambert laughed, seeing things going the right way. 'On the map, it's spelt C-a-i-r-n-s, but it's pronounced Cans. Anyway, it's right off the Great Barrier Reef. And the boat – Clarkson's boat, the *Happy Wanderer* – is a twelve-metre catamaran. Presently, it is moored almost permanently at an anchorage out in the river.'

'Yeah,' said Clarkson, already thinking about his next holiday. 'I've got some time coming and the wife and I'd like to cruise some of the reef. I figure the cruise up there could be easily done in about ten days. It's about 750 nautical miles. If we sail the boat up, it wouldn't leave enough time for us to enjoy much of the area. So you sail her north. Take your time, say two weeks. That way, you'd have time to do some fishing along the way. Then, in a couple months, I'm thinking about spending Christmas up there. My wife would like that.'

'And,' Lambert cut in, 'I know just the person to go along as crew. You been in touch with any of your old crew? I didn't think so. Well, the two women and Mr Tipton caught flights back to the US as soon as I returned their passports. Yeah.' He held up a hand before JC could ask questions. 'You'll get yours too. No matter where we looked, we couldn't find a way to link any of you to Webster's drug gang. We tried, but there you are. Free as a bird. Oh, I'm still keeping an eye on you. As long as you're in the country. But don't worry about that. And here's a good opportunity to return the favour.'

Already, JC was shaking his head. 'Don't tell me. You're going to send one of your officers along to act as crew to watch over me.'

Lambert shook his head. 'No. Afraid none of my people have the time or the inclination to take a holiday right now. Uh huh. It's your old pal, Harry Bridges, I'm thinking about. He's been spending a lot of time over in Fortitude Valley. A tough part of town, Fortitude Valley. Harry seems to fit in, though. Anyway, I hear he's looking for something to do and you two seemed to get along pretty good.'

JC slowly ate his meal, trying to get over the feeling he was being used. The feeling wouldn't go away and the mud-crab somehow didn't taste as good as before.

What the hell was he getting himself into?

Chapter Fourteen

By the time the dinner was over, with Inspector Lambert picking up the tab, JC and Clarkson had worked it out. Two days later, he met Harry and the two men hopped one of the river ferry boats out to Clarkson's boat. After checking out the *Happy Wanderer,* they spent a couple days laying in groceries. After lifting the anchor and washing off the river mud, they were on their way north. Harry was feeling good, and with a cold beer in his hand, he started reading the charts they'd found on board.

'Hey, good buddy, thanks for getting me involved with this. I was getting a little tired of all the Aussie bullshit going on there in Fortitude. A lot of would-be bad asses. Wouldn't last five minutes anywhere in LA. But look here, according to what someone's written on the margin, there are places to stop for fresh veggies, cold beer, a swim and even good fishing. Man, I was ready to be yammering about getting my passport so I could get back to civilisation, but now, I think this little side trip'll be good.'

On the voyage from Fiji, Harry had turned out to be good company. As he'd said, he was quick to pick up the essentials of sailing. On this cruise, JC knew it would be different. The plan was to sail only during the day, laying at anchor when the sun went down. The evenings were spent fishing or swimming off the back deck. When supplying the boat, JC had made sure there was a good supply of wine, although Harry opted for beer.

Everything went along just as planned and they were still a handful of days out of Cairns when things changed.

Talking about it later, JC remembered looking at a chart and seeing they were at the southern edge of the Great Barrier Reef. It was a place he'd read about that but had never expected to ever see. He'd seen pictures but didn't really know what to expect. World-famous and a favourite of scuba divers. Most of the photos showed strange fish and weird coral heads. The first sign of anything other than blue water was dramatic; it was an airplane passing over head, losing altitude as if making a landing.

Grabbing a chart, JC saw just ahead a couple miles was an island, Lady Elliot Island.

'Must be some kind of resort,' he mumbled, watching as the aircraft disappeared. Reading the labels on the chart, he saw they had entered the Coral Sea.

'Hey, Harry,' he called to the man who was lying on the netting between the hulls, 'we're in the Coral Sea.'

Harry rolled over on his back, using his arm to shade his eyes. 'Uh huh. So what?'

'No, man, think about it. The Coral Sea is where a lot of fighting happened back in World War Two. You know, the US beating up on the Japanese. Hell, they named one of their ships after this piece of ocean. An aircraft carrier, I think.'

'Yeah. So are we heading in towards shore for the evening soon?'

Studying the chart, JC saw they were making good time. Looking ahead, he saw the beginning of the reef. On the chart, it listed the hundreds of little islands. The first was Lady Elliot Island, but there were a lot of likely places after that to spend the evenings before arriving at the transient moorage at Cairns Harbour.

They anchored a little early that afternoon, rounding to the north side of Lady Elliot Island. Sailing past, keeping one eye on the depth sounder, they could see a series of low-lying buildings along a stretch of beach. Sailing in the gentle breeze, JC steered a course off shore, coming back to a suitable depth after passing the northern tip of the island.

Harry was quick, once the anchor was set and they'd dropped the sails, to cast a plastic lure. Dinner that night was barbecued fillets of some kind of strange-looking fish.

Talk about paradise. The weather was tropically warm under pure blue skies. Sailing away from the island the next morning, JC was happy. The ocean, as far as could be seen, was calm, almost flat, with only slow rolling waves gently rocking the hulls as the boat ghosted along. Land was out of sight to the west and, once away from the island, there wasn't anything but the undulating water and a few clouds far away over near the horizon.

The chart showed a series of reefs ahead and they decided which one to head for with the outlook for a repeat of the previous night; set the anchor and relax.

Spend another evening watching the stars come out while enjoying a glass or two of good Aussie wine and cold beer. Both Harry and JC thought they'd found heaven.

For the next couple days, that was the pattern. Choose one of the little islands for anchoring, catch a few fish and relax.

Things changed dramatically when they were only a day or two out of Cairns.

Drifting along, JC was watching the depth sounder to make sure they didn't discover any unmarked reefs. At the time, Harry was standing forward in the bow, waiting for the signal to drop the large Danforth anchor.

'Hey, JC,' he called back, his voice breaking with excitement, 'you aren't gonna believe this, but there's a couple people out there in the middle of the ocean, standing up to their butts in the water waving at us.'

Chapter Fifteen

Joyce and Keith Marsh had been glad to get away. A week off, away from everything. A week of walking on the beach instead of sidewalks, stopping for coffee and taking their time to enjoy it, relaxing. It had been Keith who suggested they take one of the day trips out on the reef.

'It doesn't get much better than this, hon,' Joyce Marsh whispered to her husband as they sat with the other tourists on the dive boat, heading away from land out into the emerald green water. 'Gawd, I've really needed to get away. Your idea of coming up here was just what the doctor ordered. Thank you very much.'

Keith and Joyce were from Brisbane. She was an accountant with one of the city's larger real estate firms. Thirty-two-year-old Keith had been a long-haul truck driver until being laid off. Not finding another job was only one of the issues the couple were facing on a day-by-day basis. Both wanted children but so far, no matter what program they tried, nothing was happening. To add pressure, the housing market in the state's biggest city was suffering. Having a good view of the financial part of today's real estate market made it clear to Joyce, there would have to be cost cuts in the very near future.

Keith leaned over and kissed his wife's cheek. 'Baby, if you recall, this is very near where we spent our honeymoon. A different reef and we didn't go out on a dive boat, but if you remember, we had some good fun.'

Feeling her face flush, she glanced sideways to make sure nobody had heard him. Of course, she remembered. That time they had only been snorkelling, not wearing full-body wetsuits. Drifting along on the surface, watching the schools of tiny, colourful fish flashing one way and then another, she had nearly lost it when she felt a hand rub along her inner thigh.

'God.' She had choked, bringing her head out of the water and spitting out the mouthpiece. 'Don't do that. I thought something was going to get me.'

Keith laughed. 'Something is going to get you,' he said, hugging her close.

The reef they had been swimming over was only chest-deep for him. Being shorter, she wasn't able to put her feet down. Letting her fins float up in the weak current, she found her legs encompassing his muscular body.

'Ah,' he said quietly, holding her close and leaning his head down, meeting her lips with his.

'Keith, don't. There are people around us.'

'Nope. I've been watching. They are all staying over on the other side of the dive boat. I think the dive master knows we're newlyweds and he's leaving us alone.'

'Oh,' was all she could say as she felt his fingers tug at the edge of her bikini bottom.

Slowly, pulling her body closer to him, he entered her. Not moving but letting the slight motion of the water move them, they hung there for a long few moments.

Smiling into her brand-new husband's eyes, Joyce had felt her climax grow.

'Yeah, I remember all about that trip, love. But don't go trying to do anything this time. I don't think these wetsuits have any openings. I know you, you'll get all horny and want to play, but you're just going to have to wait 'til we get back to the resort.'

Keith laughed and touched her cheek.

To most people, his wife probably wasn't thought of as being beautiful, but he knew she was. Even after being married this long, he still couldn't believe his luck. He knew what he was, a big brawny, lug of a man – not overweight but only because he worked at it. It went with the business – sitting behind the wheel for long stretches, not really getting any exercise. And then the food at the truck stops. No wonder your average trucker carried a big belly. Well, he didn't have to worry about that now. He didn't have a steady run to make any more.

Damn, he felt his shoulders sag. Not being able to find a job was killing him. It wasn't that he wasn't looking. He frowned, thinking about the number of applications he'd put in. Long-haul truckers were having it tough all over the state. Hell, everybody was having it tough. About the only jobs available were out at one of the mines.

They had talked about that, him taking one of the driving jobs. Fly in, fly out. Work three weeks at the mine, then home for a week. A lot of people were doing it.

'We aren't having it that tough, hon,' Joyce had argued. 'I don't think I could take it, not having you home for three weeks at a time.'

He hadn't fought it. But having to live on her salary didn't sit well with him. Sooner or later, something would have to break.

Not now, though. This long weekend was for her. Getting out of the rut she had to be feeling, all the hours she'd been putting in. Thinking about it wasn't going to help either. He might not be putting food on the table, but, for Christ's sake, he could make this trip something for her to remember.

'Okay, people,' one of the dive instructors called out. 'We'll be dropping the hook shortly and doing our equipment check. You all remember how that goes, don't you?'

Each of the dozen or so divers, all wearing the same black rubber wetsuits, nodded.

To make this trip extra special, Keith had suggested they take one of the scuba diving cruises. Neither of them had ever done any real scuba diving. Cairns was one of their favourite holiday spots, but every time they came up, the closest they had gotten to water was snorkelling. This time would be different.

That meant a session at one of the scuba diving schools before being allowed to go out to one of the reefs. They opted for the one-day extended session rather than the two- or even three-day sessions. According to the brochure, the shorter course gave them what was called a 'tourist diver's' license. All lessons were held in a modern training facility located right next door to Marsh's hotel. The morning session was spent in an air-conditioned classroom, learning about the scuba equipment. Breaking for lunch, most of the students walked down to one or another of the half-dozen or so nearby restaurants. After being inside, coming out into the heat and humidity made sitting inside a real pleasure.

Coming back from lunch, Keith wondered how many had followed the 'no alcohol' ban. The thought of a nice, icy glass of beer almost got him, but Joyce, knowing her man, made it clear. They had ordered iced coffee.

Back at the school, the students found themselves being fitted for wetsuits. Again, Keith had wanted to help his wife into hers, but he knew better than to make the offer. Suited up, the group moved out to a couple large pools.

The instructors were good at their job, and soon everybody knew how the various pieces of equipment worked. Laughing and learning, they became comfortable with the lead weight belt and the feel of the scuba tanks strapped to their backs. Keith was amazed at the amount of gear they were using. It appeared to all be in good condition, which made him feel safer about it. Late in the day, the class was taken down to the harbour for an hour or so in salt water.

Dinner that night was a celebration; they had all become qualified scuba divers and would be taken out on the reef the next morning.

The motor catamaran was outfitted for diving, with scuba tanks and other gear all in place. Everybody was in high spirits, laughing, joking and watching the water.

'Good morning,' one of the dive masters greeted the group. 'On this day trip, we'll be visiting three spectacular reef sites. These have been chosen to give you all the visual diversity of the Great Barrier Reef. We'll be out for about seven hours, five of those on the reefs, having you back in time for afternoon tea. Or cocktails. Now, here is what to expect. Once we're anchored, for those wishing to snorkel, we will have five of our staff available to answer questions and ensure your safety. The certified divers will be taken to the other side of the vessel. Again, the dive masters will be on hand to make sure you all experience the underwater world of colourful marine life in safety and comfort. Go ahead and relax; it'll take a little over an hour to reach our first reef.'

'Oh, Keith,' Joyce said, smiling up at her husband, 'this is so good. I'm already planning on how to make the evening equally memorable.'

Keith felt his chest fill. How damn lucky could one man be?

The diving itself was as advertised. Schools of fish of all sizes and colours flitting around and through the remarkable structures making up the reefs. The fish didn't seem to be afraid, swimming away in a flash if someone's hand got too close. Keith tried his damnest to sneak up on one huge grouper, the big fish's mottled black and grey skin looking rough as the reef it swam over. The man never got close to the beast, and Joyce, swimming along behind, watched, laughed into her regulator's mouthpiece.

It was after they had chased the fish that Keith thought to stick his head above the surface to see where they were and where the dive boat was. What he said made his face go white. The boat was a long way off and looked to be moving even farther.

'Honey,' he called, and looking around and not seeing his wife, ducked quickly underwater. He didn't see her at first, then, from the corner of his eye, he saw a movement and found her, holding on to a piece of reef, watching something.

Swimming over, he touched her and pointed up. Quickly, they came to the surface.

'Did you see it?' she asked, excited, 'an octopus. I saw an octopus. It was beautiful and then it went into a little hole and disappeared.'

'Joyce,' Keith said solemnly, 'we've got a problem. Look.' He pointed, watching as the white dive boat sped up, going up on a step, with white foam pealing back from the bow.

'What?' she asked in panic, 'where are they going? They can't just leave us here.'

But that was exactly what was happening.

Chapter Sixteen

'Easy, love, don't worry,' Keith said, trying to keep the panic out of his voice. 'They'll do a count and come back. Don't get upset. Remember? That was one of the things the dive master did, took a head count as we went aboard and they would do another when leaving to go back. Don't panic, they'll be coming back. You watch.'

The couple floated, holding their heads up, watching as the boat continued away from them. All too soon, it disappeared in the distance.

'Oh, God, Keith. What'll we do? It's not coming back.'

Looking around, Keith felt his stomach knot up. Everywhere he looked, there was nothing. The ocean, as far as he could see, was flat and empty.

Glancing at Joyce, he knew he'd have to do something. She would be counting on him. 'Okay, the first thing is to move over to more shallow ground. We can't keep floating here. We don't have much air left, so it'll be better to be able to stand on something firm. But, love, don't worry. If they miss the count going in, there will certainly be a count once the dive boat reaches the dock. Someone will notice we're not on board.'

'No, they won't. We didn't know any of the other people, so they won't notice we're not on board. And if that dive master didn't count before the boat took off, what makes you think anyone will do a better count later? Keith, we're going to die out here.'

'C'mon, let's find some solid ground.' Taking her hand, he started swimming slowly back to where he thought the boat had been.

Hitting an outcropping of stone with a flipper, he stood up. Now with the ocean lapping at his waist, he took time to look all around. Still nothing.

'Oh, my God,' Joyce moaned, leaning against his bigger body. 'We're going to die out here. They'll never find us.'

'Stop that, Joyce,' he said angrily, 'whatever happens, panicking won't make it better. Now, there's no reason to keep these tanks on. Let's drop them. It's still a couple hours before dark. Someone's sure to come pick us up and when they do, we'll give them hell.'

Quickly, they helped each other out of the harness holding the scuba tanks to their backs. Holding on to each other, they lifted one foot at a time to pull off their swim fins. Keith was glad their wetsuits included thick rubber booties. At least the coral wouldn't be cutting the soles of their feet.

For a long time – to Joyce, it seemed to be hours – they stood, holding onto each other, the water lapping against their bodies. When they had first stood up, the water came up to their waist, as the day wore on, the level slowly came up and was just under her breasts when she noticed the change.

'Keith, what'll we do when the tide comes in and we can't stand here any more?'

He'd been thinking about that but hadn't wanted to say anything. Another thing he hadn't wanted her to think about was sharks. Somewhere, he'd read that the most dangerous shark was the Great White. He also seemed to remember reading that Great Whites liked the colder water farther south. It wouldn't do any good to mention sharks or jellyfish or anything else to Joyce.

'For once, I'm glad we didn't have children,' Joyce said after a long, silent period. Her voice was, for the first time since they had been left behind, quiet and calm.

'What? What do you mean?'

'Well, think how bad it would be if we were leaving children behind.'

'Oh, Joyce. Don't think like that. Don't give up. We aren't dead yet.'

'Uh huh. I was just thinking about something. Remember a couple years ago, a couple were left behind by a dive boat? They made a movie about it. I don't think the couple were ever found. Remember?'

'No, don't do that. We can't give up. Look, turn this way a little. Your face is starting to get all red. Sunburn. From the sun's rays bouncing off the water.' Inching around until he was facing west, towards the setting sun, he spread her hair out to cover the red skin of her neck.

'Water,' she said, almost sounding dreamy. 'That's what I've been thinking about. You know how long it's been since we had a drink of water?'

'I'm counting on you, honey. We've been having our problems but we're still together and still able to fight them off. It's impossible, but don't think of anything negative.'

'Always the optimist. That's one of the things I love about you, Keith, you always go looking for the silver lining.'

Keith was still for a moment. She felt his body stiffen. 'What is it, Keith? What did you feel? Not a shark, was it? Oh my God.'

'No, honey. Look there. It's a sailboat. I saw it a little bit ago but thought it was probably a cloud. But it's not. It's a sailboat. And it's coming this way.'

Joyce turned around and seeing the white smear off in the distance, giggled. 'It'll save us. We have to wave so they'll see us.'

'Not yet, hon. It's too far away and we're not a very big item in this wide, wide ocean.'

God, he prayed silently, let there be someone on board keeping watch.

Chapter Seventeen

Both Harry and JC had to put their backs into it, getting the pair out of the water. It didn't go smoothly. They had been standing in the ocean so long, fighting the ocean's gentle movement that their bodies had stiffened. Plus, the skin on their hands was all wrinkled and pale. The redness of their sunburned faces was bright against the wet blackness of their wetsuits.

'God, thank you,' the woman started blubbering, her words coming all broken as her teeth chattered. Shock and hypothermia, JC figured. People don't understand about hypothermia. One doesn't necessarily have to be in cold water to suffer. The body's temperature only has to drop a few degrees and over a period of time – and not a long period either – the internal organs begin to close down.

'Thank God, you came along when you did,' said the man, his voice sounding weak and thin.

The woman was hauled on board first, Harry and JC each grabbing one of her hands and lifting her onto the tiny dive deck at the stern. Swinging her up and into the vessel's spacious cockpit, they quickly let her go and reached for the man. He was barely able to grasp on as the boat was drifting. Another second and he'd have been out of reach and someone would have had to go swimming.

While they were bringing the man on-board, the woman had collapsed onto one of the cushioned seats. Soon, the two were huddled against each other, shaking and crying.

Harry stood, watching, but JC knew the couple were still in trouble. All day in the water without water. Dehydration was a danger. As quickly as he could, he was opening bottles of water and handing one to each of them.

'Take it slow,' he warned, holding the woman's bottle down when she started to choke. 'Your body wants water, but take it easy and slowly let the water do its work. We don't want you getting sick and throwing up, do we?'

Harry, looking down at them, frowned. 'How'd you get out here all by yourselves?' he asked.

The man did choke before lowering the water bottle to answer. 'We were left behind. We were on a dive boat out of Cairns and got separated. When we looked up, the boat was moving away. They left us behind.' Reaching around, he gave his wife a gentle hug, bringing her head down onto his shoulders. 'I'm Keith Marsh and my wife's name is Joyce. Man, if there's ever anything we can do for you, all you gotta do is ask.' Holding his wife close, he spoke into her hair, 'See, love, I told you we'd be okay. They would have missed and send out boats to search.'

'Uh, maybe,' Harry said, shaking his head, 'but we're not part of any search party. And looking around, I don't see any other boats anywhere.'

'Oh, then they don't know we're missing?'

'That isn't very important right now,' JC cut in and motioned towards the open cockpit, 'how about this. You two work yourselves below, taking it slow and easy. Help each other out of those rubber suits. There's a toilet and shower down in that hull. Should be plenty towels up in one of the lockers. Take your time. There's enough fresh water for a quick shower and it'll make you feel better. Meanwhile, I'll go down the other hull and see what I can find in the way of clothes. There must be something. We'll settle in for the night, have a meal and a good night's sleep. There's a nice double berth down there too. You're safe now and in the morning you'll feel a lot better. Meanwhile, I'll radio the harbourmaster and let them know we've picked you up.'

Watching them move slowly and stiffly, almost as if in pain, he wanted to help but thought better of it. Let them deal with it. Getting their muscles working would be a good thing.

Harry had taken the wheel and turned the boat away from the shallows. The catamaran didn't draw much water, only about a couple of feet, but grounding her against the coral wouldn't please anyone.

Glancing at the chart at the nav station, JC found the next nearest coral reef. 'Hey, Harry, what say we head up to Sudbury Reef? It's going to be dark in an hour or two, and I don't think much of trying to make it into Cairns in the dark. We can anchor up and go in early tomorrow.'

JC wasn't the only one on board, wondering what else could go wrong.

Chapter Eighteen

Getting the pair out of the water didn't go smoothly. They had been standing in the ocean so long, fighting the ocean's movement that their bodies had stiffened. Plus, the skin on their hands was all wrinkled and pale. The redness of their sunburned faces was bright against the wet blackness of their wetsuits.

'God, thank you,' the woman started blubbering, her words coming all broken as her teeth chattered. JC knew they'd been in the water for a long time. Even as warm as this part of the ocean was, hypothermia was a danger. People, he knew, didn't understand about hypothermia. One doesn't necessarily have to be in cold water to suffer. The body's temperature only has to drop a few degrees and over a period of time – and not a long period either – the internal organs begin to close down.

Watching them move slowly and stiffly, almost as if in pain, JC wanted to help but thought better of it. Let them deal with it. Getting their muscles working would be a good thing.

Harry had taken the wheel and turned the boat away from the shallows. The catamaran didn't draw much water, only about a couple of feet, but grounding her against the coral wouldn't please anyone.

Glancing at the chart at the nav station, JC found the next nearest coral reef. 'Hey, Harry, what say we head up to Sudbury Reef? It's going to be dark in an hour or two and I don't think much of trying to make it into Cairns in the dark. We can anchor up and go in early tomorrow.'

Calling the harbourmaster on the VHF radio was interesting for JC. Apparently, nobody had noticed when one of the dive boats had come in with two fewer people that it had taken out. Once he explained where the two scuba divers had been found, and the name of the charter dive company, which was painted down the side of both wetsuits, the harbourmaster got all excited.

'We'll be ready when you come in, *Happy Wanderer*.' The voice on the other end sounded excited. 'I expect it'll be best to have the pair checked out at the hospital. And I'm sure the sheriff's office will be interested in hearing what they have to say. Yes, sir, I'd say there'll be people waiting for your arrival. Over.'

Glancing over, JC smiled at Harry. 'Uh, yeah, Harbourmaster. They seem to be in pretty good condition, but I can understand how there'll be people interested. We'll make contact as soon as we can guesstimate our arrival. This is the *Happy Wanderer*, out.'

'Boy' – Harry chuckled – 'it sounds like our arrival is going to be a big thing. Maybe we'll be called heroes. Be given the keys to the city. Wouldn't that be something?'

'Well, you can have the keys. All I want is a good dinner with a nice wine, a night's sleep in a bed that doesn't move. We get rid of this boat and I'll have to start thinking about getting myself back to California. Have you given any thought about that?'

'Naw. Get my passport back and who knows? Whatever happens, it'll happen without my worrying about it. Always has. Anyway, I've got other things on my mind. Man, did you take a close look at the body of that woman? That wetsuit fit her like a second skin. Mmm, nice ass and those tits. Wowser.'

'Yep, old Keith is one lucky guy.'

'Old Keith, let go of her for a minute and I'll ace him right out of the picture. And I'm just the man can who do it, too.'

It wasn't long before they reached Sudbury Reef. When the depth finder indicated they had about twenty feet of water under the hulls, the anchor was dropped. JC motored back, setting the hook and shut off the engine. With the sails down, for the first time since picking up the two divers, the two men sat back, relaxing and toasting each other with bottles of beer.

'Who would have thought,' Harry said. 'Of all the things I've done in my life, this is the first time I've been an actual hero. Man, now that's something to brag about.'

JC nodded, sipped the beer and relaxed. On the internet, he had learned that the Great Barrier Reef ran about 2,000 kilometres along the upper east coast of Australia. The reef was made up of thousands of coral islands. Protected by all kinds of environmental organisations, the Great Barrier Reef was a world-class diving paradise. The reef itself was protected but apparently, those people coming out to it to dive weren't.

'Well,' Harry said after a few quiet minutes, 'this isn't getting dinner.'

It didn't take him long to toss out a baited hook and it wasn't long after that before he brought in enough fish for dinner. While Harry cleaned and filleted the fish, JC lit off the stainless steel barbecue.

When the young couple came up on deck, wearing shorts and T-shirts JC had found in a locker, they looked much better. They had each had a shower and a quick lie down on the queen-sized bed. Nothing was said to them about the welcoming committee they'd be facing the next day. Better, JC thought, not to give the pair more to stress out about.

Chapter Nineteen

Later, with the meal out of the way, the dishes were cleaned up and their guests were off to the port side queen berth. Harry and JC relaxed in the cockpit with the rest of a bottle of wine.

'I have to admit.' JC smiled lazily over at the other man and thought back to his comment about the woman in her wetsuit. 'You do think highly of yourself.'

Harry laughed. 'You bet. You know, back when I was in high school, I was known as Harry the Horse.'

'The horse. As with drugs? Heroin?'

'Nope. Back in those days, I was never involved with drugs. Huh uh. No. It was Harry the Horse because I was, and still am, built like a horse.' Setting back with his legs stretched out, he laughed and patted his crotch. 'I've got a lot of what every woman wants.'

JC could only shake his head. Either the man was a bragging fool and believed what he was saying, or he was just a foolish joker. 'I suppose you never fail with the women?'

'Oh, I don't score a hundred per cent of the time. Huh uh. You remember those two girls on board when we came down from Fiji? They were one of my failures. Nope. Tried, but I wasn't able to get them apart long enough to show them what they were missing.'

'Yeah, Sandy and Lucy. A couple of good-looking women. Good sailors, too. You didn't try to seduce them, did you?'

'Hell yes. Well, not chunky one, the Dollarhide woman. They were a couple, you know. Muff munchers. Uh huh, and don't look so shocked. I worked my butt off, trying to get the little one, Sandy, off by herself. But old, hard-assed Dollarhide wouldn't allow that.'

'I must have missed all that. Don't recall any conflict at all.'

'Yeah, you were too busy being skipper. Didn't matter, though. That damn Dollarhide woman let me know in no uncertain terms to keep my hands and my eyes off her girlfriend. Had a winch handle in her hand when she said it. I decided it'd be best not to bother any more.'

Sitting there in the dark, looking up at the night sky, JC smiled. Harry the Horse. What a fool! But maybe his bravado was what it took. God only knew his own experiences with women wasn't anything to brag about. He just didn't seem to have had much time for women. Even back in college, or to tell the truth, as far back as high school. In those days, he was kept busy on the family farm. Each year, Mum planted a huge garden. As far back as he could remember, as the eldest of three boys, it was his morning job before school to go spread chicken feed around the yard outside the hen house. Afternoons, after the homework was done to his mum's satisfaction, the kids would have to spend time hoeing weeds.

'You like it when eating what comes out of the garden, don't you?' his mother would say whenever he or his brothers argued. 'That means someone's got to take care of things before I cook them up. So, if you want to eat, you got to weed.'

A few years later, when he was big enough, it was his job to help his dad, stretching fence, cutting hay, feeding stock and all that farm stuff.

That didn't mean he and his siblings didn't get to play baseball or do other after-school activities. Even after getting his driver's license, JC was able to take a girl to the Friday night dance once in a while. Not that it did him much good. Once, he almost talked his date into the back seat of his sedan. Almost. Veronica was her name. She didn't mind jerking him off, and once in a while would suck him off, but other than letting him play with her breasts, she didn't allow anything else. Not him, or from what the other boys in his class said, anyone else. The question he asked himself years later had to do with those dates with Veronica. Did getting a blow-job or two mean he was no longer a virgin?

College was a lot harder than high school. He had to really work hard to keep his grades up, and high grades were important if he wanted to keep his scholarship. No time for partying, which meant no time to chase any of the girls. When it was all over, along with his diploma, he felt a certificate announcing his virginity wouldn't have been out of line.

Travelling up and down the west coast on a variety of expensive boats, always with a pick-up crew of boat-bums, one would think sex would be as common as opening a bottle of wine. After all, about half of those willing to sign on as members of the delivery crew were young women. But once again, things didn't work out in his favour.

Not often, anyhow. True, JC was no longer a virgin, and it was also true that a few of those women travelled with him on more than one job. Until he met Janine, none represented a long-term relationship.

Thinking about Janine was a lot easier now than it had been a few weeks ago. He remembered the day she came on board. The boat he was to deliver was a forty-foot full-keel double-ender ketch. A beautifully outfitted vessel, it was berthed in Victoria, BC. The new owner wanted it delivered to San Francisco. After flying in and inspecting the boat, he'd hung the usual help wanted notice on the bulletin board outside the harbourmaster's office. Janine was the third person to show up.

That eight hundred mile cruise was one of the best he could remember. Gentle winds and lots of blue skies. And Janine. He had scheduled the watches, so she had the evening watch, from four to eight. He took the eight to midnight. She was waiting for him and from that night on, they shared the aft stateroom.

Twice more in the following month, they travelled together; a power boat to Cabo San Lucas was the best. They spent a week at a resort down at the tip of Baja California. Almost like a honeymoon.

Then came the delivery to Maui.

'We have to talk,' Janine said when he started telling her about that upcoming trip. His heart stopped when he heard those four words. No good could come from a "we have to talk" statement.

'Okay,' was all he could say. I mean, what could he say?

'Is this the way you see your future?' she asked, looking up at him, reading his face. 'I mean, yes, it's nice, sailing here and there and living on expensive yachts, but do you have plans to do something else with your life?'

He'd never thought about it, so couldn't answer.

'Look,' she went on, still watching his face for a reaction, 'we've had a good time, but if we're going to get serious, well, I guess I don't see it as being on someone's sailboat.'

Serious. How serious was he? He couldn't remember exactly how he answered, but she didn't go with him to Maui. Now, lying back staring at the heavens above and thinking about the couple they had saved who were sleeping comfortably down below, he wondered if he wasn't missing something. Not getting married, but being part of a couple. Before he could work his way through that thought, Harry sat up.

'Wow,' Harry said, pointing up at the darkness. 'Look at that, a shooting star. Did you see it?'

'Nope,' said JC, not bothering to look where he was pointing, 'missed it.'

Silence once again covered the vessel. Shaking his head in the night, JC vowed to stop thinking about women and sex. For a time, neither man spoke, both settling back sipping the wine, relaxing with the slow, gentle movement of the boat.

'Look over there,' Harry said almost dreamily, 'towards those three stars all lines up. See it? Something moving across the sky. Steady and in a straight line. Think it's a satellite?'

Again, JC didn't bother to look. 'No, I can't find it. Could be, though. There's a lot of stuff floating around up there.' He poured a bit more wine into his glass. 'Did you see that movie, *Gravity*?'

'No. I haven't been to a movie in a long time.'

'All about a woman up at the space station. The station gets wiped out and she's left hanging. Scary stuff.'

'Uh huh. Now that woman diver, did you see her tits? Now that is scary stuff.'

JC sat quietly, nursing the last of his wine. Somehow, he didn't think it was important to respond. They would be in Cairns in the morning and turn the boat over to the owner's representative. At that point, Harry would go his way and he'd go his. Wherever that way turned out to be.

What he didn't expect was the greeting awaiting them.

Chapter Twenty

JC had decided not to sail into Cairns that morning. Raising the sails and going through the process of tacking their way into the harbour was the way for people on holiday. The lazy trip up the Queensland coast was finished and the two Americans' holiday cruise was over. For certain, Marsh's long weekend was also finished. While Harry kept a close eye on the water depth, JC used the diesel engine to power their way around the heads and up the river.

At the same time he'd used the laptop to get information about the Great Barrier Reef, he'd looked up Cairns. Not a big town, at least by the American standards. With only about a quarter of a million population, the three things important to Cairns were tourism, the damage left by the latest cyclone, the last one colourfully named Yasi, and, of course, the Great Barrier Reef.

The Marsh couple were up early and looking a lot better than they had the night before. After a breakfast made up of the last of the eggs, pork sausage, toast and orange juice, it was obvious the pair were a bit anxious. Keith was wearing a pair of JC's board shorts and an old, faded Rolling Stones T-shirt. They hadn't been able to come up with anything small enough for his wife. Joyce

Marsh had to settle for her bikini, which she'd washed the salt out of, and one of Harry's long-sleeve shirts. JC had to agree with his shipmate, she was a luscious-appearing woman.

'What do you think we'll run into when we get into port?' Joyce Marsh asked between mouthfuls of scrambled eggs. 'Did the harbourmaster say anything when you called him yesterday?'

JC nodded, considered how much to tell them. 'Well, yeah. He said he'd have some medical people there to check you out. I guess there'll be a charter boat owner chewing his nails.'

That caused the woman to frown. 'You think there will be newspaper people? That scares me. I really don't want any fuss.'

'Hon,' Keith said, taking his time and enjoying a second or third glass of juice, 'there's nothing to be scared of ever again. We've been close to dying and came out of it all right. Myself, I'm not sure whether I'm pissed at the dive company or just disgusted. Cap't, what do you think?'

Being the skipper of this boat meant, JC was discovering a lot more than just knowing how to control the direction the boat was going. 'I don't know,' he said after thinking about it a moment. 'I've never been in this kind of situation before. The harbourmaster seemed to enjoy the information that one of the dive boat companies screwed up. I'd say he'll take control of things once we reach our mooring.'

Coming in under power, JC eased the throttle back, paying close attention to other boat traffic and then boats within the harbour itself. Spotting where the harbourmaster wanted them to go wasn't hard; the man standing on the dock was waving his arms and pointing. Behind him, a crowd of people watched. Lots of people standing both around the dock and lining the neighbouring walkways.

'Well, looks like we really have a welcoming committee,' Harry muttered, nodding towards the officials.

JC, busy working the engine into reverse and bringing the boat to a stop against the floating dock, didn't look up until someone grabbed the mooring lines and made her fast. That was when he saw what Harry was talking about. For the second time, when bringing a sailboat up to the dock, JC looked up to find a familiar face among those waiting patiently on the dock.

What the hell was Inspector Lambert doing here? And out of uniform.

Chapter Twenty-One

'No,' said Lambert, later, doing his best to appear sincere, 'I'm not here about your rescuing those divers, although I think that was noteworthy. No, sir, I'm here because Noel couldn't make it. Something came up with one of the cases he's working on and I've got some holiday time coming. So he asked if I'd be here to secure his boat. Although,' he looked away before going on, 'I did say I'd be keeping an eye on you two.'

The inspector had cut the two Americans out of the crush of people, leading them off to one side. Nobody seemed to notice, all eyes and ears were on Keith and Joyce Marsh.

'It appears you two caught a lot more than a heap of fish on the way up here,' Lambert said. 'I reckon they were lucky you came along when you did.'

JC wasn't about to let his question go unanswered. Before the AFP officer could start explaining, the American asked about his passport.

'No worries, mate,' Lambert said, his smile fading a little. 'I've got them at the office. They are yours. But' – again the hesitation – 'I don't think you'll be able to jump on the next plane out.'

'And why the hell not?' Harry asked, a big frown corrugating his forehead. 'What kind of bullshit you pulling now?'

'Not just me. It's the district magistrate. He has already set a date for a hearing on the charter boat, leaving that couple out on the reef. I've been asked to make sure you're both available.'

'And what,' JC asked, 'are we supposed to do while all this is going on?'

Harry jumped in on that. 'Yeah, what the hell are we supposed to do – twiddle our thumbs? Man, I've been looking forward to a few cold brews and a meal someone else fixes. How long are we supposed to sit around playing with ourselves?'

Lambert shook his head. 'The charter people are working with their insurance agent right now. The judge thinks there's been a crime committed and he wants time to do the research on that. I reckon the company's insurance will cover your costs, but I don't know. You'll have to deal with them on that. But' – he held up a hand before either of the two men could cut in – 'there isn't any reason you can't take some casual work while waiting. To keep you from being bored, I mean.'

Harry didn't like that. 'Casual work? Like what?'

'Well, you said something about a thirst for beer. I happen to know the pub over at the Crown Hotel is looking for a bartender. You ever worked behind a bar?'

'Man, I didn't come up here to pour drinks for a bunch of tourists.'

JC cut in, letting his anger show. 'How long will this take, you think? Remember, even if you're holding our passports, we are still on a visa. I think both of us have done enough lolly-gagging around. I've got work back in San Diego I could be doing.'

'Hard to say how long it'll be. The judge has set the date for a hearing, next Thursday. But it's likely there will be a trial scheduled. Could take another two to three weeks.'

Two or three weeks. Back in California, it was early summer. According to what he'd been told, June in Australia was still part of winter. You wouldn't know it. JC frowned, wiping the sweat from his brow. Late June in Cairns and the daytime temperature was pushing the mercury to the mid-80s. Standing outside the restaurant after enjoying lunch, the heat felt like a heavy weight on his back. How did people living here stand it?

Harry had grumbled but after thinking about it, decided sitting around on his hands wasn't good. He'd tried to make connections after arriving in Brisbane, but nobody'd talk to him. Hell, he'd done what he'd been hired to do, watching that fool Webster, making sure the shipment went where it was supposed to go. Was it his fault someone had talked to the cops? Try telling that to someone. No dice. So now he was deeper in no-man's land. Well, standing behind a bar would be the best place to find out how things were being run here in this podunk town.

He was put to work almost immediately as the day bartender at the Crown Hotel pub. The pub manager didn't mention a visit he'd had by the man, who, after showing his AFP card, asked for a favour. It didn't matter. He needed an afternoon bartender, didn't he? So when the Yank came calling, he got hired. Not because the federal officer requested it, but because he was the only person to ask for the job. That meant, as a pub manager, he could look forward to getting a favour from the officer. You never knew when that kind of favour would be important. Especially in a place like this.

JC, on the other hand, wasn't too excited about looking for work. Not even part-time, or as Lambert called it, casual. Called temporary employment back in the States, here, especially in the hospitality area, people were hired as "casuals", meaning they'd be here today and might show up tomorrow. Backpackers, mostly. Young men and women bumming their way around the world, working on a "casual" basis to make a few dollars as they go. Waiting tables in some restaurants didn't appeal to JC.

'Hey, Mr McCoin,' it was Inspector Lambert again, waving as he came up the street. 'Wait up. I may have some good news for you.'

The police officer was wearing tan khaki pants and a colourful Hawaiian shirt. Somehow, JC thought the man looked uncomfortable. It could be because he was out of uniform. Or possibly because of the heat. Even in the light pants and shirt, he looked like he was baking.

'Crikey, it's going to be a hot one today,' Lambert said, sounding like he was panting. 'I'll bet most of those who are able will be spending the afternoon at the beach. How about a cup of coffee? My shout.'

'My shout?'

Lambert chuckled. 'Yeah. It's what Aussies say. You know, my treat. I mean, I'll pay for the coffee. C'mon.' Turning into the restaurant JC had just left, Lambert didn't give the American a chance to turn down the invitation.

'Okay,' JC said after they had ordered their coffees, 'you said something about good news. Don't tell me, you're going to give me my passport and let me go back to California.'

'No, not that kind of good news. The hearing is still as scheduled. No. Look, when I was making the phone calls, trying to find out about you, I remembered reading that you are a certified PDI Dive instructor?'

'Yeah, I've got my PDI certificate. It's in the folder along with my passport and visa.'

'Right. So you've got a job. Over at the Royal Crown Dive School. They're always looking for certified teachers, especially foreigners who can teach other foreigners. I guess it helps if the instructor has the same language, or at least the same accent. Anyhow, I happened to be talking to one of the school's administrators and, well, I mentioned you being a dive instructor.'

'Teaching people scuba? Yeah, I can do that. But isn't that outfit the same one that has the charter business, taking tourists out onto the reef? The same one that left that couple behind?'

'Yes. But you wouldn't be going out as a dive master. It's teaching the tourists at the dive pool. Think about how nice it'll be when it's hot outside, you'll be in the pool.'

'Uh huh. And once again, you have Harry and me, where you can keep tabs on us. Haven't you found out we had nothing to do with that cocaine in the *Sea Cloud*? Why are you still hounding us?'

Lambert pursed his lips and nodded. 'I'm sure you didn't have anything to do with that, but, well, it isn't doing any harm, getting you a casual job. At least until the hearing.'

JC shook his head. 'If I'd known this was the way it was going to be, I'd have let those two make their own way into the harbour.'

Chapter Twenty-Two

The young woman could only grimace as a stream of blood spurted from the bird's neck. Watching two beautifully feathered roosters go after each other, feathers flying, men screaming and too soon blood soaking in the sand, was the price she had to pay. Almost too high a price, but then she remembered what she hoped to gain. Nothing was too high for that.

Melissa Graves, Class of 2000. Member of the university yearbook staff, honoured in volleyball and tennis. Dreams of becoming a professional photographer. Dreams that were shot down, when in her first year at uni, she discovered how much work there was in learning to be a photographer. Quickly, she changed her major to journalism.

Mel Graves, twenty-nine years old, red hair, thick and covering her shoulders, green eyes and clear complexion. Mel Graves, still somewhat attractive, still single, still with a dream. Mel Graves, her name in fancy black type at the top of her CV. The list of accomplishments, long and, as it turned out, meaningless.

Right out of school, still with the dream strong in her heart, she had begun her search for the job that would give her what she was meant for – the top position. Rejection after rejection was the wall she ran into. There hadn't been anything in journalism school about how hard it would be. No warning at all.

It wasn't until, months later, she learned what her professors hadn't mentioned. It was when turning her down, that one managing editor explained how things worked.

'That degree you studied for, sweated blood getting, is like a fishing license; one buys a license and then has to go out and learn how to fish. Okay, so you have your degree. Lots of people have one. Until you can show me what kind of journalist you are, I'm not going to give you a desk. Sorry, kid, but that's the breaks. You're a reporter? Go report.'

Obviously, this guy had watched too many American films.

So, go report. On what? And for who? Whom?

'Look, Mel,' Robert, at the time her true love, explained over a glass of Chardonnay after she spilled her tearful story, 'going into the biggest newspapers in the state and expecting to be hired wasn't the brightest idea. You have to start at the bottom and work up. You must be able to show that you can write a coherent news story. Collect your clips of stories published. And not the kind you wrote in school. Real stories. Don't frown at me, I'm trying to help.'

'Sound's impossible,' she snapped. 'I'm unable to get a job until I can prove I can do the job and can't prove I can do the job until I have a job.'

'It's not like that at all. The best thing is to work building your clip file. Check out the neighbourhood free newspapers. They often accept things from people. Get published. Mel, dear. It's either that or have a relative already on staff. Or,' he said, taking her hand and smiling gently, 'forget all this and marry me.'

Robert didn't know it but his time with lovely Mel was short. Not that he wasn't good in bed, and he had a good job and didn't mind picking up the tab for dinner, but he was dull. Another black mark was his desire to get married. Start a family. Buy a house. Ugh! There was too much life to live to join the world of married life. That wasn't for her.

The stories about the local bank manager donating five thousand dollars to the youth soccer team was the first story. The Free Weekly Rag didn't pay her for it but they printed her name under the headline. Over the next two years, her clip file grew with stories, each carrying her by-line, and finally she landed a job. A real-paying job. Not with a big city paper, no. With a three-times-a-week community newspaper.

Five years later, still with the little community paper, she was getting desperate.

So what was she doing at a cock-fight? An illegal cock-fight? And with an inexperienced girl photographer to feel responsible for. What was she thinking? Was her personal goal worth all this? Yes. That was the whole point. A future as a second-class journo working for a series of bogan publications had never been on her list. Until she'd come across those letters her grandfather had written, she'd never really thought about her future. But now she had a plan. Or at least the beginning of a plan. And the first step was to get to Cairns.

The opportunity presented itself when she approached the editor of a regional lifestyle magazine. According to that man, his publication had the biggest readership in Queensland. For a girl raised in Brisbane, travelling by train up to Cairns was not normal. That far north was another world. She wouldn't have been surprised if someone asked for her passport. But a job, any job, was a job. A good one if it got her closer to her goal.

'Look, you want a job,' Carl Musgrave, the editor of the *Sun Life Magazine* said after looking Mel up one side and down the other, 'show me you can do the work. Go get the story. You want to write about the attack on Broome during World War Two? Forget that. Never mind about the attack on Broome. In the first place that's history and won't be worth ink until they celebrate the 75th anniversary. In the second place, Broome isn't in Queensland, it's over on the west coast in Western Australia. So your proposal has merit, but not now and not for *Sun Life*. But, cock-fighting is right now and it is in Queensland.'

Mel had taken her idea for a story on the attack on Broome to *Sun Life Magazine* because the publication's offices were just down the street from hers at the community paper. The germ of the idea came when she found a ribbon-tied packet of letters in a box of photos, letters and other memorabilia. It was just luck that she found the letters. Reading them to see if there might be a story idea, she was instantly excited. The letters had been written by her grandpa, Alexander Baranoff. She had never met the man, he'd died before she was born. But the family history was full of stories about her father's father and how he had won the Second World War all by himself. The letters had all been addressed to his wife, Mel's grandmother, Clarice. Mel did have fond memories of Grandmother Clarice.

Even as a young girl, being in the same house as Nana Clarice meant everybody was laughing. Mum called Nana Clarice a wild child. Mel wasn't sure what that meant or even if it was a good thing. But she loved her Nana.

Upon her grandmother's death, it had fallen on Mel to clean out the family home and get it ready for the real estate agent. The box of papers and things had been shoved aside and nearly forgotten. Looking for something else in the back of a closet, she had come across the tattered cardboard box. Not remembering what was inside, she tore off the strip of crusty-aged tape holding down the cover. Inside among the faded photo albums, she found the letters.

For the most part, the letters were simply those of a man to his wife complaining about being separated. Complaints about the people he found himself flying rated right up there with the kind of gripes anyone in the military had during wartime. According to her grandfather's letters, he had been flying a DC-3, ferrying VIPs from a place in the Dutch West Indies. Only when she read the letter that talked about when his plane had been shot down did Mel really get interested. Maybe there was something she could use in the man's story.

Mel didn't know where the Dutch West Indies were, but that would be easy to find. Might add to the story she was thinking about writing. Give it more of a historical feel. Quickly, she read the next letter and the one after that, but no mention of being shot down was made. Not until about the last letter in the packet. Looking at the postmark, Mel saw it was nearly three months after being shot out of the sky that Baranoff explained how he'd learned something interesting about that event. Something that almost changed his life and now, many years later, might change his granddaughter's.

Chapter Twenty-Three

'*Being shot out of the sky wasn't a pleasant experience,*' her grandfather had written. '*However, the reception I got wasn't what you'd expect either. Clarice, all I can remember of that trip was how hard it had been to pull my passengers out and get them safely to shore. We had come down on flat wetlands, a hundred metres or so from the shoreline, right next to the mouth of a little river. My co-pilot, a young man named Eddy Young, had been killed when the first wave of Jap Zeroes made their run at us. Of the nine passengers, four were wounded and two of those died that night. We were able to save most of the survival gear the plane was equipped with and actually had a fairly easy time of it. Thankfully, I'd been able to get off a Mayday call and a flying boat rescued us the next day.*

'*I don't remember what directions I was able to give with that call for help,*' he wrote in the letter, '*but the flying boat was right there early the next morning. As far as I could tell, the nearest landmark would have been the mouth of a smallish river. Nothing like as wide as the Brisbane River, but it was certainly as muddy brown. Later, someone told me there was a small aboriginal village up that river. A bit, can't say I remember the name of it though.*

'Anyway, one fact does stick out in my mind and that was how my airplane disappeared over night. That morning, in full daylight, after checking the condition of the men, I took a long look around. The first thing I noticed was that the plane was gone. I had apparently put her down close to the edge of the tidal wetlands and sometime in the night, probably when the tide came it, she'd slipped down into deeper water. Well, it was unlikely that the plane would ever have flown again anyhow. But I wasn't worried about that. No, getting the wounded men to the hospital was, as far as I was concerned, the most important thing. The plane wouldn't be missed. When we reached Broome and off loaded the wounded, a military man with a lot of gold stars on his jacket shook my hand and thanked me for having saved some of his people. American he was.

'Another man, all important looking in his three-piece wool suit, came to me and asked about the box. You know, it was only then that I remembered being handed a cloth-covered box, about the size of a cigar box, before taking off from Bandung. I'd shoved it under my seat and forgotten about it. I had to tell him it'd gone down with the plane. He shook his head and started telling me how I'd been responsible for it. He got all red-faced and angry and I'm ashamed to say I did too.

'I wasn't exactly yelling when I told him I hadn't had time to worry about any damn box. That my first duty had been to get my passengers to safety. It was clear he didn't like that news. He let me know he wasn't happy. Later, when I had to explain about losing the box to couple *other men, I came to understand there had been something important in that cloth-covered box. It was explained to me that there was. The men identified themselves as officials from the Commonwealth Bank. The box I'd been entrusted with had been containing diamonds belonging to a couple of Dutch businessmen. Somehow I had the feeling the bankers didn't totally believe me when I once again told them of the tide taking the airplane.'*

'*Well,*' he wrote in the letter, '*I got over my anger pretty quick and really had put that whole matter out of my mind. Never thought about it again. I had other things to think about. Losing my co-pilot and good friend, Eddy Young, really had a bad impact on me. That was when I decided not to fly that route any more. If you'll recall, you'd been after me to come home but I thought it was important to help ferry people trying to escape the Japanese invasion. But after being shot down and Eddy getting killed, well, I had a change of heart. Such a thing can change a man, you know. I'd known Eddy for a long time. He had flown in the right-hand seat with me on three or four trips. Flying with someone else, well, it just wouldn't be the same.*

'*Anyway, to get back to my story, losing my plane, and your letters, made me rethink things, so I decided it was time to come back home. So, remembering how we'd talked about buying that block of land outside Brisbane, when I deposited my last pay-check, I asked about a loan. The bank clerk, a young man, made me wonder why he wasn't in the army. Well, he got all flustered. Said he'd have to talk to the bank manager. Well, I wasn't asking for all that much, but thought the young man probably didn't have the experience in such things. The manager came out and I could tell he wasn't happy. Fact is, he was downright snippy. Almost made me mad enough to change banks right then and there.*

'Well, that's how I discovered my bank account had been marked. Even though I was only thinking about borrowing a third of the sales price, that manager got all indignant. He demanded to know where I had gotten the cash for the rest of it. Let me tell you, he wasn't the only one getting tight under the collar. I got to say, I did my own share of finger pointing and talking loud. My account, I told him in no uncertain terms, was big enough; maybe I didn't need his money after all. Clarice, I felt bad about it after, but he wasn't treating me like a valued customer. Well, as you know, the bank finally did make the loan. I learned later, the bank people had treated me that way because there had been someone higher up who remembered that little box and thought I'd pocketed it. Yes, they hadn't believed me when I told them my airplane had washed away. And all the time, Clarice, the joke was on them. The box and the diamonds had to be still in the airplane, underwater, out there in the Gulf of Carpentaria. Far as I know, they're still there.'

After reading the letters, Mel sat back and thought about how having a box of diamonds would improve her life. No more writing garbage stories for a throw-away small town newspaper.

The idea of the diamonds still being somewhere underwater wouldn't leave her. Even the sight of bloody roosters dying while the crowd of men yelled and hollered didn't make her think about giving it up.

Chapter Twenty-Four

Just as she'd learned in journalism class, all good stories started with research. It didn't take much effort to find where Bandung, Dutch West Indies had been. Today, nearly seventy years later, Bandung is in West Java, a province of Indonesia. Her research turned up a lot of information about the attack on Broome by the Japanese. There were even reports about the shooting down of her grandfather's passenger plane. The three Jap Zeros had been based in **Rabaul, Papua New Guinea**. She even found the name of the pilot who had led the attack, Lieutenant Nakamura Miyano.

Knowing that much and remembering what her grandfather had written, it was easy to judge where Lt Miyano and his other two pilots had spotted Baranoff's DC-3. From the letters, her grandfather had almost pinpointed the location, near the mouth of the Norman River. But knowing, or thinking she knew, and getting there to look for the wreckage were two very different things.

One way might be to treat it as a feature article for a magazine. Let the publisher pay her costs. That was the idea she took to *Sun Life Magazine*. Only to be shot down. Just like her grandfather.

'Cock-fighting is illegal,' editor Musgrave had said, 'but it is big business. Just a few months ago, the cops raided a farm over in Mount Isa. Arrested eighty people, mostly men, confiscated $100,000 and four vehicles. The RSPCA gathered up three dozen roosters. Okay, it may be against the law, but cock-fights are held. Go show your chops. Find out where, who, when and how much. And take that new girl with you. She's supposed to be a photographer. Get me the story and get pictures.' Picking up the phone and not looking her way again, he started talking a mile a minute to someone on the other end. Mel hadn't heard it ring.

Well, if Musgrave was willing to pay her to go look into cock-fighting, at least he'd be paying her and the photographer's way north to Cairns. Even if it was by train. She'd never been that far north, but looking it up on Google Maps showed how the city was almost straight across the bottom of Cape York from the Norman River. The river was flowing out over the wetlands where her grandfather's plane had gone down. Oh boy. Things were looking up.

Mel wasn't too impressed by the photographer Musgrave had sent. A young woman, a girl actually, who looked a lot younger than Mel thought she'd ever looked.

'Samantha Edgerly,' she said, shaking Mel's hand softly. 'Mr Musgrave described you perfectly: a little older than me, red-haired and looking tired. He didn't tell me very much about what kind of story I'm to shoot. Guess you just point me in the right direction and I can do the rest.'

Something about the photographer made Mel take a closer look at her new partner. Samantha Edgerly was clean – too clean. Her squarish face was the kind, Mel thought, worn by women with two kids and a hard-working husband. But she came prepared; two very serious-looking cameras hung from straps around her neck. The long lens of one hung down to the bottom of the girl's tan-coloured canvas vest. The vest, the type with lots of little pockets – the kind only photographers or fly-fishermen wore – still had the creases left from being packed in a box. Under the vest, the girl's blouse had a soft pattern of pastel coloured squares, all tucked into a long dark grey wool skirt. The bottom of her skirt was only inches above the tops of her thick-soled hiking boots. Those leather-topped boots were so new they didn't have the appearance of ever having trod a dirt track. Samantha Edgerly was a rookie.

'How many stories have you gone out on?' Mel asked.

Samantha's smile slowly faded. 'Not many.' She hesitated then, with frown lines filing across her smooth forehead, added, 'actually none. But' – with excitement lifting her eyes – 'I won an award at Uni for a series of shots I took at the annual LGBT's Mardi Gras Parade.'

'So Musgrave hired you based on the Gay and Lesbian Mardi Gras Parade? Are you one of his staff photographers?'

Slowly shaking her head, Samantha's eyes once again dropped away. 'No, I'm not on the staff. When I applied, Mr Musgrave said he didn't have any openings for a photographer, but if I come back with good photos, then maybe he'll go on using me until something opens up.'

'So he's got you going along with me, more or less, as a kind of trial run,' Mel said. Boy, what a clever guy that Musgrave was, getting the story complete with photos for little cash money, a couple of train fares and a couple of promises of future employment. Maybe. But, wait a minute, did it really matter? Wasn't it an idea to get someone to pay her way up to the north end so she could go after her grandfather's diamonds?

'Okay then, Samantha Edgerly, let's get a good story with a lot of fighting chicken photos for our chicken-shit editor.'

Chapter Twenty-Five

After arriving in Cairns, it didn't take her long to learn that Rooster Jackson loved his chooks. Something of a local character, she'd been told after asking about chickens. Jackson owned a farm back in the Lamb Range, a couple kilometres on the other side of Speewah, a wide place in the road about twenty-five kilometres inland from Cairns. In one of the first pubs she'd come to, a heavily tattooed, long, stringy-bearded bikie laughed when Mel asked about cock-fighting.

'Sheila, don't go messing with them boys. Uh huh. Good ol' boys won't have nothing to do with that stuff. It ain't sporting, ya know?'

It had cost her two glasses of beer just to get that much. Mel had walked into the pub, paid for a pot of beer and carried it out to a table on the patio. She had to think.

When she had gone in, there had been three or four men at the bar. They watched her as closely as if she'd been some kind of poisonous snake. Or a walking, beer-drinking lovey dove. She was used to that. Everybody knew men up in the far north rarely had real manners when it came to women.

Taking her empty glass back for a refill, she saw only one man remained. The bikie. She couldn't remember seeing a motorcycle out on the street. Glancing through the window, she could see a couple of rust-bucket utes, but no sign of a motorcycle. Ah, well, he was wearing the tats, greasy ponytail, oily black clothes and heavy leather boots. So, what if he didn't have a bike. But if anyone knew of illegal activities, it'd be a bikie, wouldn't it?

She offered to buy him a beer if she could ask a few questions. That meant putting up with him checking her out again. This time really looked her over, closely examining her breasts. Gawd, what she had to go through to get a story.

'Okay,' he said finally, smiling weakly and for the first time looking directly into her eyes, 'ask away. Gotta tell ya, though. Answers depend on what ya wanna know.'

Mel nodded at that and wondered how she could put the beer on an expense account. As if she had one. Her mention of cock-fighting killed his thin smile. For a long minute, the rough-looking man simply stared at her. Then, with more of a smirk than a smile, he emptied his glass. Putting the empty on the bar, he glanced up at her and nodded. She waited a beat, then motioned to the bartender, who was ready with another glass. Mel was drinking with the small glass, called a pot. The beer she was buying for her new friend came in pint glasses, twice as big as hers.

'Thank you,' he said after taking a big swallow. Nodding again, he pursed his sun-cracked lips. 'Old Rooster Jackson loves his chooks. He sells eggs at the Saturday market and outa his driveway. Won't sell the meat, though. Says his chooks ain't for eating. Loves them, I tell you. Well, he says if you want a hen to lay eggs, ya gotta keep the girls happy.' The bikie smirked at that. 'Only natural, ya know. Anyway, for Old Rooster, that means having a rooster or two around the place. Uh huh. If there's anyone in this part of the state what knows about roosters, it'd be old rooster himself.'

Mel smiled her thanks and was headed for the door when the bikie chuckled. 'But you just watch yourself, you go asking questions like that. Cock-fighting is something them Asian men like and they don't let anything bother them in their sport. You go talking to ol' rooster; better take somebody-guarding boyfriend with ya.'

Chapter Twenty-Six

Rooster Jackson's farm wasn't hard to find. There actually wasn't even a village to drive through – just another pub with rooms for the weary traveller or heavy drinker. Mel didn't bother buying a beer and the lady behind the long, polished bar didn't let it bother her.

'Eggs? Yeah, you'd want Rooster's place. On out the pavement there,' she said, pointing, 'about four or five Ks. Look for a dirt track off to your right. Sign on the fence, "eggs". The man's got 'em, fresh enough to still be warm. Don't go asking about anything else, though. The old fart'll talk your arm off, he gets a chance.'

The bartender might have known what she was talking about, but the frail-looking old man who came out to her car when she drove in didn't waste any time. She was taken by the man's blue eyes, clear and bright, surrounded by harsh, sun-baked, leathery skin. This man lived most of his life outdoors under the tropical sun.

'Eggs?' his voice crackled, sounding a lot like the chooks muttering to themselves everywhere she looked.

'Yah, I got lots of eggs. And getting more every day. How many dozen you want? Five? Ten?' Mel held up two fingers. She'd find someone to give them too.

'Two? Bah, not worth walking out here for. Okay. Four dollars.'

When the old man turned back towards the porch, Mel opened the car door and stood by the front fender, casually looking around. The house was like the man – old, needing some colour and leaning a little to the south. Chooks, mostly brown but with a scattering of white ones, were everywhere. Not just dozens, more like hundreds. Too many to count. Just everywhere.

The eggs he handed her were in an old cardboard supermarket carton. The fingers of the hand she dropped the gold coins into were curled, wrinkled and the nails needed cutting.

'There's a helluva lot of chickens running around,' Mel said, giving him her best, most innocent smile. Just a little housewifey out to get the family some eggs. 'How can you find all the eggs they must be laying?'

'Ah, ya learn where they leave 'em. I don't look more'n once a day. Takes me a couple hours to walk around and pick 'em up. Anything else I can help ya with?'

She had to ask, 'I'm curious about the roosters. Most of these are hens, aren't they? I'm told you have roosters too.'

'Yah. Gotta keep the girls happy, ya know?' His smile was the typical male-making-a-sex-joke-of-it smile. 'They're mostly in pens out back. Don't let them run around so much. Not good for the hens, ya see, if ya want eggs.'

'I was talking to a fellow down in a pub in Cairns. He was the one who told me where you were. Said you were the person to talk to about cock-fighting. You use your roosters for that?'

His smile disappeared. 'Can't. Against the law. Don't want those people from the animal rights gang coming out, causing me grief.'

'But there are cock-fights held, even if they are illegal, aren't they?'

'Oh, I don't know. I guess. That's a big deal for some folks. Hell, in some places cock-fighting's part of the religion. Least that's what I was told. I don't know.'

'Well, the truth is, Mr Rooster, I'm a freelance writer. Always looking for a story. You know, stories about things happening out of the ordinary. I heard about cock-fighting and thought that'd make a good article.'

'Hah! Yeah, and get people in trouble too. No, thank you.'

'That wouldn't happen,' she said quickly. 'No names, no addresses, nothing that would lead anyone here. I've done some research on the, um, sport. And yes, in some places, fighting cocks is a religious event. But there's also a lot of betting in some cases.'

Rooster held up his hands, warding her off. 'Not here. I don't let anything like that go on here. And I don't know where they do.'

'Look, Mr Rooster, I'm not starting trouble. All I need to do is see a cock-fight. Just to get the feel of one. Then I can write my story and do it honestly and informatively.'

The old man frowned, shaking his head. 'This is what you do for a living?' Mel nodded, hoping he wouldn't ask about who published her stories. 'Then you get paid for such things?'

'Well, not a lot, but yes. It's how I pay my rent.'

'Ya got to understand, selling eggs doesn't hardly pay my rent. What'd it be worth to ya, for say, half an hour of watching a cock-fight? That is, if'n I knew where one was gonna be held. Understand, you'd have to keep outa the way, not get too close and not put nothing in any story about where the cock pit was. What'd that be worth to ya?'

Mel gave it a quick thought. A good story might mean a job. A full-time job. A job that might be needed if the search for grandpa's treasure didn't work out. Okay, how much is that worth to ya, Melissa? she asked herself. 'Fifty dollars. And I wouldn't use any names or anything that would identify anyone. I promise.'

Jackson looked around the yard as if counting his hens. 'All right. I'll trust ya. Fifty dollars and ya don't stay longer than a little bit. You come here Friday night. The fights start at about ten. Well, after dark. Don't drive into the yard. Hell, it'll be packed with cars and utes anyway. Park out there a ways and walk in. I'll wait for ya. But understand, these boys are serious about it. They can get really mean; they think someone's gonna screw up their fun. It ain't just the fighting cocks what get bloodied, ya know? I saw men whip out a cane knife when a fella don't deal straight on a bet. Ya better be prepared to run like hell, if ya don't play it right.'

Chapter Twenty-Seven

Harry hadn't wanted to work in a pub, pulling pints of beer and not snarling at the pricks on the other side of the bar, calling him a Yank like it was a big joke. But as with most times, his luck was holding.

'Look, man,' said the pot-bellied manager after looking Harry up and down. 'I've had people behind the bar try every trick in the book to cheat me. It didn't work. I'm just warning you ahead of time. Don't bother. The place pays me pretty good to do my job, and if you take the bartending job, you'll get a fair pay packet. But anything doesn't come up right, we'll both be out on our asses. And I wouldn't like that. It's as easy as that. Okay with you?'

Harry figured he could short-change any bar at anytime, anywhere, but only nodded.

'Right. Then you do the noon-to-six shift. That's opening to when things get real busy. The start of the dinner rush. I got a sweetheart of a back-packer, a Kiwi, helping me for the evening. Today I'll come in early and show you how to set up for later. Now, just pour beer and be nice to the paying customers' – the manager turned and started walking away, then stopped – 'oh, I forgot. Gabbi'll be in. He's a young Abo. Pretty steady worker. He'll help with sweeping up, wiping tables and setting the kegs up. You got any problem, working with Aborigines?'

Still not saying anything, Harry shook his head.

When he showed up, Gabbi didn't appear to see anything different. He came in, didn't pay any attention to the new white fella behind the bar and went about his work. As he did every day, he walked the length of the bar room and out the door that led into the hallway. Harry watched, expecting the young man, really not much more than a boy, to at least make eye contact. Didn't happen.

After the chubby, sweating manager had left, Harry had walked around, looking things over. The back door opened into the short, wide hallway part of the hotel. A broom closet across the worn carpeted entryway was filled with brooms, mops, pails, brushes and cases of toilet paper rolls. That was where Gabbi was headed. Returning to the bar room and still not paying any attention to anything or anyone, started sweeping the bar room floor.

Sand, that was the problem – sand being brought in on the feet of customers who had just come up from the beach. Most tourists, in the heat of the day, wore no more than they had to. That meant cheap plastic flip-flops on their feet. Flip-flops covered with beach sand. Harry, standing behind the high bar, watched as the young, brown-skinned man pushed the broom around, piling up the gritty dirt. Not once, from the time he walked into when he scooped up the piles of sand that he dumped out the main door, did he look in Harry's direction.

The young man was just barely drinking age, Harry judged, which was eighteen in Queensland. He waited to see if, once the sweeping was done, the kid would ask for a glass of beer. Surprise brought a smile to Harry's hard face when, after putting his tools away, Gabbi walked behind the bar, tapping each keg to judge their fullness, and again, not paying any notice to the bartender, then through the little door at the end of the bar that led to the storage room.

When customers came in from the sun-glaring street outside, Harry forgot all about the young kid. Moving to greet the two men, he came to a quick halt, frowning. 'What the hell're you two doing here?' he asked, his snarl stopping the pair as they reached for the high bar stools.

'Well, looky here, Ruckman, if it ain't Harry the Horse. Never expected to see you here, man. What the hell you doing in Cairns? And behind the bar?'

Harry glared. 'Maybe, just maybe I was sent up to find out what the hell you two are up to. Ever think of that, Dobby? The question is, do any of the big men know where you are? Or what trouble you're causing?'

'Hey, don't get all pissy, Harry, my man. It's no big drama. The word I got was that the big men aren't too happy with you. No, sir, not after losing that shipment of coke you were supposed to be protecting. Yep, from what we hear, you're lucky to still be breathing. The man himself, Webster, is right now sitting in the watchhouse there in Brisbane, not sure he'll live long enough to go to trial on that drug bust. The one you let happen.'

Harry's body tensed with anger. 'You're forgetting yourself, Dobby. The big men and I are tight. They know there was nothing I could do. Everything was working out until that damn Webster got scared and brought in a bunch of strangers to float his boat. It's finding you here that bothers me. I've got a bloody police inspector watching me. He gets news of a couple two-penny druggies and it'll only make things worse. What're the big men gonna say when I tell them you're up here?'

Dobby smiled. 'That's when you'll learn we're up here doing our job. Me'n Ruckman here are setting things up. Maybe you ain't in so tight as you thought. You don't know. Now,' he went on, obviously feeling safe, 'how about a couple pints of mid-strength?'

Chapter Twenty-Eight

Pushing against the storage door with the hand truck carrying two beer kegs, Gabbi stopped cold when he heard Dobby call for beer. He couldn't face those two again. They were the first white fellas he ever had trouble with and he didn't know what to do. Except stay away from them.

Gabbi Dingo didn't want to get rich. He certainly didn't want to get into any business with the big city men. Nope. No way. His father might have left out a lot of things in teaching his son about life, but when it came to bad druggies, the warnings were clear. Don't.

His pa, a long-haired hold-over from the 1970s, had taught him everything. His ma had died when Gabbi Dingo was born and he didn't have any memories of her. The only women in his life, until he was about fifteen anyway, were a couple old women. One, Joord, was his mother's sister. Least that was what his pa told him one day.

They had gone down river and out to where the tidal flats ended. It was out in the deeper water where the fishing was good.

'You been messing around with that Bulingarr girl, ain't ya.' It wasn't a question, so Gabbi Dingo didn't answer. 'I reckon you're at that age, starting to look at women. Least ways the young ones. Man, whatever you do, don't.'

That had always been his pa's order to anything: don't. Like the time he asked about his mother. 'Don't' was all his pa said, then got up from the table and went out to check the irrigation canals.

It was Joord who told him, not only about his mother but about his pa too.

'Your pa, he came down the river one morning. I don't think he even knew the town, Karumba, was even there. We were out doing women's work, collecting roots, berries and the like, when there he was walking along the path like he owned the world. That was a few years back. He didn't come into town on the road or on one of those airplanes like other people did. I don't know how he found that path there by the river. Your mother, Nellie, saw him first. Okay, so later, when he started farming over there at Jacky-Jacky Creek, it was Nellie who went out to help. Nobody cared much about them, or paid them much attention until your pa brought in his first crop. Huh, I'll tell you, those white fella's over at the airport sure liked what he had. But that ain't what you asked, is it?' Gabbi Dingo didn't want her to lose her story, so he didn't say anything.

'Well now, you came out squalling. We tried – us women who'd gone out to help her. But there wasn't anything we could do. She just kept bleeding. You were hungry, I'll tell you. Right from the first. There were a couple of girls nursing already, so feeding you wasn't a problem. Your ma was buried and the right ceremony was held. Be sure of that.'

'Where? Where was she buried?'

'Now that ain't for you to know. You ever seen a burying ground any place around Karumba? If there is, it ain't for us Aborigine people. Nope. That's a white fella's practice. Your ma was taken care of our way, and where she is doesn't matter to nobody no more.'

Gabbi Dingo didn't know what to say, so he didn't say anything.

'Your pa now, he's done a good job bringing you up. He's taught you all he knows about growing the smoke. Over the years, he's made a good living, selling his smoke to the men over at the airport. Oh, he could sell more, if he wanted. He always said he didn't want to get too big or have too many people know where he was.'

That was the problem now, Gabbi Dingo had gotten too big. He'd started a while after his pa had died. On the old man's death bed, he'd promised to go out to the nearest high school and graduate.

'You did good at the school here, boy, but you gotta think of what you're gonna do. Can't be like your pa and grow dope the rest of your life. You gotta get an education so you can find a job and it's gotta be out there in the white fella's world.'

Gabbi Dingo didn't see any reason for that. He and his pa had always had everything they needed, didn't they? So after the funeral ceremony was done, he settled in and did what he'd been doing all his young life:

tending the farm. It was his now. He didn't need anything else.

But Joord had heard that promise and one day asked when Gabbi Dingo was gonna leave the village. The nearest high school was over on the east coast, across the cape in Cairns.

Rather than argue, he loaded up a pack with his clothes and another with bags of smoke. Catching a ride over to Cairns, he waved goodbye to Joord. He figured he could come back over before the plants he'd just recently put in the ground were ready to harvest.

According to his pa, that was what he'd come to Karumba to do. The story his pa told him painted a picture of what he'd been like before coming across the cape to Karumba, where he ended up pitching his well-patched tent and setting out his seeds.

'Yeah,' the old man said outa the blue one day. They had been out digging in the ditches and stopped while his pa rolled a smoke. Gabbi didn't say anything; just waited to see what his pa was going to say. It wasn't often his pa talked about what happened before. Gabbi figured his pa was feeling pretty good, to be telling his story. 'I was looking for someplace people would leave me alone. What happened was, one day I was laying around the beach there at Cairns, talking to my mates, you know? We were smoking some fair weed. There wasn't much good smoke around, but what we had, along with someone's homemade brew, was good enough. Anyway, the talk was about things beautiful. I hadn't been up in the tropics long and when someone mentioned a Morning

Glory cloud, I started laughing. Where I grew up, down in Brisbane, my ma had Morning Glory vines growing all along the porch. I thought the idea of a cloud like that vine was funny. My mates set me straight. The Morning Glory cloud was a real, unique natural phenomenon, they said. Some even thought it was a sign from the spirit world.'

'Karumba,' his pa said, 'then as now had been an Aborigine fishing village. Located as it was a few kilometres up the Norman River, the village was small and quiet until a bunch of white fellas came to town.

'They went to the village elders and worked a deal, giving them a piece of land down near the river mouth. Hell, the elders didn't have no use for that land, it was too close to the tidal flats. But the white men quickly cut out a landing strip and before you knew it, there were a couple big buildings. The landing strip was going to be a refuelling and maintenance depot for some regional air service. They even paved the old dirt track down off the highway. It was the mining company that upgraded that, all the way across from Cairns. Covered it with bitumen. Built a couple bridges across some creeks and made it so trucks could make it no matter what the weather. Between the mining company and the airport, Karumba got pretty prosperous, so the elders thought they'd done good.

'Well, maybe so,' Gabbi's dad had explained, 'but they weren't paying any attention to the beauty around them. Not a bit. Anyway, all that happened before I heard about the Morning Glory cloud. I wanted to see what the

Morning Glory cloud was all about, so I hitched a ride and got as close as I could.' The older man took a deep pull on the thin-rolled smoke and smiled at the memory. Not wanting to interrupt his pa's thoughts, Gabbi Dingo sat and waited.

'Ah, now that's good,' his pa said after a bit. 'Let me tell you, that cloud is something. We've never been out on the gulf at the right time of year, or you'd have seen it. It's a long roll of a cloud, looking like a joint some god rolled up. The first one I saw was miles long and not very high. It was coming in off the water fast, rolling along a few hundred feet off the ocean. And there were half a dozen or so of them. One after another. Seeing that, I decided this was going to be home. I went back up the river and found me a spot, this one here, on Jacky-Jacky Creek. Boy, life couldn't be better. And it'll stay that way, as long as we don't want to get too big for our britches.'

Which is what Gabbi Dingo had done.

Chapter Twenty-Nine

That was when the two white fellas took Gabbi aside. 'Now look at it this way,' the big man had said. He had introduced himself to Gabbi Dingo, but the young man couldn't remember the bigger man's name. A white fella, he had big, wide shoulders, keeping his black T-shirt tight across his chest. Dobby, that was it. A strange-sounding name.

Gabbi Dingo had a good steady group of customers, mostly friends he'd made while attending Cairns State High School. Over the four years he'd been selling, his customer base had become stable. Each school holiday, he'd catch a ride across the winding road to Karumba, where he'd spend as much time as he had, cultivating his crop.

His pa had laid out the patch, digging irrigation canals and planting trees to shade the tender marijuana plants as they grew ever upwards, reaching for the sky and the sun. Gabbi Dingo had learned the lessons his pa had to teach and the bags of dried bud he took back to Cairns were according to his customers, the best they'd ever had.

'Now here you are,' the big man, Dobby, said.

'A young man just out of high school. Do I have that right?' Gabbi Dingo nodded, not wanting to speak to this man.

'Okay, so you're bringing a few kilos of good Maryjane to town every so often and selling it to a bunch of your friends.' Gabbi Dingo wondered who this white fella had been talking to. 'And that is good. Good for you, making a few dollars, and good for your friends. Now you see, that was before we came to town.' Smiling, the big man glanced to one side.

Leaning with his shoulder against the trunk of an old palm tree, a second big man wearing the same kind of black T-shirt as Dobby, stood, his hands clasped, hanging loosely in front. 'That's my partner, Ruckman. We are here in Cairns to open up a new operation.'

Gabbi Dingo had been sitting on a bollard near the city dock, enjoying the sunshine and thinking about what to have for lunch, when someone got between him and the sun. It was Dobby.

'From now on, you'll sell your dope to us. You don't sell your stuff to bartenders and your mates at school. We'll pay you for all you can deliver. It'll make you a rich man, trust me. Your friends, like everyone else, can deal directly with either me or Ruckman. Once we get all set up, that is. There's a lot of holiday people coming into Cairns. Tourism is the coming thing. Did you know there's a small airline planning on bringing Chinese tourists directly to the Cairns airport? Yep, no reason for them to fly into Brisbane or Sydney. That means two things. Chinese love to gamble, so it won't be long before there's a casino here. And we'll be ready to supply their other needs. Drugs. Girls. Boys. Any kind they want. Yeah, mate, we got our contacts and there'll be a lot of money to be made and you're getting in on the ground floor.'

Gabbi Dingo had heard enough. He stood up and looking the big man in the eye, shook his head. 'No, sir. Count me out. My pa told me not to get too big, and so I'm not going to do it. I'll keep growing my little patch and selling enough to stay happy. But I'm not interested in getting any bigger.'

Dobby's smile grew bigger. Gabbi Dingo could see, though, while the lips curved, the big man's eyes stayed cold and hard.

'You don't understand, mate. We ain't asking you to join us. We're telling you. Any dope coming into this area from now on, comes to us. Now you've got your plantation, or patch, as you call it. Fine. But you ain't selling any to anyone. You are with us or you're out of business. And before you say no, understand what I'm saying. You're with us, or well, you see how it is. We can't have you just hanging around.'

Gabbi Dingo frowned.

'Man, you just don't get it, do you?' Dobby said, 'Tell me, how many young men disappear up here each year? Who's to say you didn't just take a long, uh, yeah, a long walkabout?' He lifted his hand, throwing a thumb over his shoulder pointing out to sea to make his point.

Gabbi knew he was caught in a hard place. He didn't want to have anything to do with these city men. Hearing that voice, he quietly pulled the hand truck back and let the door swing silently closed. He'd wait until they left. The new white fella bartender seemed to know the city men, although it didn't sound like they were friends. Maybe he'd ask the new bartender what to do.

Chapter Thirty

Back in town after talking to the chicken farmer, Mel Graves stopped at the pub at the Crown Hotel for a late lunch and cold beer. That was one of the best things about living where the daytime temperature, even in the so-called winter, was in the upper twenties to low thirties. Hot, humid and unless a person was in the water or in a pub enjoying an icy cold beer, it was hard to live with. The air con' in the Crown Hotel Bar was turned up too high.

Late as it was in the afternoon, other than a young Abo who was scraping the top of a grill back in the kitchen area, Mel and the bartender had the place to themselves. Maybe, she thought, people who lived here got used to the heat. Yeah, like in twenty generations or so.

'Nice day, out there,' the barkeep said, smiling as he put the frosty glass of beer down on a coaster. Mel liked men and really liked it when any halfway hunk of a man paid that extra little attention. Like this one did, quickly looking her over as she walked in, then making good eye contact. Any staring at her breasts would be done on the sly. Even the fact he was bald – not a shaved head, but actually bald with a fringe above his ears and a short ponytail, even with that, she felt good. Maybe it was getting out of the heat that made the difference.

'Uh huh. Nice cold beer, though.'

'Yeah. And now's the best time to just sit and relax. After the lunch rush and before the before-dinner crowd shows up. You visiting? Somehow you don't look like a tourist.'

Mel chuckled. 'Yeah, a visitor. Not a tourist, though. I've got some work to do. But with your accent, I wonder, you're a little old to be a backpacker.'

The man smiled. 'Uh huh, nope. Just a guy spending a few days out of the tropical heat working behind the bar. And what kind of work would you be doing? From what I've seen, the cops in this town are pretty mean when it comes to young women working the tourists.'

'Well, I'm not working any tourists. I'm a reporter and I've got a lead on a story' – she sipped her beer, not wanting to hurry – 'your accent, you Canadian?'

The man laughed. 'What's that all about? People hear me and ask if I'm Canadian or American. Can't people tell the difference?'

Mel smiled and nodded. 'It's just people not wanting to hurt your feelings. Look,' she smiled as she explained, 'if you are Canadian and I asked if you were American, it might hurt your feelings, to be mistaken like that. But asking the other way around – well, everyone knows, you can't hurt an American's feelings. That's all. Just people trying to be nice.'

The bartender laughed.

'Say,' she asked, 'you're a pretty big guy. Looks like you can take care of yourself. How'd you like to make a few dollars?'

'Now what kind of scam are you running?' he asked, his smile becoming a still fixture on his face.

'No scam. Look, I've got an opportunity to get close to a story I want to do. I'm a journo. It's a good story, but means I'll have to be in a certain place late Friday night. And that's not the time or place for a woman alone. I'd like to have a strong-looking man watching my back. Mine and that of another woman, my photographer. It'd be worth, say, fifty dollars for just taking a ride late Friday evening. What do you say?'

The man's smile was the kind; you just knew his thoughts were not the kind a girl would feel comfortable with. 'Nope,' she said quickly. 'On second thought, never mind.'

The bartender held up both hands and his smile changed. 'Ah, don't mind me. A luscious redhead asks if I want to make some money, what do ya think I'm gonna think? Okay, so tell me. What do I do for a couple hours to earn fifty bucks?'

'Fifty dollars to drive us to a farm and back. While there, I'll expect you to look tough and mean. Give it that "don't muck around" kind of look. Fifty dollars and we'll be back in town before midnight.'

'Look tough. Am I going to have to back up that look? If we're talking about getting into a fight, then the price goes up.'

'Fifty dollars and no fighting.'

He looked at her for a long moment before nodding. 'My name's Harry. Fifty dollars. We taking your car?'

'Yep. I'm Melissa and I've got a rental. I'll pick you up.'

Chapter Thirty-One

After telling Samantha what she'd set up, they still had some time to kill. Always the photographer, Samantha took her cameras and equipment bag and disappeared. Just as with Melissa, being this far north was new to her. New meant good possibilities for photos, photos she might be able to sell. Looking around town, she decided the harbour area might be interesting. Boats, just as with babies, always made good pictures.

Born, raised and educated in Queensland, if you'd asked her, she'd tell you how it was Captain Cook who discovered Australia. Walking along a long finger dock in the Cairn's harbour, she discovered that historical fact wasn't entirely true. The vessel that had caught her eye was an old-timey wooden three-masted sailing ship. The only boat like it she'd ever seen was a replica of Capt. Cook's famous ship, the *Endeavour*. This one, according to the information sign, was the *"Duyfken"*. Taking a series of photos, both from the dock and then, after climbing the ramp, from various angles on board, she quickly shot up a roll of film. It was the little signs found attached to the ship's railing.

Cook, according to what every school student was taught, visited Australia in the mid-1770s. He named bays, rivers, mountains and other features all along the way. Then he went on to do scientific things before ending up in Hawaii, where the natives killed him. And maybe, being cannibals, ate him. But according to this, the *Duyfken* sailed along the Australian mainland in 1606.

Disappointed, Samantha walked back down the dock, thinking about what she'd learned. Looking back at the wooden boat, she frowned. Very picturesque, but quite possibly not worth shooting. Something like that, she chided herself, would already be overly photographed. Probably not images any publication would pay for.

Leaving the waterfront, she strolled towards a park. The Esplanade Swimming Park, according to one sign. Walking across the lawn and seeing people swimming in the huge pool, or lying in the sun alongside, she shook her head again. Too popular and certain to have been photographed dozens or even hundreds of times.

Damn, being a photographer with dreams of making a living with pictures wasn't going to be easy.

Melissa was also strolling around town. She wasn't searching for something new, though. Her mind was replaying what she'd learned from her grandfather's letters about the diamonds. Mentally making a list of what she'd have to do now that she was this close.

What were the chances, she asked herself, of finding an airplane after it'd been lost in deep water for seventy-some-odd years? Probably not good. Even if she knew about where it'd gone in, what good would that do? Stopping for the light at an intersection, she glanced across the street and saw something that made her smile. The Cairn's Scuba Dive School. Any search for a cloth-covered box left behind in the cockpit of an airplane lost in deep water would call for diving, wouldn't it?

Crossing with the light, she decided to find out more about learning to become a scuba diver.

Chapter Thirty-Two

When Inspector Lambert had mentioned an opening at one dive school, JC hadn't jumped at it. He had no desire to take on a job. That's what he told the inspector. Until he was given his passport and could leave the country, he was satisfied with being a tourist.

'Look,' he said, trying to get the federal drug cop to understand, 'you wanted your buddy's boat brought up here and now it's here. There was, as I recall, a promise of the return of our passports. I don't really care if Harry is happy tending the bar in that pub or not, but I'm not interested in employment. So, how about my passport?'

Inspector Lambert nodded in agreement. 'You're right,' he said calmly, 'you've held up your end of the deal and Officer Clarkson is happy. He and his wife are planning on taking a sailing holiday up here towards the end of the year. Probably over the Christmas holidays. Myself, I think December is the wrong time of year to be this far north. You might not realise it, but Cairns isn't that far south of the equator. We're in the tropics and that means September through the first few months of the year is summer. Just backward to what you're used to up in America. December will be a hot month. Too hot, I reckon, to holiday.'

JC wasn't having any of it. 'Yeah, and if you ask me, it's too damn hot here now and this is only, what do you call it, spring?'

'Well, yes, I suppose. End of June, first of July. But you see, our spring doesn't hit until June, but that doesn't matter. Not when it comes to the heat and humidity. Up here, those two factors are always something to suffer through. Usually, this is the wet season for the northern parts. The end of the cyclone season and the middle of the rainy season. Guess we're just lucky now, not to be bothered by flooding.'

JC wasn't having any of it. 'All that's fine and dandy, but it doesn't change anything. Hot, humid, rain, flooding – your weather report doesn't cut anything with me. All I want is my passport so I can hop on the next flight outa here. Now, how about it?'

'Yes, the matter of your passport. As I recall your visa, yours and Harry's were good for ninety days. That would take you to, let's see, about the end of August, wouldn't it? You see, there's still the issue of all that cocaine coming in on the boat you were in charge of.'

'Hey, wait a minute' – JC held up his hands, warding off this new attack – 'I had nothing to do with that. Didn't even know the drugs were on board. It was the guy who hired me, Webster. Didn't you arrest him?'

Lambert stayed relaxed as he nodded. 'Oh yes. As we speak, Mr Webster's sitting in the Brisbane watch house, waiting to go on trial. But you see, he isn't giving us anything. That's why I'm not so keen on handing you your passport. I'm of the opinion that if I hold on to them

– yours and Mr Bridges' – then the opportunity is greater for other crims involved in the shipment to come forward. Drug smuggling is a major problem for us, you know. Having this opportunity to discover the names of other players is too good to pass up.'

'What names? The only names I know of, or even knew of after leaving Fiji, were those of the crew and your Mr Webster. Hell, you can go clear back to when I left San Diego. Or Maui. You know the names of everyone I've met or even talked to. What are you expecting – that one morning I'll wake up shouting something about a dream where I recognized the head drug importer?'

Inspector Lambert smiled. 'No, I don't expect that at all. However, you have to admit there is a lot better chance of someone being named with you and your friend, Harry Bridges, being close by than if you two were allowed to leave the country.'

JC shook his head, frowning in disgust, then, it came to him. 'Ah, wait a minute. Yeah, I get it. It's not me you're waiting to stumble, it's Harry. He's the one you're waiting to screw up. Okay. You could be right. What do I know about the man? Nothing. I wouldn't have hired him in the first place. It was Webster who all but ordered that to happen. And then you worked it out to have him make the trip up here. Uh huh. You know something about Harry Bridges and want to keep him under your thumb.' He nodded before going on. 'Okay, so keep his passport and give me mine. Old Harry and I don't exactly get along when we're not on the water. If you're waiting for him to tell me anything, don't hold your breath. It'll be a cold day in hell before he gives me more than a bottle of beer. If I have the money for one, that is.'

The inspector smiled and held his hands out, palms up. 'You caught me. I knew you were too smart not to figure it out. Yes, it is your shipmate, Harry Bridges, that I want to keep here. Just for a few more days. There is something going on that I think he is part of. He's run into a couple of hard men – men we've long known as being part of a huge drug-running cabal. Well, with those two in Cairns. Harry Bridges knows something is happening. He may even be part of whatever it is. But don't kid yourself, he's no fool. There's a reason he's behind that bar. Looks to me, he's found himself a reason for staying in Cairns. What makes me suspicious is that he hasn't once asked for his passport. Not once even mentioned it. Nope, just took on the job at the Crown Pub. Now there's a place. Have you been in there yet?' he asked, then seeing JC wasn't answering, went on.

'Look, it's simple. I don't want to scare him off. If I let you fly out, he'll know he's under investigation. Right now he isn't sure. It could be you I'm watching. After all, you were in charge of that sailboat and he might think I'm under the impression you had something to do with the shipment. You see? Now, I've worked out a deal with that dive school. Go on over and talk to them. Take the job they'll offer you. It's only for a short while. I'm positive your mate, Harry, will do something that I can use to lead me to bigger players.'

JC shook his head. What could he do? Without the passport, he couldn't fly out. And to tell the truth, he kind of liked living in Australia. Better down in Brisbane, but weather aside, this little town wasn't all that bad.

If only that damn Bridges would hurry up and do whatever the drug cop was waiting for him to do.

Chapter Thirty-Three

Inspector Lambert wasn't as confident as he wanted JC to think he was. If he was ever going to get back to the Sydney office, he was going to have to do something that would make the hierarchy forget the black marks on his record.

He was a good police officer; he knew he was. So he got a little ahead of himself, wanting to take a rat bag pack of galahs off the street, but had overlooked a few things. Cleaning out the local chapter of a motorcycle club should have earned him a promotion. But no. A high-priced silk had punched holes in the arrest. Half a dozen tattoo-covered, dirty criminals had walked, leaving the AFP looking like a bunch of boofheads.

In Lambert's view, there were three things wrong with the present system. First were the money-grubbing solicitors. It seemed this class of the legal world knew how to use every sneaky bit of weak-kneed law. Anything that would get their scummy clients off. Worse were the weak-tea judges and magistrates. Catch a crim with his hand in the till and what happens? The judge feels sorry for him and lets him walk with a warning.

The last group was, in Lambert's eyes, the worst of the lot. The pollies filling the commissioner's office. Politicians and bean-counters, not honest police officers.

The ones who decided Inspector Lambert was too impetuous. As one comment ending up in his personnel file stated, Lambert obviously felt it was not necessary to follow official procedures and processes. It was that file he had to correct.

It was high office politics that got him transferred up to Brisbane. The top dogs making sure their skirts were clean, passing the blame down to the lower levels, to where complaints could be ignored. That was what he was fighting and there was only one way to win the battle. He had to show he was better than the pols at the commissioner's office thought he was. Unconsciously, he nodded, agreeing with himself in this silent discussion. It was that reason behind his request for holiday time. Time to be away from Brisbane; time for him to come up to the top end.

Even being the new bloke in the Brisbane district, it hadn't taken him long to realise something was up. First was when his best snitch down in Sydney had called to tell him about hearing that Dobby was seen catching a Qantas flight out of Sydney. Dobby had been one of the lucky ones. Laughing at all the attempts to set him up, he didn't bother hiding the fact he was one of the Sydney cartel's stand-over men. Everybody in and out of the drug world knew that.

Lambert and his crew had known all about Dobby. The man's full name was Pascel Doblones. Probably, a common name wherever he'd come from, but there in Sydney, he became Dobby. He had shown up in Sydney a few years back when Carlos Daimler came to meet with some of the big men. Sydney's crime lords. Again, mostly men well known by the authorities but who were never able to be brought to trial. Since coming out of the AFP Academy, Lambert had made catching these people his private goal.

Carlos Daimler wasn't a known name and had never held a place on the AFP crime scene list but it didn't take long to discover he was on Interpol's watch list. According to the international police, although it had never been proved, it was believed the man was the head of a South American drug cartel. At the time of the meeting, Dobby, not long out of his teens, was one of Daimler's bodyguards. For some reason, when Daimler left to go home, Dobby remained behind.

Now a watched man, it was believed by the AFP Drug Squad that Daimler was in Australia to set up a delivery system. Left behind when Daimler caught a flight back, Dobby was suspected of being the drug lord's eyes in Australia. Now, a few years or so later and a paper Australian, Dobby was still high on the list of men Lambert wanted to put behind bars. True, the man had been arrested a number of times but had never served one day in prison. All thanks to the slicks hired by the city's big men. A company, one of Sydney's most prosperous legal firms, made successful by representing members of both of the largest bikie gangs, the Bandidos and the Finks. When on his hog, Dobby wore the colours of the Finks.

And now here he was in Cairns. A long way from the Sydney docks. There had to be something big happening and Lambert was going to be ready for it. For sure, even if the inspector had arranged it himself, he had to believe Harry Bridges being here was part of whatever the something was. Harry was too far up the food chain, even now, after the fiasco of the cocaine bust. With Dobby and his shadow in town, it all added up to something. That something was the inspector's opportunity to clear his reputation and get ordered back to Sydney. And Harry was the link. Which meant making sure the other Yank, JC, stayed close by. Just for a while.

Chapter Thirty-Four

JC had never seen it rain so hard. Rain fell in huge drops, wave after wave of them blasting like machine gun bullets against his back. The weather, he was discovering, could change in a heartbeat. From sweltering heat and humidity to rainfall so hard, it felt like being plummeted by gravel. And still, the temperature had to be in the high 90s. Sweating while being drowned. If this was what living in the tropics was like, they could have it. He'd take San Diego any day. All it would take was to get his passport from that damn drug cop.

Just as Lambert had promised, the owner of the Cairn's Scuba Dive School had welcomed JC like a long-lost brother.

'You have any idea how much business you and your mate brought to my school?' Rob Jacobson said, shaking JC's hand. 'Man, people are the weirdest. You find a couple tourists out there on the reef, left behind and desperate and what happens? All the other tourists want a piece of it. But first, they have to qualify. Before you brought those people in, diving on the reef was just something visitors might do. Like taking a sailing cruise. But now, whooee. Can you have a job? You better believe it. I've got four trainers and they can't keep up. Not since you guys showed up. When can you start?'

From the moment he'd brought the sailing catamaran up to the dock it had started. The television people were waiting on the dock like vultures, cameras aimed at the *Happy Wanderer* as JC eased her in. Before anyone on board could do more than catch their breath, the questions came roaring out at them.

'What was it like? Here, look this way. Did you think you were gonna die out there?' The media people were yelling their demands and questions.

'How long were you in the water before getting picked up? Look here. Smile. No, not like that. Look relieved. Look scared. Were you scared?'

'What did you talk about? Did you pray?'

The questions stopped when a man stepped out in front and held up his hands. Half a dozen uniformed police officers lined up, pushing the journalists back. The man holding his hands up, not needing a loud speaker, explained there would be time for all that later.

'C'mon people, give these folks a break. You know me. Greg Lockhart, the Cairns Harbourmaster. There'll be time for all your questions and to get the video, but not right now. We've got some official procedures to get out of the way first. So lighten up, will ya? These people have just been through a horrendous experience and having you yelling at them won't make it any easier.'

That was when JC saw Lambert. The drug cop wearing khaki pants and a brightly coloured Hawaiian shirt stood beside the harbourmaster, but with his back to the crowd, facing JC and the boat. His smile was thin and humourless. Catching JC's eye, he nodded and pointed off to one side.

Getting the sailboat secured and helping the Marshes step over onto the dock, JC and Harry busied themselves, putting everything right. All the sails had been dealt with while motoring in and Harry had packaged up their personal gear.

'Hey, Harry,' JC said, keeping his voice low and looking around the lounge area as if making sure they had everything. 'Don't look up, but that damn Inspector Lambert is up on the dock waiting for us. Let's turn the boat over to him, get our passports and get the hell out of Dodge.'

By the time they were ready to step off, nearly everybody had left the area. JC saw that the Brisbane drug cop was patiently waiting. 'This is the second time we've been met by that guy,' JC said, 'sure, hope this time doesn't end up with us in handcuffs.'

'Naw, this time we're the heroes,' Harry said, setting his canvas carryall on the dock. 'Maybe he's got our passports in his shirt pocket and we can get out of this place.'

It didn't work out that way.

Chapter Thirty-Five

In spite of himself, JC found he enjoyed his new job. The first couple of days were spent getting used to the school's procedures. Those days seemed long and dull. When, for the first time he found himself facing his little group of tourists, his spirits lifted. These people wanted to learn, they were excited about it. That made teaching them what they needed to know about diving fun.

By the time he'd given a brief lecture on safe diving procedures, he could start them out developing scuba skills. And that began the first day in the pool.

If Lambert had come by and asked, he'd have to agree, somehow it felt better wearing a wet suit and being in the pool than even at the helm of a sailboat. More freedom. First, though, before his group got wet, they had to learn about their equipment.

'A good diving course,' he started out explaining, following the school's script, 'will teach you to anticipate possible problems and avoid them. Some things will become second nature to you underwater. Things like the rule to always keep breathing, don't hold your breath, and to adjust your buoyancy. It won't take long and these will become straightforward techniques. At the end of the course, you will receive a scuba diving certificate.'

'What about sharks?' one of the younger tourists asked.

'Yeah,' piped up another. 'And jellyfish. I was down at the beach yesterday and noticed a warning sign saying something about the danger of jellyfish. What's that all about?'

JC smiled. 'There are a lot of things to be wary of and, yes, sharks are on that list. Now, I'm as new to the waters here as you are, so all I can do is read what the school has to say about jellyfish. There are, and I'm quoting, a great variety of jellyfish living in the Great Barrier Reef. Well' – he stopped reading and smiled at the group – 'I can't tell you more than that. I have heard people call them stingers. Apparently, the stings from jellyfish are painful. I'd say the best protection is your wet suit. Now, let's talk a bit about the equipment you'll be using.'

The rest of the day went fast and all were ready for a break by the time they had been in the pool for an hour.

The rain had ended sometime during the day. By the time JC and most of his group of students came out into the sunshine, all signs of the earlier downpour had vanished.

'Hard to believe it,' he said, looking around and expecting to find the street gutters filled with run-off. Not a wet spot was seen anywhere. The humidity was heavy, though, and when someone suggested a cold beer, few didn't agree.

Most, he learned, were staying at the hotel next to the dive school. Probably part of a package deal. With the training taking up two long days, it only made sense. Sitting around a table in the hotel pub, the talk was about what they'd learned, about diving.

And questions about finding the Marsh couple. 'Boy, that's scary,' one of the students said, a young man JC had pictured as a super confident salesman. Funny how a person's profession could typecast him. Or her. Take a bank manager out of his three-piece suit and rep tie, put him in a wetsuit and he would still be counting the value of everything. A hot-shot salesman would still be a hot-shot salesman even when naked as a jaybird. 'I'll bet it surprised you,' the salesman student said, 'to find them out there all alone.'

'Hmm' – JC nodded – 'well, not something you'd expect, that's for sure. But I've got a feeling the charter dive boat operators are making doubly sure it doesn't happen again.'

'When you finish with us, will we know what to do if we're left behind by some idiot dive boat driver?' someone asked, earning him a round of chuckles.

JC had to smile as he shook his head. 'Nope. I don't think anyone can teach that. But again, I don't think the charter people will take any chances.'

Another student, the red-headed woman, took a sip of beer and laughed. 'Guess the only one who could teach you what to do,' she said, 'would be your priest. I imagine all anyone could do would be to pray.'

He'd noticed her before, when he first faced the group. Most of the would-be scuba divers were tourists, a bit of sunburned and tired-looking. Typically, people coming north from one of the big cities were pale and laughed a lot. Relaxing in the change of environment would do that, JC figured. Sitting behind a desk, wearing 'dress-for-success' suits for months at a time, then arriving in Cairns would be like coming to a different planet. Instead of suits and ties, pulling on a pair of board shorts and a colourful T-shirt and a guy's attitude changed. Take away his hard leather shoes and let him walk down the street in a pair of rubber thongs and you had a different person. Adding a dose of heavy sunshine only made it more obvious.

The redhead wasn't like that, though. Every red-headed person he'd ever seen had tons of freckles plastered over egg-shell thin skin. The kind of skin better kept out of direct sunlight. Especially the kind of sun blanketing this part of the world. Except when it was raining. But this girl, uh, woman, her face wasn't like that. More lightly tanned. Wearing a form-fitting black rubber wetsuit, just as everyone in the class, he couldn't see how much of the rest of her body was tanned. He noticed she had a well-shaped body, though. No, the tanned face and something else – he wasn't sure what – made him think she wasn't a tourist.

Checking the list on his clipboard, he tried to determine which female name went with her. Only one was single, Melissa Graves. All the others were part of a Mr and… part of a couple. He wasn't a bit put out to find she wasn't part of Mr and Mrs. But now, she was asking about wreck diving.

'All the brochures talk about diving the reef,' she was saying, 'and all the colourful fish seen out there. How different is it to dive in a sunken boat. Aren't there a bunch of wrecks left over from the Big War? Will we get to dive any of those?'

JC shook his head. 'Now that's something I don't know about. Remember, I just arrived in town a day or two ago myself. Diving the reef is as new to me as it is to you. Or diving wrecks. What I know about is scuba diving. You'll have to ask someone else about diving any wrecks.' Seeing her frown, he went on. 'I can tell you that diving wrecks, any wrecks, whether from WWII or as you Aussies call it, the Big War, can be very dangerous. Personally, I've never had the urge. My diving experience has focused mainly around harbours and the boats floating in them. But I imagine Rob Jacobson back at the dive school would know if there is any wreck diving available.'

'I saw a doco about that,' one of the woman students said, 'somewhere up in Indonesia, I believe, some island where there'd been a major battle with lots of ships sunk there's a lot of diving on the wreckage. I don't know where, but I do recall how spooky it looked, seeing ships all covered with plant growth.'

'I learned in class,' said another member of JC's dive class, the youngest diver-to-be. A person had to be at least twelve and this young man didn't look much older than that. 'It was about the attack on Darwin,' he said, 'back during the war with Japan. The Japanese bombed that city and killed a lot of people, but I don't remember anything about ships being sunk in the Darwin harbour.'

Mel, wishing she'd never asked the question, tried to think of a way to change the subject. She certainly didn't want the talk to focus on the war. 'So,' she asked quickly, 'what are we in for tomorrow? More in the pool training?'

'No,' JC said. 'We'll start in the pool, but after the lunch break, we'll move out into the harbour. That'll give you a chance to see what things look like down there.'

'And that'll earn us the certificate we need to go out on the reef?'

JC nodded. 'Yep. Tomorrow we'll spend some time streamlining your swimming skills, learning buddy diving techniques and being in the harbour, get a feel for the kinds of fish life you'll find out on the reef.'

'And if we don't want to go on a charter dive boat,' Mel asked, 'the certificate is good in other places?'

'Yes, you'll be certified and qualified for diving up to twelve metres deep. Anyone wanting to go on and become a fully certified dive instructor or dive master can do so. The school has trainers for that, but all I'm doing is getting you to the twelve-metre level. What you'll need to go out reef diving. And that certificate is good for a year. So if you time it right, you could use it to dive other reefs and lagoons.'

Or, she said to herself, in other Australian waters. Places where there are at least one WWII wreck.

Chapter Thirty-Six

Friday evening, no one had much to say after leaving town. Samantha, cradling her ever-present pair of cameras, sat quietly in the back seat of the rental. She and the red-haired reporter had picked up the man. Until then, she was comfortable, simply going out on an assignment. After being introduced to the big man, she was starting to wonder about what she'd gotten herself into. What kind of a story was it that a muscle-bound man was hired to act as a bodyguard? She didn't say anything but had given the Graves woman a dirty look. For certain when she got back to the magazine, she'd have a lot to tell their boss, that editor guy. Meanwhile, she'd keep her mouth shut and do her job. Get the best shots possible and prove she was someone the magazine needed on permanent staff.

Mel was also quiet, thinking about the diving lesson. Wearing the tight rubber wetsuit had felt strange, restrictive. But once in the pool, her mouth filled with the rubber mouthpiece, and remembering to breathe naturally, she discovered a new kind of pleasure. Scuba diving opened up an entirely new world. Even if it was only the bottom of the swimming pool, the experience was almost thrilling.

Shaking her head, she frowned. Now wasn't the time for that. There was the story she'd have to write. It shouldn't be too hard, she'd drafted a lot of articles on the basis of a lot less than she'd be getting tonight. This one she wouldn't have to make up things for. Maybe, glancing over at Harry sitting silently in the passenger's side, she'd even mention having a bodyguard. That fact alone would add some colour to the event. The one thing she wouldn't write about would be the diving class she'd taken. No reason for anyone to know about that. The magazine wasn't paying for it, and its editor, Musgrave, hadn't had any interest in the plane being shot down, so he didn't need to know. Covering her pert little butt. Just in case the search for her grandfather's lost diamonds didn't pan out, she would still have something to fall back on. Christ, the idea of a lifetime as a writer for small market newspapers and magazines with limited readership made her cringe.

Driving inland on the narrow, paved state highway at night wasn't as pleasant as it had been when she'd come out during the day. In daylight, the forest of tall trees and masses of low brush made an almost solid wall along both sides. Streaks of sunlight, coming through the tops of the trees made the shade spread out from those trees even darker. In the light given off by the car's headlights, all she could see was the roadway. Pure blackness covered everything else. Spooky.

What lights to be seen were from houses somewhere off to the side. What kind of life would that be, Mel asked herself, living out here in the rural aloneness? She didn't want to think of the kinds of animals there would be out there in the night, foraging for their food. She'd read about the growing number of domesticated dog packs that were terrorising the countryside. And pigs. Feral pigs. Nothing, she'd heard somewhere, was as dangerous as a herd of pigs that had gone feral.

The pub she'd stopped to ask directions at when she came out the first time was dark as she drove past. Slowing down, she leaned forward, looking for the dirt road that led out to Rooster Jackson's place.

'Another five kilometres or so,' she said, the first words spoken in the car since leaving Cairns. Neither of the others commented.

Mel's throat felt dry, making her wish she'd brought a bottle of water. When she made the drive over to the Gulf of Carpentaria, she'd have to remember to take a couple bottles. Hard to say what kind of water she'd find when she finally reached the mouth of the Norman River. Learning the name of the village hadn't been hard, it was the only one listed on any of the maps. From Google Maps, she'd been able to see how the village itself was a couple kilometres upstream from the river mouth. Closer to that, farther along the river towards the Gulf from the little village, was what looked like a single strip airfield. Google didn't offer to name the airfield or mention who used it. When she spotted it, she'd thought about flying over. But now, having given the whole thing a lot of thought, she decided learning how to dive and driving over was the best way. That way, she could take her time in making the search and not be bothered by anyone knowing what she was doing or where she was doing it. Yeah, that would be best.

Driving up to Rooster Jackson's chook farm, she saw it was dark, not a light showing. Her first thought was that the old man had lied to her. Then, a bit past his place, she spotted the line of vehicles parked alongside the road and understood. The old man wouldn't want anything as illegal as a cock-fight in his front yard. Move it down the road a bit and he's out of it. A sly old fox.

Stopping short of the parked cars, Mel grabbed her bag containing notebooks and extra pens, opened her door and got out. She hesitated, then decided it would be best to lock the car. When the lights flashed, she noticed Harry standing with his hands at his side, waiting for her. Samantha, standing next to him, was holding one of her cameras in one hand, ready to start shooting. Both were watching her.

It was quite obvious there was something going on, both sides of the dirt road were lined with dusty cars and utes, the dust and dirt hiding dents and rust.

'Okay,' Harry said, his voice low and quiet, 'now tell me again what we're doing?'

Mel nodded. 'It's a cock-fight. We're going to spend as little time here as possible. Sam here will take as many photos as she can while I'm just looking and listening. This kind of article almost writes itself. All I have to do is make it authentic. See what kind of people will be there, get an idea of how things are done. Both of you keep close to me and be ready to leave. I'll let you know.'

'Cock-fights legal here?' Harry asked.

'No, but they go on. If someone's interested, it isn't hard to find one.'

Harry nodded, finally taking his eyes off Mel and looking around. As if he could see anything in the darkness. The only lights were coming from down the road and were faint. 'Yeah, just like back in the States. They're illegal there too, but any time there's people who want to bet, someone'll figure out a way to do it. Things like that happen. This cock-fight, there'll be a lot of betting?'

'Oh, yeah. Lots of money changing hands. I'm told most of the people who go to those things are from Indonesia and China. People like that.'

Harry chuckled. 'Yep, any time you got a Chinaman, you got a gambler. I don't think there's anyone in the whole world who can beat the Chinese when it comes to gambling.' He paused for a moment. 'You know, I heard somewhere there are plans to build a big casino in Cairns.' He pronounced it with the "r" sound, Carrns.

Mel frowned. 'I haven't seen that many Chinese people in Cairns.' Cans.

'Not right now. But from what I'm told, once the casino is built there'll be direct flights into town, bringing in Chinese tourists. Uh huh. Don't worry. Like I said, if there's someone who wants to do some betting, there'll be someone'll there to make it easy for them.'

Mel didn't say anything. If some developer was planning on building a casino, that meant someone with a lot of money was behind it. Flying in tourists would mean a lot more money coming in and a lot more jobs. Now that would be a story to break. Shaking her head, she smiled to herself. If I wanted to go on working for some daggy magazine, she said silently, I'd be just the person to do it. But, huh, uh, not this sheila. I got other plans.

Chapter Thirty-Seven

After parking alongside the single-width track, a ways down the road from any of the other parked vehicles, Mel watched Harry as they left the cars and walked towards the lights. She mentally nodded. He'd do. This guy was as big, maybe, as say about 90 or 100 kilograms? It was probably his swaggering walk and his tats and ponytail, made people think he might be a bikie. She hoped whoever they ran into at the cock-fight would see the hard side of him and not cause any trouble. All she wanted was for the girl photographer to get good photos, to which she'd add the text filled with colour and she'd have earned her money. Money that would maybe get her to a wrecked airplane that her grandfather had left behind.

With the big man beside her and Samatha, Mel felt safe as she walked down the road. Turning between two dust-covered utes, both probably white when new but now faded to a dull light grey under the dirt, she stepped over a shallow ditch. Lights strung on wires that had been run from tree to tree illuminated a large opening in the scrub forest. Men were standing tightly packed, three or four deep in a wide circle, facing towards the centre.

It was hard for her to estimate how many men were there. The bodies were continuously moving as they excitedly watched what was happening in front of them. Moving, their arms, their heads bobbing, fists clenched holding wads of money, yelling as whatever was taking place happened.

The movement and yelling died almost instantly as Mel watched. As men shuffled around, some handing over money and others taking the bills, two men carrying wire cages stepped into the ring. At once, the ring of noisy betters formed again, the men yelling and waving their hands, making and taking bets. The noise under the bright lights and the dust bellowing up from the inside of the circle made the woman flinch.

The crowd of men weren't tall, but Mel, being even shorter, couldn't see the ground inside the ring.

'Hey, Harry,' she asked quietly, 'can you see what's happening?' She didn't notice when Samantha, her camera held up in her left hand, finger of the other hand ready to push the button, stepped over to one side.

'Uh huh,' the big man said. 'Those guys just brought in a couple chickens. Roosters. They're holding them, facing each other. Geez…' The yelling increased, masking Harry's words.

'What's happening? C'mon, Harry, tell me.'

Harry frowned. What the hell did she want him to do – give her a blow-by-blow description? That wasn't what he'd been hired on to do. *Okay*, he thought, *let's see*. 'The dirt of the pit looked to be sand, deep sand by the looks of it,' he said. 'Those lights up there in the trees, they pretty well light up the pit. Yah, there's a couple men carrying roosters stepping in. Wait a minute…'

The lights hanging from wires in the nearby trees were directed at the pit, which was nothing more than a pen surrounded by a crude wood fence. Men stood tightly packed around the fence, close together but still with room enough to wave their arms and yell, making their bets. In the centre, two men crouched, each holding a big rooster, their wing feathers clipped and thin spikes fitted to their spurs. Bright, shiny steel spikes, maybe two inches long. The crowd standing surged forward a bit around the ring, cheered as the two men released their birds.

Harry watched speechless at the roosters, one's black feathers sparkling in the dusty lights, the other no more than a flash of orangey-red as it flew in attack. 'The black,' someone yelled, waving a fistful of money, 'the black.'

'Done,' another voice rang out and all the while the two fighting cocks were flying at each other, spurs glinting in the harsh light. More yelling, more handfuls of money and colourful Australian bills being waved around. Then suddenly, as if a switch were flicked, the crowd went silent. Blood spurted from the chest of the reddish feathers as the bird crumpled and after a couple beats, its clipped wings went deathly still.

The crowd, surging a little this way and that, parted for an instant just as the spur on one bird's leg sank into the chest of the other. It was in that flash opening that Mel was able to see the blood spurt, disappearing into the dusty sand.

Noise instantly filled the night as the betting men surged to either collect their winnings or fight to see the next two contestants being brought in.

Faintly Harry heard Mel screaming at him. 'Damn you, what's happening?' He didn't know the words to tell her what he'd seen. How quickly it had happened. How excited he'd become.

Tearing his gaze away as the loud yelling continued to roll over the brushy area, he looked down at her. 'They let loose those birds and bam! They were at each other. You shoulda seen it. The feathers were flying as those roosters jumped up, slashing away. And like that, one fell back, blood spurting and the other, well, that one just walked away.'

'I've got to get on something so I can see better,' she said, glancing around. 'Look, over there on the other side, there's a tree. You lift me up so I'm on that big branch and I think I'll be able to see everything I need. C'mon.'

Stepping back into the darkness, outside the glare of the hanging lights, Mel's eyes hadn't quite adjusted when she bumped into someone.

'Sorry,' she said automatically.

'No worries, lady,' a gruff man's voice said. 'Just stand right there.'

Mel looked up to see the man she'd walked into wasn't one of those dusty men watching the cock-fight. This man was as big as Harry and wearing a cap – a billed cap with a blue and white checkered band. Police.

Harry, coming close behind her, started to push past when he also saw the uniformed man. Glancing beyond the policeman, he saw more of the same.

'Oh, shit,' he said quietly.

Chapter Thirty-Eight

New and even louder voices started yelling. 'All right. Don't anyone move.' Someone had a loud-hailer. 'This is the Queensland State Police. There is no place for you to go, so stand where you are.'

At the first sound, the men around the dirt patch started to scatter, only to run into what appeared to be a solid wall of blue-uniformed shirts, police officers armed with nightsticks, pushing back.

Harry grabbed Mel's arm, pulling her back a little as the officers tightened up their ambush. 'What'll we do, lady?' Looking over his shoulder he thought of simply fading back into the night. But he couldn't leave her here by herself. *And where is the other one? Ah, hell*, he thought, letting himself relax. Nothing he could do about it. Anyway, she had the car keys and this wouldn't be some place he could hitch a ride from. Damn.

'We stay, Harry,' Mel said, standing on tip-toe and looking around. 'You see Samantha? Damn, I hope she's okay. Look, there's nothing to worry about. Once I explain what we're doing here, that we aren't part of it, we'll be all right. We're about the only whites here, and once they see I'm a reporter and you're with me, we'll be okay.'

That proved good thinking, but it all took time. Slowly, after all those not wearing a uniform had been rounded up, they were taken one by one from the crowd. Mel watched as each one was questioned, his ID checked, and then led away. More lights had been brought in by the police and she could see where the men were taken. To a bus. A police bus with a screened window, painted with the blue and white chequerboard, stripe the length of its body.

'I got some really great shots when the police arrived,' Samantha said excitedly. Mel had been busy watching as things developed and hadn't noticed the photographer come up. Standing next to her, camera still at the ready, the young woman's face was glistening.

'I took nearly a whole roll before the raid started, too. Man, this one is going to be something.'

Before Mel could comment, she noticed one of the uniformed men striding towards them. Quickly, thinking of the story she was writing in her head, she read the nameplate on the shirt of the officer who finally faced her. Robert Conway.

'Officer Conway,' she started to say before the police officer even looked up.

'It is Constable Conway,' he growled before looking up and glaring directly into the woman's eyes. 'Now, all I want to hear from you is, what're you doing out here in the bush with a bunch of crims?' he demanded. 'Don't tell me, you're in the market for some of old man Jackson's eggs.'

Mel decided the best defence was to be blunt and not give in. 'No, officer,' she said, putting as much starch in her words as she was able, 'I've already bought all the eggs I can use. No, I'm a reporter, working on a story for *Sun Life Magazine*. The story is about illegal cock-fights. This' – she nodded towards Samantha – 'is my photographer, and the gentleman beside her is Harry. Uh, what's your surname, Harry? I don't think I ever asked.'

'Bridges,' Harry said softly, keeping his head down. 'Harry Bridges.'

'I hired Harry as protection,' she went on forcefully, not showing the fear she was feeling. 'Now you can call my editor, Carl Musgrave, if you don't believe me.'

Conway sighed and shook his head. Disgust was strong on his face. 'Oh, crickey, just what we need, the media. Okay, stay right there and I'll get the senior sargent.'

Mel watched as the police officer walked over to where another uniformed officer was talking to Rooster Jackson. When the Senior Constable explained, pointing back towards Mel and Harry, the officer nodded and held up a hand to stop the chook farmer's words.

'But, dammit, I tell ya,' the older man went on, speaking louder as the officer walked away, 'this ain't on my place. I don't know nothing about what's going on here. Fact is,' he was almost yelling, 'I was thinking about calling you about the cars and trucks blocking up the road.'

Neither police officer paid any attention.

'Conway,' the ranking officer said, after looking first at Mel and then Harry up and down, 'will you see that our friend, Farmer Jackson, gets a seat on the bus. You know, I think we finally got him this time.' Constable Conway nodded, turned and walked back to the old man.

'Now then, my senior constable tells me you are members of the media. Is that correct?'

Mel nodded and took a deep breath, ready to assert herself. The uniformed man didn't give her a chance. 'I am Senior Sargent Louis Crabb. Be warned,' he said, holding up a hand after identifying himself, 'you three are being charged with participating in an illegal endeavour. Anything you say will be noted and possibly used when you appear before the bench. Yes' – his smile barely lifted his lips – 'but to be clear, just claiming to be working for some dink magazine won't get you anything. You were found at an illegal event, a cock-fight. Taking part in cock-fights and betting at cock-fights are all unlawful activities and all carry penalties, fines and, in some cases, jail time. Now, let's hear what you have to say.'

The righteous anger Mel had been feeling was like a balloon with a hole poked in it. Harry, on the other hand, was scared. It wouldn't do him any good with the bosses to get thrown into a cell.

Chapter Thirty-Nine

Like the drive out to the cock-fight, the trip back to town was done in silence. After listening to the woman, the senior officer merely nodded. Glancing at Harry, he frowned, waiting to see if the big man had anything to offer. Harry didn't look away; only shook his head slightly side to side.

'All right then,' Senior Constable Crabb had said. Glancing around, checking to see that all was proceeding as it should, he looked back at the pair. 'I am going to let you go your own way, for right now. Each of you will be issued a notice to appear on a charge of taking part in an illegal and unlawful activity. It wouldn't benefit the law to place either of you in the bus with the others, so I'll release you on your own good behaviour. You'll be notified as to the date and time of your appearance before the magistrate's court. Wait right here and I'll have Constable Conway come gather information and issue the appropriate summons.' Turning abruptly away, with his hands still clasped behind his back, Crabb walked away, leaving Mel seething. She felt sure if the officer had shown a little courtesy she could have talked her way out of it.

Down the dirt track, heading for pavement and Cairns, and still angry, Mel gritted her teeth, wanting to scream and pound the steering wheel.

Sitting quietly on the passenger's side, Harry stared unseeing out into the night. He'd been put into a no-win situation. Even if he had his passport, he couldn't simply buy a ticket out of town. Trying to explain to his bosses how he had come to the attention of the local cops wasn't something he wanted to do. Bad enough having that damn federal drug cop watching his every move. To make it more frustrating, he knew it was his own damn fault. He'd had plans for this red-headed woman and look what it got him. What the hell had he been thinking? This whole deal had a bad smell – the smell of trouble. Even back in the jungle lab, where they were cooking up the coke, it had seemed pretty slip-shod. Trouble, ever since he'd gotten involved with that load of coke, there'd been nothing but trouble. And now he's facing charges of being in a cock-fight. Can you believe it? A pissy-assed cock-fight? He would have to come up with a damn good story and be ready with it. Certainly, with Dobby and his thick-headed mate in the picture, it wouldn't take long for the news of getting arrested to get back to the higher-ups. He could count on those two stumble-bums, reportedly in Cairns to organise some mickey-mouse drug deal, to spread the word on his being caught in a cock-fight. The bosses wouldn't believe it.

Mel's hands gripped the steering wheel hard, her knuckles white. Driving too fast for the narrow dirt road, she felt the rear wheels slide in the sandy soil as she rounded a curve. Slow down, she told herself but still breathing heavily, it wouldn't do to pile up and have to be rescued by the state police sure to be coming along behind her. But then, thinking of the police and getting the notice to appear, her anger grew and her foot pushed down the throttle.

Well, she got her story, didn't she? Yeah, right. With a nice little sidebar about getting arrested and facing possible jail time to go with it. Hope that damn kid picture-taker got some good shots. Damn, why hadn't Harry pulled her back into the trees? They could have just ghosted away, couldn't they? But no, she had to face the police down. After all, she represented the media, right? What a pile of crap!

Well, one good thing came from this fuck-up. For a while, she'd been thinking about getting Harry to take her over to the Gulf. All along, since learning about her grandfather's sunken plane, she'd had a bad feeling about making that trip by herself. A strong woman she may be, but common sense said there were times and places to ask for help. That part of things would be one of those times. But tonight he showed her he wasn't the man for that job. She'd find someone other than Harry to watch her back while she searched for her grandfather's downed airplane. No. She'd pay him his fifty dollars and that'd be the end of it. At least until they had to go before the magistrate.

Chapter Forty

Melissa had just had about enough of the all-too talkative girl photographer that the foolish, demanding small magazine editor had foisted off on her.

'Look, Ms Reporter-in-Waiting,' Samantha said, trying to sound in control. 'I didn't sign up for getting arrested when I took on this job.' All the way back from that fiasco of a cock-fight, she'd planned what she was going to say to this smart-arsed woman. The opportunity didn't come up and after a quick shower, she'd stretched out on top of the bed sheet, continuing the one-sided dialogue. The day's heat hadn't lessened much and she fell asleep feeling sweaty, her mind churning with her argument.

Mel, too, had a bad night. Lying awake, tossing and turning, thinking about what having something like an arrest on her record would mean. She had showered just before turning out the light and trying to sleep, but the heat of the day hadn't dropped even a little bit. How in the hell did people stand it? Sticky. Covering herself with the thinnest of sheets, it wasn't long before the material was twisted like a snake around her. Unable to shut her mind off, her imagination painted scenes of jail, she gave up. Getting out of bed and hoping to catch a breeze, she pulled the bare wooden chair over to the open window.

Sitting with her arms on the window sill, gazing out over the roof of the shack below, her eyes finally grew heavy and she slept. Only to wake up when the hot morning sun burned her bare shoulders.

She wasn't able to get past the sick feeling in the pit of her stomach in the early morning either. Not able to look food in the face, she tried for a cup of coffee, only to push it aside. This couldn't go on.

The person to talk to would be the bartender, Harry. He was the type of man who would have some experience with the law and courts. That's what took her to the Crown Pub, arriving before it opened. Even from the street outside, the smell of stale beer hit her empty stomach, queasy and roiling like the waves rolling over the tidal pools she'd swum in during the diving lessons. Turning away, she found herself facing Sam, the photographer.

It obviously had been a bad idea, telling young Samantha that she too had been hoping to turn the cock-fighting story into something more than it was. Not mentioning the goal of searching for her grandfather's airplane was about the only part of that discussion she'd shown any smarts about.

'We have to talk,' was the young woman's morning greeting, sounding hard and demanding. 'I can't deal with this. What are you going to do about it?'

As usual, a pair of professional-looking cameras hung down the front of the woman. Her tan vest, with many of the little pockets bulging with who-knew-what, covered the blouse under it. *God*, Mel thought, *even early* in the morning she's dressed like she's on her way to some place important to take photos of it. Glancing down, she saw the girl's hiking boots were dirt-streaked.

'Back up,' Mel said, holding up her hands as if ready to fight the other woman off. 'There's nothing that says I'm responsible. And I don't have any more idea of what's going to happen than you do. So don't come attacking me.'

'I was there because of you. You and that crazy story about people who kill chooks and bet on it. If this is the way journalism works, I don't want any part of it.'

Shaking, both because of her empty stomach and getting angry, Mel let her voice become an echo, hard and demanding. Gritting her teeth and making her jaw hard, she silently promised herself she wouldn't cry. 'For someone whose claim to fame was a series of high school photos, you're the one who asked for a job. So back off. Don't rely on being new to the business, either. That's the name of the game. Every reporter who's ever been worth his salt has at one time or another come up against the legal system. Don't you know that? Guess those kinds of things aren't taught in picture-taking class.'

'Photo-journalism. Not picture-taking. And where does it do you any good to have your name and mug shot hanging on the wall? How does that make your story, or for that matter, my photos worth more? Can we expect any legal help from that dumb magazine? Bet not. So what are you planning on doing about it?'

The same question had been on Mel's mind too, but she wasn't about to admit it. Not to this... this child.

Feeling the tears welling up, Mel abruptly turned away and walked blindly into a man coming up behind her.

'Ah,' Inspector Lambert said, a big smile lifting his lips and making his eyes sparkle, 'just the two women I was hoping to see this fine morning. Good morning to you both. I apologise for bumping into you, but, well, I stopped by the hotel and was told you'd both left early. Let me introduce myself.' Pulling a card from his jacket pocket, he held it out so the women could read the text. 'I'm Inspector Colin Lambert of the Australian Federal Police. You, I'll wager' – nodding towards Mel – 'are Melissa Graves. And your companion would then be Samantha Edgerly. Senior Sargent Crabb's description of the two of you is spot on.'

'What is the AFP's interest in us?' Mel asked cautiously.

'Well, none really. I'm stationed down in Brisbane, but find myself up here in Cairns on business. I happened to be in the local police watchhouse when Sargent Crabb mentioned the cock-fight and how two members of the media had been arrested. I took an interest. Now, finding you two here, I can relay the good news. Next on my list is to talk with the bartender, Mr Bridges.'

'What good news,' asked Samantha, cutting in.

Lambert smiled. 'You'll be happy to know, I had a long conversation with Senior Sargent Crabb and was able to convince him not to press any charges about finding you at that cock-fight.'

Mel felt the heavy load lift from her shoulders at the news. 'You got him to change his mind?'

Lambert's smile grew as he nodded. 'I've known men like Louis Crabb for a long time. He's a small-town policeman. Now, in this case, for you, it even gets better. He and I have attended a number of conferences put on by the Australian Federal Police for state police officers. I was able to remind him of one of those events. With that personal background, he was finally open to my argument. Yes, it took a little, uh, shall we say, pressure? But I was able to argue the benefit of having the media at the scene. Getting a story published, especially with photos' – he flashed a smile in Samantha's direction – 'would help show the public the negative side of such things as cock-fights.'

'And he's going to forget it?' Samantha asked, sounding as if she didn't believe the inspector. 'We won't be having to appear in court?'

'That's right. I'd make sure Louis gets a copy of the magazine when it comes out, but, no, there'll be no court appearance.'

Mel's relief brought a huge smile to her face. 'That goes for Harry, too? He's not part of the media, but he was working for me. For us' – she nodded to the other woman – 'I had hired him as a kind of bodyguard.'

Lambert nodded. 'That was a little harder sell, but Crabb finally gave in. None of the three of you will be facing any charges.'

Samantha stuck out her hand for Lambert to shake. 'Thank you, Inspector. I was really worried.' Looking sideways at Mel, she went on, 'I don't suppose there's any more to this assignment, is there?'

'No. We're about done. I'll write up my story and when you head back south you can take it with you. Turn it in along with your photos.'

Samantha frowned, not liking that. 'When will that be? I'd like to get out of here as soon as possible.'

'Another day or so won't hurt you. I'll get on it right away.' Flashing a smile at Lambert, she shook his hand and offered her thanks for his help.

'And that,' Lambert said, 'takes care of that. Oh, I'll still have to talk with Mr Bridges. This kind of duty is one of the better parts of my job.'

The inspector's job was going to get even better than he had hoped.

Chapter Forty-One

Lambert watched as the two young women walked away from the locked pub door. Since his divorce, he'd focused on his work and hadn't attempted to open the door to any kind of social life. After all, it'd been his being tied to the job that had been the cause of Bronwyn leaving him. Too many missed dinners, too many telephone calls in the middle of the night, calls getting him out of bed and out of the house. It wasn't anything new. Typical of a lot of policemen. Probably no easier for the women wearing a badge. But what the bloody hell was he supposed to do? He didn't know. Back when he'd met Bronny, he'd just graduated from the academy. She'd been proud of him, thinking he was fair dinkum in his starched uniform. That feeling lasted for a while. It was only a short time after the excitement of the wedding had faded that the reality of being a copper's wife set in that things changed.

The first sign was her complaint about his firearm. Having a gun in the house scared her, she said. He'd kept his weapons secured in a locked desk drawer, but that wasn't good enough. When he started carrying the TASER, she acted as if he'd stepped in dog poo. That was when she started in on him, demanding he remove his equipment belt and lock it in the closet by the front door.

Over the next year or so, things only got worse. The breaking point had been his being on duty on their second anniversary. She couldn't understand why he didn't stand up to his boss and demand the time off. Not for the first time she'd brought up the pain she'd felt when he'd been called out early on Christmas morning. That had happened their first Christmas and she never got over it. Probably a good thing they hadn't had children. But now, watching the two women walk away, he decided he'd been locking himself away too long, become too involved with his job. Catching himself watching the way their butts moved, he quickly looked away, embarrassed.

Glancing across the street, he spotted Harry standing at the curb, talking to two men. The two drug runners, Dobby and Ruckman. That made the police inspector smile. Maybe he'd been right. If he waited long enough, ol' Harry'd step in it.

Hoping they hadn't seen him, he quickly turned around the corner and almost ran head-on into Gabbi Dingo.

'G'day, officer,' said the young man, smiling and stepping back.

'Ah, good morning. Gabbi, isn't it?' Lambert frowned. 'How'd you know I'm a police officer?'

'Mr Harry, there behind the bar. I heard him tell a couple of his mates about you.'

'Harry and his mates, eh? Well, I was just on my way to talk with Mr Harry, but saw he hadn't opened the pub yet. Are you opening it up?'

'Me? No sir. I sweep out and bring up new kegs. I don't know anything about opening the doors. But Harry'll have them unlocked pretty soon.'

'Well, guess I can talk to him now, then.'

The two went back around just as Harry was opening the double doors. Gabbi hesitated when he saw the two men follow his boss inside. Ever since they had threatened him and ordered him to bring his dope to them and only them, Gabbi had done his damnest to stay away from them. Now there they were, going into the pub and he'd already told this policeman that he was late for work. The police inspector didn't notice the young man's hesitation. Gabbi didn't know what to do. He didn't want to be late for work but more importantly, he didn't want to be talking to those men. Not with the policeman or Harry there.

Not seeing a way out, he followed the inspector through the pub door. Putting his head down, he followed the inspector, keeping the officer between him and the bar. Stepping quickly, he headed for the hallway and the broom closet. The three men, seeing the AFP officer, didn't pay any attention to anything else.

'Good morning, Inspector,' Harry said quietly, and going around the end of the bar, he stopped only long enough to switch on the hot plate. 'Haven't had time to heat the kettle, but if you'll wait a minute, we can have coffee.'

Lambert smiled. How he'd like to be sitting here, listening to what these three had to talk about. Harry saw the smile and frowned. This visit, he felt, wasn't going to be good for him. Damn, those two for showing up this morning.

Dobby, flicking a glance at Ruckman, nodded to one side and moved away. His partner, not taking his eyes off Lambert, followed.

'Good morning to you, too, Mr Bridges.' Lambert took his time and giving Dobby and Ruckman a long look. He finally nodded and turned back to the bartender. 'Just wanted to let you know, Harry, the kerfuffle over the cock-fight has been taken care of. There won't be any charges brought against you and the two magazine women.'

Harry, leaning against the bar with both hands spread out flat on the shiny wood, felt a wave of relief. That was one worry he'd done away with. 'Well, that's good news,' he said, and then thought he'd better put on a good face. 'Truth to tell, I always thought it was a muck up. That reporter and her mate were just doing their job and I was there to protect them, you know?'

'Yes,' said Lambert, smiling, 'that's what Senior Sargent Crabb decided. I've already talked to the two women and now I've told you the good news: I'll go see about a bite of brekkie.' Turning towards Dobby and Ruckman, Lambert nodded. 'Be seeing you,' and walked out.

Gabbi, standing out of sight behind the door to the storage room, waited silently. He could be patient. Sooner or later, the two hard arses would have to leave. Maybe, he thought, it was time for him to be leaving himself. Time to get out of Cairns and back to his little farm. After working this morning, he'd ask around and see if anyone was heading west out of town. Normally, he was able to get rides all the way over to Karumba, although sometimes it took more than a day or two to make the trip. But with those two men threatening him, being long gone was likely the best thing.

He didn't know it, but this time he'd be able to make the trip in one afternoon.

Chapter Forty-Two

JC was surprised when he learned the red-headed student had been the one with Bridges at the cock-fight. The story about the arrest quickly got around town, he heard about it when he went to the news agents to get a newspaper.

'What is there,' the man selling the papers asked, his smile softening his question, 'about you Yanks that you're always getting into trouble with the law?'

JC shook his head. 'Don't know what you're talking about. Far as I know, I'm not in any trouble with anyone.' He handed the man money for his paper.

The man chuckled and handed over the change. 'Naw, not you. The other one. Bartender over at the Crown Hotel Pub. Didn't you hear? He and a couple women reporters got themselves arrested last night.' Seeing he had JC's attention, he stood a little taller and continued his story. 'Yeah, from what I hear, they were somewhere out in the bush, at a cock-fight, you know? A cock-fight. Doesn't make sense, does it? You ever been to a cock-fight?' JC shook his head, folded his paper and started to turn away. The news agent wasn't finished.

'Cock-fights and bull fights. Two things I've never understood. Now, I've gone down to the arena whenever they hold a night of a mature boxing that I can understand. And were you here when that rodeo came to town? Boy, that was something – men getting out there to ride those bulls, some bigger than… well, bigger than any cow I'd ever seen. Yeah, that I can see the sport in, but cock-fighting? Nope. Don't make no sense at all.' He stopped only when another customer bought a newspaper.

JC nodded and quickly left the little store.

Reading newspapers had never been one of his habits until he found himself here in this strange place. The heat and humidity made him comfortable only when in some place with a lot of air conditioning. The pub was one such place, but not the one where Harry was working. He'd had enough of that man. It was Harry's fault that the federal policeman was still holding the passports. Staying in his hotel room was out, there wasn't even a TV set and he couldn't sit still very long with only a radio to talk to. So it was down to a café for breakfast, and rather than simply sit and stare, it'd look better, he thought, if he was reading a newspaper while killing time and cooling down.

That's where Inspector Lambert found him.

'Good morning, Mr McCain,' Lambert said, pulling out a chair and sitting down, even before JC could invite him to do so.

Glancing around to make sure he wasn't overheard, the inspector leaned forward and lowered his voice. 'Have you heard what your best mate, Harry Bridges, has been up to?' He sounded as if whatever it was pleased him.

JC decided he'd see what this drug cop had to say. He shook his head. 'Whatever it is, I hope it's bad enough that you'll be handing me that passport with my name on it. I'd really like to go back to the States.'

'Ah, no. I'm afraid that isn't the case. But,' he said, his voice once again full of happiness, 'I can report that Mr Bridges has been arrested.'

'Arrested? Then how about that passport?'

'Arrested, not charged. Plus, I'm afraid I've had any charges that might have been brought against him dropped.'

'You're just full of good news this morning, aren't you? So what did your' – emphasising the "your" – 'Mr Bridges get in trouble over.'

Quickly, and still keeping his voice down, Lambert told JC about the cock-fight and subsequent police raid. 'I had to talk fast to convince Senior Sargent Crabb that it would be in his best interests not to press charges. I was able to impress upon him the one thing I learned early in my career, which was not to upset the media.'

All JC could do was smile and shake his head. Somehow Harry Bridges had always struck him as a loose cannon. Getting involved in an illegal cock-fight seemed to prove it. But the red head? Just goes to show, he said to himself. You can never tell about women.

'Uh huh,' he said after sipping his coffee, 'so, to protect your reputation, you got Harry out of the slammer.'

'Well, no. Not my reputation. I still believe he's up to something. Something I can put him away for good, for a long time. And at the same time, bring to a halt whatever drug deal he's gotten himself involved with.'

'That doesn't make any sense at all. You're the one who got Harry and me up here in this hell hole. Harry didn't come up to Cairns to do any drug dealing, he came up to deliver your friend's boat. So what makes you think he's dealing?'

'Simple. First, I'm convinced your Mr Bridges was part of the drug deal that the boat you brought over from Fiji was carrying. All right, there was no evidence of that. But now he's here and who does he meet up with? Two men long known to be part of the importation of illegal drugs into Australia. Those two just happen to be here in Cairns. That is what makes me sure Mr Bridges is going to step in the mud. And I'm going to get him when he does.'

'And the two women who were arrested at the same time at that cock-fight, are they part of Harry's gang, too?'

Lambert frowned. 'You're not taking this seriously, are you? No. Ms Edgerly and Ms Graves are simply two members of the media. No more. Apparently, they had hired Bridges to act as a bodyguard. But they made my argument with the local police work. Don't you see?'

JC nodded and finished his coffee. He stood up. Time to begin day two of his diving instructions.

Looking at the list of names on his clipboard, he thought about what the federal drug cop had said about Melissa Groves being arrested with Harry. Or, as he claimed to be known as, Harry the Horse. Smiling, he shook his head and watched the dive group as they went about adjusting their tank harness straps. The black rubber wetsuits were like a second skin. In most cases, it was a sight better not to notice, but with the Groves woman, the rubber suit looked smooth and well-rounded. Nice, he thought, a well-shaped mermaid with a tank on her back. He remembered her asking about wreck diving. Wonder what that was about, he asked silently. Probably nothing. Just a question. Time to stop daydreaming and get to work.

'Okay, gang,' he started out, 'let's get in the water and practice what you learned yesterday about buddy breathing.'

Daydreaming or not, he found himself watching her wet-suited body as she walked towards the edge of the pool.

Chapter Forty-Three

'We gotta talk,' said Ruckman as he and Dobby walked away from the hotel pub. Dobby had wanted to talk with that bartender, Harry the Horse, but he couldn't see what it'd been about. Dobby had explained they were going into the pub only because he wanted to see if Harry the Horse would have anything to say. He'd heard about the bartender getting arrested and thought it was the funniest thing he'd ever heard. Certainly, Dobby had said, it was something more to pass on to the big men down in Brisbane.

But Harry hadn't done much more than glare at the two men before growling at the kid bringing beer kegs out of a back room. Dobby was surprised to see the kid was the same aborigine dope dealer he'd had a talk with a couple days ago. He wondered if Harry was trying to move in on that little deal too.

Deep in thought about the way things were going, he ignored his partner until they finished their morning glass of beer and were walking back down the street. 'We gotta talk,' Ruckman said, stopping at a cross-walk to let a bus go by.

'What d'we gotta talk about, mate?' Dobby and Ruckman had been a team for a long time, ever since old man Daimler had told Dobby to stay behind after finishing whatever business he had come down to do.

Dobby hadn't liked that. And he certainly didn't like the nickname these damn Aussies had given him. Pascel Doblones was his name, dammit. But when he complained, the old man laughed it off. 'Naw,' he'd said, 'let the natives enjoy themselves. Your job is to protect our interests down here. I figure you can do it a lot better if they think you're one of them. So let them joke around a bit. Make sense?'

Well, hell. If the old man said, 'Jump,' a smart man merely asked, 'how high?' So he became Dobby and Ruckman got to be his right-hand man. Ruckman wasn't real smart but, like most men in the business, he knew what was best for him. Doing what Dobby said was what was best. Don't worry about things, let others do that. Just do what you're told. That was what's best. Always.

So, what's to talk about? 'You tell me, Ruckman, old mate. There something bothering you?'

'Dobby, yeah, there is. You know what we're up here in this hell-hole for. I was there when the big men down there in Brisbane told us. Told you. Go up to Cairns, they said. Set up things so when stuff starts coming in, we'd be ready. Okay, so the stuff ain't coming in for a while. That's good. You said that yourself. Ain't no rush, you said. Remember? So we got time to, uh, yeah, organise. That's what the big men told us, right? To get everything set up. Get it all organised. Right?'

'Ruckman, old horse, that's what we're up here to do, just as you say. So what's your point? I mean, yeah, that's what we're doing, getting things organised. Okay, so nothing's moving yet. The big men know what they're doing, don't they? You bet. Yeah, stuff is still coming into these parts in the old way. You know how it works. A load being flown in, a change of planes and shipped south. Nobody down there knows where it comes from, nobody up this end knows where it goes to. Simple. We ain't got nothing to do with that. It's all someone else's to worry about. So what's it about? Your problem.'

'I ain't as smart as you, Dobby. I know that. Hell's bells, I don't got to be smart. Just gotta do what you tell me. You do the smart stuff and I do the heavy lifting. That's what I was told to do when they brought you into the system. Okay? But I don't know. I mean, this mucking around with the kid. It doesn't make any sense. What kinda thing is it gonna be, dealing with his few baggies of dope? I mean, how much stuff can he be screwing around with? Not enough to get into a sweat about, you ask me.'

'There you are, Ruckman. Ain't nobody asking you. Yeah, this kid from some black man village is nothing to bother with. Right now. But when things get going, every little bit will matter. You 'n me, man, we ain't nothing to those on up the ladder, you know? We're at the bottom rung. Okay, so how do we do better? Come on, do we wanna stay at the bottom, doing the grunt work forever? I don't. When I was working with the old man, Daimler, I was seeing how things worked. Let me tell you, Carlos Daimler wouldn't let anything go that he didn't get his share of. So now here I am, living in this god-forsaken, ass-backward country. Hell, there ain't even a decent cuppa coffee. All ya can get is expresso, or whatever. Either a lotta milk or strong enough to melt a spoon. I don't wanna be here forever. I got people back in the States, you know?'

'Ah, Dobby. I thought you liked it here. You're always saying how good the beer is, and you got yourself a girlfriend, don't ya? That sheila is right stuff; she's beautiful. I didn't know you wanted to go back where you come from.'

'Well, I do. But the old man, he told me to stay here and watch his interests. So I'm here. But I ain't where I can even watch his interests any more. No. The big men down in Sydney send us up to Brisbane. Okay, so maybe that's okay with Mr Daimler. Maybe not. I don't know. Hell, I can't even ask. So I'm thinking maybe I'm being left out on my own, kind a… But, look, if I was to show how much more I could do for him, maybe he'd send for me to come back. He was good to work with, back when I was guarding him. He'd talk to me, ya know? And I listened. I watched and listened. So here's this black kid selling a little dope. That's a good place to start. See, think about it like this. We take over his dealings. We can show the big men in Brisbane how to make a bit more. Extra from the amount of stuff we'll be setting up to deal with. That'll show them we are worth more than chump change.'

'What's chump change?'

'Ah, god. You people don't understand nothing. Peanuts. Chump change is like no money at all. Just not making any money – real money at all.'

Dobby stopped and looked at the bigger man. 'Ruckman, old sock, don't bother yourself with it. I wanna take the cream from this kid. You'll get your cut, don't worry. Then, once things are all up and running, we'll show the big men that little extra. They'll shit themselves when they see what they missed. We can't lose.'

Ruckman nodded his head to show his understanding, then pursing his lips, frowned. 'But what about that man over at the pub? The guy pulling the grog. You called him Harry the Horse. I heard that name. It was something about the trouble when the drug squad discovered a shipment of stuff. Sounded like he was the trouble. He knows the big men. You think he's here to watch us? He said he's got some federal police on his tail. And then that one comes in, you both say is a federal drug squad big man. I dunno, Dobby. Setting things up with this kid and having someone like this bartender know us, it doesn't look too good. You know?'

'I can take care of old Harry. From what I heard, he's in enough pain from that missing shipment. That'll work in our favour. All I gotta do is let the big men down in Brisbane know he's up here and that he's brought the federal police with him, and that he's been arrested by the local boys in blue. That'll take care of it. Yeah, that's what we'll do. Let them know about Harry.'

Thinking about putting the dirt on Harry made Dobby feel good. For once, he smirked, it'd be someone else getting the shaft, not him.

Chapter Forty-Four

Mel didn't like wearing the wetsuit. The skin-tight black rubber made her hips look too wide. And her butt, too big. Her boobs – well, she'd always thought they were too small, but the wetsuit separated them and she liked that. But she really didn't like the way the Yank instructor was looking at her. Not staring, but she'd caught him running his eyes over her body at least twice.

She didn't say anything, though. It didn't take a genius to realise if she was going to look for the diamonds left by her grandfather under the seat of his old plane, she was going to have to learn to use scuba gear. Being in the ocean wasn't part of her childhood. Until her parents moved off the acreage and into town, the only water she'd been familiar with was a shallow creek back of the barn. Not deep enough to really get wet. Except in the rainy season. During the wet, the creek was a growling, roiling torrent of thick, brown, dirt-laden water.

Even living in town, a small place with a single supermarket, the post office, one servo and the pub or hotel, there was no opportunity or need to learn to swim. A former boyfriend, Roy something – she couldn't remember his surname, probably didn't want to – had been an avid sailor. For him, she learned to swim. Now, for an unknown treasure, she was learning how to scuba dive. Wearing a form-fitting skin of black rubber.

'We'll start our day in the pool,' the instructor said to begin the second day of lessons, 'and after the lunch break we'll go out into the harbour.'

Mel hadn't paid attention when he'd introduced himself on the first day. Not until she learned he had been partners with the bartender when they had saved that couple who'd been left behind. Where the bartender had proved himself useless when trouble started, possibly this guy wouldn't. She still kinda blamed Harry for her getting arrested. It wasn't his fault but even now, with that crisis done and dusted, she somehow didn't think he'd done enough to keep her out of trouble. Thinking about those things caused her to frown. She'd always thought of herself as being a strong woman. One who liked men but didn't actually need them. But, to be honest, how prepared was she to go searching for the airplane? Wasn't that why she was taking the dive lessons? Because she couldn't do it herself. She needed help and what would be better than a man who could dive? With that in mind, she gave the American a closer look.

She watched as he swung the scuba tank onto his back, fitting his arms through the straps of the harness. Hitching the weight belt around his waist, she noted how slender that waist looked. He wasn't the burly type the bartender was, but she really didn't need a brute to help her. Just someone like this dive instructor.

Running her hand over the smoothness of her wetsuit-covered hip, Mel smiled to herself. One thing she learned long before leaving high school was how to dress to impress. From the first of Year Seven, Mel somehow found a way to make even the dowdiest school uniform classy. Normally, the uniforms worn by school students, always designed and approved by old-fashioned-minded women and possibly even older frustrated men, had one goal. That was to make the male students appear professional and officious and the girls to look anything but sexy. At first, young Melissa's actions were simply something all the girls, or most anyway, did. They joked about it. But then she saw how the boys noticed them.

Uniforms for boys often included black pants, short-sleeved shirts, usually white, with a dark-coloured blazer and striped tie. The girls' uniforms might also include a tie, a dark blazer, a short-sleeved blouse and a knee-length skirt, although in most cases the skirt might be longer. It was Mel's habit, once out of sight of her mother, to roll the skirt up, tucking the extra material under the bottom of her blouse, at her waist line. This left her skirt's hemline as far above her knees as she could. Mel wasn't a tease; she merely liked to be noticed.

Years later, at university, with uniforms a thing of the past, her usual attire was even more casual: short skirts, brown corduroy blazers, complete with leather elbow patches and in winter, long-sleeved blouses. Always, her chosen colours supplemented her red hair. Summer weather brought out shorts and colourful tees.

Again, having the boys, now young men notice her was exciting.

Now, when working, her skirts and blouses were always well-pressed, depicting her vision of a well-dressed businesswoman. During the day, her choice of footwear was focused on comfort, low heels and even sandals. It was when dressing to go out night clubbing that she would put on the high-heels that brought her well-shaped legs to their very best. In any case, Mel was a past master at smiling, flashing her pearly white teeth and sparkling green eyes. And getting men to notice her. She didn't think this Yank dive instructor had a chance.

Chapter Forty-Five

The morning lesson progressed well. From learning about buddy-breathing to making sure they all knew the value of staying close to their dive master. As they broke for lunch, JC was thinking they were ready to get out into the harbour.

'We'll meet back here in an hour,' he told them. 'Don't take on a heavy lunch and for gawds sake, stay away from any alcoholic beverage. There'll be time for a celebration after we finish up this afternoon.'

Watching his students slip shirts on over their wetsuits, he smiled. Without a doubt, of the dozen would-be divers, only a couple would remember what he'd shown them this morning. Ah, well. They would get their certificate and go on out to dive the reef. But they wouldn't be his responsibility.

'Excuse me.' He hadn't noticed the good-looking red-headed woman hanging behind. The colourful Hawaiian short-sleeved shirt she had put on over her wetsuit was covered with palm trees, some printed right side up and others upside down. He quickly told himself it was the trees he was seeing, not the rounded smoothness of her breasts. 'I wanted to ask you a question.' She smiled, enjoying his growing uncomfortableness. She surprised herself by not feeling uncomfortable herself, as she usually did when a man stared at her boobs.

'Ask away,' he said, bringing his gaze up to hers. For the first time, he noticed the colour of her eyes. Green. A clear jade green. Don't be a fool, he told himself. Relax. Feeling a bead of sweat roll slowly down his back, he hoped his poker face was working.

'We'll become certified this afternoon. Will that mean we can safely dive anywhere?'

JC shook his head. 'That certificate doesn't cover everything there is about scuba diving. It'd be very dangerous to think so. No, the certificate is actually what's called a resort dive certificate. What you're learning here is just the basics, enough so the average tourist can go out and explore the reef in safety.'

'That means there's a lot more one can learn?'

He chuckled. Taking her arm, he started walking her towards the exit. 'It's a great big ocean out there, full of dangerous things. Almost as many as there are here on dry land. Now, if you're going to get any lunch, you'd better hurry. There'll be time for questions later.'

Mel nodded and with a smile, walked away. It would be a lot better, she thought, to get him talking when they had more time. Let him think about things now, she told herself. Soften him up.

She needn't have worried. JC, buying a banana from the stand outside the little green grocer down the street, was already thinking about things. Peeling the fruit, he frowned. Don't be an idiot, he told himself. He'd lusted after women before and each time it didn't turn out pleasantly. Oh, the sex had been good and even a couple times wonderful, but always he was left with an empty feeling. Okay, so the red-headed woman looked good, but no matter what happened, it wouldn't go anywhere.

Sure as hell, he thought, if I did get this woman into my bed, that'd be the exact moment when the federal cop came in and wanted to hand my passport over. Then what would I do? Nope, better to simply look and lust, but don't get all calf-eyed over her.

Standing in line to be waited on at the little open-air espresso stand, Mel couldn't help smiling. The American was typical male, show him a womanly curve and watch his tongue get all tied up in knots. The fact he wasn't bad-looking didn't hurt either. Made her job more interesting.

Passing her money over and taking the steaming flat white, her gloating came to an abrupt halt when she saw Samantha coming down the street.

'Wow,' the younger woman said, giving Mel a long study, 'are those tights the best knock-'em-dead slut clothes that pass for fashion in this part of the world? And rubber, too. How kinky.'

Mel wanted to throw her coffee but held back. 'Finally got out of bed?' she said, knowing it was a lame comeback. 'I'm amazed, after all, it's barely noon.'

'Meow. You're funny, girlfriend. I'll have you know I've been up and out taking photos since sun-up. Got some good shots of boats going out with the rising sun in the background. There might be a market for them, who knows. But I did come looking for you and here you are, having coffee. May I join you?' Not waiting, she turned to get in to place her order.

With the good feeling she'd been enjoying, Mel didn't see a way out of it. She'd have to somehow get this damn fool girl to go back to Musgrave to the *Sun Life Magazine* and get out of her hair.

'Well,' said Samantha, after removing the lid, dropping it into a stainless steel bin near the door, then holding her own take-away coffee and being careful not to slop it over, 'you said you'd have your cock-fighting story ready. Where is it? I'm sick of being up here in this heat and humidity. Cairns just isn't big enough for me.'

'Look, I haven't got time to deal with you now. I'm in the middle of a dive class. How about we have a drink later and I'll give it to you?'

'A dive lesson? Guess that's one way to deal with the hot sun. Okay. Over at the pub. Think you'll be finished by five?'

'Yeah, the class ends a bit before that.'

Walking back to the dive school, Mel was a bit worried. She knew she'd have to get rid of her without making her angry. If that was possible.

It would have been better to have kept her photographer in sight.

Chapter Forty-Six

'Okay, gang,' JC called out once his tourist divers were assembled. 'We'll stay here in the area of the boat harbour. Stay together and close enough to watch me. While we're under water, I'll point out various things. My aim is to watch you all, while your job is to get used to seeing what it's like. There is a slight tidal current out in the channel, so if you do feel the water moving, it'll mean you're getting away from safety. Everybody understand?'

'Yeah,' the youngest student held up his hand as if asking for a toilet break, 'are we going to see any fish?'

'There'll likely be some, but nothing like you'll find when you go out onto the reef. I took a look at one of the brochures while you were at lunch. There are whales, dolphins, turtles, sea snakes and sharks out there. Not that you'll have to worry about the sharks or snakes. That's what the dive master will be there for. In here, we'll be lucky to see things like mangrove jack and flathead. I don't know what those look like; remember, I'm new to this harbour.'

The harbour dive itself turned out, for some of the students, worth the price of admission itself. Finding themselves in a world of murky water, with long strands of sea grasses flowing slowly back and forth in the weak current, was for the first-timers like entering a wonderland.

JC happened to be watching the youngster and rushed to his side when the kid spotted a foot-long silvery shape whip past. The young diver opened his mouth in a silent yell and took in a gulp of salt water. Quickly, JC hoisted his head up into the air.

'Cough it up,' he said, holding the boy's head still. He'd spat out the mouthpiece when surprised. Water streamed from his mouth as he coughed, sucking in fresh air. 'Relax now. You're okay. Breathe normally. That's it. See? You've learned something all the rest still have to face. The fact is, you can't breathe underwater if you don't keep the mouthpiece in place.'

The youngster, breathing normally, nodded. 'That was scary.'

JC smiled and placed the boy's mouthpiece against his lips. 'Okay. Now let's try it again, only this time keep your mouth closed.'

The rest of the dive went smoothly. Once the divers got over their initial excitement at being under water, they started to explore. More than once, JC had to swim over and motion one or another of the divers back towards the boat docks.

Mel took her time getting out of her wetsuit and back into shorts and a t-shirt. It was an old one, worn thin with the Third Blind Eye band logo so faded it was almost unreadable. Once again, looking down at her chest, she was happy about her breasts. They weren't huge, but she'd never had trouble getting a good bra. She was sure the nicely rounded mounds would catch the Americans' attention.

He noticed. She'd waited, making sure she was the last one out of the dressing room. All the other students were milling around as JC signed each certificate, making them certified scuba divers. One by one, holding the document in one hand and shaking the instructor's hand with the other, they left the school. Happy graduation. Most agreed with the idea of meeting at the pub for a celebration drink. Mel stayed back and was the last to be handed her graduation diploma.

'There you go,' said JC. He'd seen her standing back and was prepared when she finally came forth. He would not, he vowed, look at her chest. But he did. 'Oh, by the way,' he continued, handing her a colourful brochure. 'I picked this up for you. Remember, you asked about what that diving certificate gave you? In there is a list of the best five scuba diving sites in the world. You can now, with that piece of paper you're holding in your hand, go to any one of these places. They'll all have dive boats and dive masters more than glad to take you out. You'll notice,' he said going on, 'the Great Barrier Reef is the number one site. In the world.' She didn't bother telling him she had no plans to go reef diving. 'Well, anyway,' he said, still working to look only at her eyes. 'I wanted to show it to you to, you know, reassure you that what you spent learning to dive was money well spent.'

Mel took the brochure, glanced at it and shoved it in a pocket. 'Okay, thanks. Now, can we talk a bit?' she asked. 'I've got a proposal to make.'

'Well, all right' – feeling a bit deflated – 'I like the idea of being proposed to.' Damn, he didn't want to say that.

Following her out of the building, he watched how her shorts covered her smooth bottom. No visible panty line there.

Whatever the young woman had on her mind, he was sure it wasn't going to be what he had on his. As it turned out, he was right.

Chapter Forty-Seven

Leaving the school, they walked over to the lawn surrounding the city's swimming lagoon. JC had brought his lunch down there a couple of times. He had read the bronze plaque giving the history of the popular area. The lagoon, shelters, landscaping and stylised fountains in the centre had all been funded with state, federal and local funds. The names of the city's mayor at the time and a number of the council members were listed as having taken part in the ribbon-cutting event.

It didn't take a genius to understand how the huge lagoon came to be so popular. The shoreline all along the northern coast was actually shallow tidal flats. In order to find water deep enough to swim, one would have to wade a long way off shore. It just wasn't possible for swimmers to get out into the ocean. Plus, according to the info sheets provided to instructors at the dive school, there were always the stingers – jellyfish of all kinds, all able to cause pain. One kind, with a name he couldn't pronounce if he could even remember it, was very bad and could cause death. Except for the one with a strange name, some experts advised pouring vinegar on the stings to stop the pain, others suggested urinating on that spot. Reading that and visualising the crowd it would draw – him standing there peeing on someone's arm or leg – he decided to go for the vinegar solution if the need ever presented itself.

Whatever the remedy, many communities along the northern coast, according to that same printed sheet, had erected "stinger nets" around swimming beaches. Here in Cairns, instead of stinger net enclosures, the city fathers created the lagoon, installing a concrete wall between the open ocean and the large saltwater lake. Around that lake lawns, benches and small open-shelters were placed. JC and Mel chose a bench in one of the open-air shelters. The solid wall behind them gave some protection from the breeze that had sprung up. From where they were sitting they had a good view of the swimmers.

'Okay, then,' JC said, settling back and looking across at all the kids splashing around in the water, 'what is this proposal all about?'

Mel sat for a long minute, thinking, trying to decide exactly how much she should tell him. It wouldn't do to bring the diamonds into the picture. After all, what did she know about this man? Hadn't he been mates with that bartender? Maybe she should look elsewhere for the assistance she needed. But he did have the best qualifications. And he did seem to be a lot friendlier than Harry, the bartender.

'I have a little story to tell you,' she said after a bit. 'It begins a long time ago.'

'In a land far, far away,' said JC, cutting in. 'Is this some kind of fairy tale?'

'No. It's about my grandfather. It starts in about 1942 or so, close to the end of the war. I can't remember exactly, but at the time he was piloting an airplane and was shot down by a Japanese plane.'

'Ah, and you know where his plane crashed and you want to go dive it.'

His comment shocked the woman. 'How… how'd you know that?'

'Well, easy. The other day you asked about diving wrecks, remember? And now you bring your grandfather's airplane into the conversation. Adding one and one equals your proposal. You want to go diving on the plane your grandfather crashed. No can do, Ms Graves' – Stern-faced he shook his head – 'in the first place, WWII ended, what, seventy-some-odd years ago? Any aircraft left in salt water that long, well, there won't be much left. For sure, if your grandfather was killed in the crash, his body would be long gone. I hate to be the one to tell you, but there it is.'

It was Mel's turn to shake her head. 'No, he wasn't killed then. Fact is, he came home and lived a long and fairly prosperous life. He and my grandmother. My father was born after the war, actually.'

'So it isn't your grandfather you want to find. Just his plane?'

'Yes. According to his letters, which I found in a box when my parents died, almost everybody on board the airplane that day was rescued. Only a couple people were shot and killed when the Japanese plane strafed his plane. His co-pilot was one. After he was rescued, my grandfather told his wife, my grandmother, that he'd had enough of flying. He returned to Brisbane and they bought a small holding where they raised their family.'

'Okay, and why do you want to find his plane? For sentimental reasons? Do you have any idea how dangerous that would be? Think about it. An airplane is mostly aluminium and steel. Well, in seven decades that steel would rust out, or most of it would anyway. What's left would only be held in place by the marine growth that grew up around it. Not a good place to be diving around.'

She wasn't going to be so easily talked out of it. 'Have you ever dived a wreck? Didn't someone say something about a popular diving spot being a place up in Indonesia where the bottom of a bay was covered with planes sunk during the war? If it's so dangerous, how can it be so popular?'

JC had to smile at her argument. 'I honestly don't know. Wreck diving isn't one of my pleasures. Look, all I do is deliver boats. Up and down the west coast. The American west coast. All kinds of boats. When I have to check out the bottom of a boat for some reason, I strap on a scuba tank and go diving. That's the extent of my experience. Whatever you are thinking of doing, I'm not your man. Sorry.' And, remembering how she looked in that wetsuit, he was sorry.

'Okay. But you do know about diving. I can't go off by myself. Even if I find the plane, wouldn't it be better if a qualified dive instructor was with me?' Looking the man eye-to-eye, she saw him shake his head. 'This is important to me,' she went on, 'and all it'll take is a couple days. A day to drive over, a couple days searching for the plane and the drive back. Say three or four days. What do they pay you at the school? I'll make up any money you'd lose.'

JC turned his attention to the swimmers out in the water. A few days. That's what his boss back in San Diego, Ralph Lewis, had said. Take a little delivery job down to Australia, he said. Just take a few weeks. Uh huh. And look where he ended up. In the far north of the damn state. Sun too hot to be out in, the air so humid you can't breathe and with a federal drug cop holding his passport. Now this woman wanted him to go wreck diving. Sure, just take a few days. Sure.

Well, hell. Thinking again of her body, what could it hurt? Spend a few days with her and who knew where it could end?

Who knew where?

Chapter Forty-Eight

Samantha Edgerly wasn't happy. She'd done what she'd been hired to do – get photos for a story being written by that frizzy-haired journalist. But could she submit those shots? Not until Ms Journo got her shit together. Okay, so wait a couple days, she says. Now it's time; we'll talk later this afternoon. At the pub. Samantha didn't like being shifted around.

Finishing her coffee, she decided to walk down by the harbour. Maybe get a few shots of something down there. Boats and children – there's always a market for good photos of those kinds of things.

It wasn't to be. Maybe because of the temperature or the humidity, there was nothing happening down at the docks. Even the boats tied to the various floats were still and unmoving. Too damn hot to move, even for boats sitting in the water.

'I'll bet that water is too hot to swim in,' she muttered to herself. Stripping down to her bikini would be inviting sunburn, so that was out. And she'd bought that bikini just before being sent up here. The tiniest of swimmies and something sure to light someone's fire. But not up here in this hell-hole. Okay, then. Back to the pub to wait for the all-important other half of this assignment? At least it'd be cool in the air con.

Samantha was past the dive school when she glanced over towards the saltwater lagoon. Even from the back, she recognised Melissa. Walking with some man. Interested, she stopped and watched as they disappeared in one of the shelters.

'Wonder what little Miss Ginger is up to.' Smiling to herself, she casually strolled across the lawn towards the back of the shelter. Silently, she stood against the corner. Out of sight of either of the two in the shelter, anyone seeing her would think she was simply standing in the shade, watching the swimmers. Careful not to move against the shelter wall, she listened.

'Wait a minute,' JC said, getting his mind off her body and working again, 'your grandfather didn't die in the crash. The plane crashed in the ocean. What's so important about that plane that now, a lotta years later, you want to find it? Didn't you hire Harry Bridges to help you get that cock-fight story for some magazine? That got him arrested, didn't it? Is that what this is – information for a magazine article?'

Mel knew this question was going to come up. She had thought about using the idea of research for a magazine article. But what would he say, when she didn't take along the photographer? Or when she came up holding the cigar-box package? If that is, she was able to find the package her grandfather had shoved under the pilot's seat. What then? No, the only thing to do was to play fair and give him the truth. Or at least part of it.

'It's not about a magazine article,' she said, after thinking about it one last time, 'it's a treasure hunt. My grandfather left something in the plane that could be valuable.'

'Treasure,' said JC, not sounding convinced. 'Uh huh. Sunken treasure lost in a WWII battle with the evil Japanese.'

'Something like that. It had a lot of value seventy years ago, so it'd be worth more today, don't you think?'

'Yeah, depending on what it was. Sitting at the bottom of the ocean wouldn't be good for most things. Like drugs or art.'

'It wouldn't be at the bottom of any ocean, either. I know where he came down. It was near the mouth of a river. The Nelson River. Nobody else knows that. And it wasn't art or drugs he was carrying. How about gold? Would seventy years in salt water bother gold? Or… or diamonds? Sea water wouldn't damage any of that, would it?'

'Is that what you want to go searching for? Gold or diamonds?'

'And you'll get twenty-five per cent of whatever it is. What do you say?'

JC was looking her straight in the eye. Her green eyes. *Might as well ask for the moon*, he thought. So far, he didn't have anything to lose. Who went looking for sunken treasure in this day and age? 'Fifty-fifty,' he said. 'No more, no less.'

Not what she wanted, but half of something was better than not getting any of it. She nodded her agreement.

Samantha, having heard most of what had been said, smiled as she quickly walked back towards the street. Glancing over her shoulder to make sure she wasn't seen, her smile turned into a smirk. A story about treasure. Well, sweet cheeks could deal with it herself; take her own damn photos. Treasure hunting. My gawd, if that's the best the witch could do and if that guy she was talking to fell for it, then good luck to both of them.

'I may be new to the game of journalism,' Samantha told herself silently, 'but I'm no fool. Or maybe old red is just after that guy. Yeah. Dressing like a tart and promising treasure. What a pair of dorks!'

Booking a seat on the Brisbane-bound Sunliner, the photographer felt better about things. With a bit over an hour before her train left, she decided to have a glass of wine at the hotel pub. Yeah, she'd be gone by five and wouldn't have to listen to her former partner try to explain the article she was supposed to have written. Nodding, she was happy with the decision. What could be better? She'd write a note explaining how she'd waited long enough and then send a copy to that editor. That'd get her clear when she turned up with the photos and there was no story. That beefy bartender, Harry, let him give it to her. Her first photo essay on a pretty good story. It'll be better than anything Ms Graves could come up with. Treasure. Gawd, how dumb.

Samantha Edgerly never knew how close she came to a real big story.

Chapter Forty-Nine

Harry didn't say anything when Gabbi got to work. Hells bells, it wasn't his job to chew the dumb kid out for being late. His job was to pour beer and be nice to customers. Pulling pints of beer was the easy part, being nice to scum like those two sitting over there, was asking too much.

Dobby and Ruckman had been sitting there, nursing their pints of mid-strength for the past hour. Harry thought they must be waiting for something. Neither had said anything after calling for the beer and didn't seem to be paying anyone any attention. It had to have something to do with drugs. As soon as he could, after arriving in Brisbane, he'd called the contacts he'd been given. That was supposed to be the end of it. Webster would deliver the cocaine, he'd get his payment and fly back to South America. Yeah, as easy as that. Except it didn't work out like that did it. No, the damn cops were waiting. So what could he do but make the phone call and let them know. What happened? Was he paid what they owed him? No. He'd been given the run-around. First, he'd been directed to an address in Fortitude Valley. It was those two sitting over there who'd met him at the door. Smirking, and after making sure he wasn't armed or wearing a wire, had opened the door. The men he'd met inside, they probably weren't at the top of the food chain either, but they certainly scared the crap out of him. Convincing them he'd had nothing to do with the cops waiting for the sailboat hadn't easy. They didn't want to believe he wasn't screwed up.

Well, hell. Harry knew how it worked. Everybody had to cover their asses. The men he met had to answer to someone higher up. That's the way it went. He'd been with that shipment since it left the jungle laboratory. He had no clue as to how the coppers learned it was on board. Not being very high up helped; they believed him. After a while. But now, here are those two muscles from that gang. What the hell were they here for? Not to keep an eye on him, he hadn't known he was coming to Cairns until that federal drug cop had told him about it. No, they were here for something else. Maybe that's what they were waiting for now.

Not knowing what was going on, Harry did what bartenders always did: he washed and polished the glasses that had just come out of the dishwasher. And watched and waited.

Gabbi, knowing he was late to work, came around the corner and nearly rushed on into the pub. Luckily, he spotted those two men before reaching the open door. They were sitting there, waiting for him. He didn't want to talk to them again. Stepping back, he stood with his hands in his pockets and tried to think of what to do. He needed the job. It was a good place to sell his little bags of products. But those two said he wasn't going to sell directly to his customers any more. And if he couldn't sell to his customers, then there was no reason to keep the job, was there?

Standing there with his head down, trying to think of what to do, he almost missed seeing the white woman coming across the street. It was one of those who had been arrested at the cock-fight. He watched as she came, heading straight for the pub. Like most white women, she walked with her shoulders back, her head held up and her stride strong. Like a goanna on the hunt for dinner. Maybe, he thought, when she walked into the pub, everyone would look at her and not see him. Then he could get into the back room, if he was quick.

Dobby's head jerked up and he quickly glanced over to see if Ruckman had caught him. Damn, sitting here, waiting for that stupid kid was too much. He could hardly keep his eyes open. Sipping his warm beer, he frowned. It'd gone stale. Before he could order his partner to get a couple glasses, his attention was caught by the woman who came in the open door. *Ah, now there's a good looker*, he thought. Recognising her as one of the women who'd been arrested with Harry, he smiled, forgetting the stale beer. Maybe there was something here after all.

He'd been disappointed when the federal policeman had arranged for Harry and the two women not to have to face charges. Telling the big men down in Brisbane about the trouble Harry the Horse was in would have been good. But maybe there was still something going on they'd like to know about.

He didn't notice the young dope dealer slide in beside the woman. Keeping her slightly ahead, he quickly went on, silently opening the door, heading for the broom locker. Gabbi hadn't seen Harry's frown.

Harry had started to growl at the sight of Gabbi coming in, but stopped when he saw the photographer. What could she want? 'Hey, miss. Come in out of the heat?' he asked, wiping the bar in front of where the woman stood. 'How about a cold beer to help you cool off. Man, I don't see how people can live up here, what with the sun beating down and the humidity. Christ, the humidity. The air feels so thick it's hard to breathe.'

Samantha glanced at the big clock hanging behind the bar, above the mirror. Yes, she had time for a glass of beer.

'I'll have a pot of light, thank you.'

Reaching for a glass Harry laughed. 'I'll never get used to that, a "pot" of "light". It took me a couple days to figure out that's a half-pint glass filled with a low-alcohol brew.' Filling the glass, he slid it across. 'On me. After all, we were almost cell mates.' His chuckle sounded false to his ears.

'Thank you. Look, I've got a favour to ask. I'm on my way out and want to leave Melissa a note. Would you give it to her when she comes in? We were supposed to meet here at five, but I've got a train to catch.'

'Of course. Yeah, Melissa. Now, if you ask me, there's a basket case. Oh,' he said, holding up his hands, 'I know you two are friends or at least you work together, but… Well, I guess I should shut up.'

Samantha sipped her beer before saying anything. 'No. We are definitely not friends. And this was the first

time we'd ever worked together. And the last, let me tell
you.' She took another drink, putting the glass down on
the bar.

Harry picked it up and refilled it, smiling at her. 'Oh,
I take it you two had a falling out?'

'You got that right' – she sipped the fresh beer –
'that slut can work by herself. Oh, no, I almost forgot,
she's got a new partner. A guy you know' – she glanced
up and smiled at the bartender – 'your sailing mate. She's
taken up with him in her search for treasure. Can you
believe that? Sunken treasure.'

Neither paid any attention to anything else and didn't
notice how Dobby had slid his chair closer. Her last
words made the man's eyes flick up. Don't say anything,
he sent a silent command towards his partner. We may be
onto something.

Chapter Fifty

'Sunken treasure?' Harry laughed. 'Don't tell me she's found a map showing a long-lost treasure. You know, X marks the spot?'

Samantha took a bigger swallow, finishing her beer. Quickly, almost like a sleight-of-hand magician's trick, Harry had another in front of her. This time it wasn't low-alcohol light but a full strength brew. The young woman, taking a sip, didn't notice the difference.

'I didn't hear anything about a map. All I heard was something about an airplane lost in the ocean and the red-headed witch asking your mate to help her dive for it. It wasn't clear' – nodding her head and drinking her beer, she looked up and smiled – 'oh, and something about gold and diamonds.'

Dobby had been leaning forward, trying to hear. All he got was the words treasure, then gold and diamonds. That's all he needed to hear. Quietly sliding his chair back to the table, he nodded to his partner. Quickly, they finished what was left in their glasses and, waving a hand in Harry's direction, strolled out to the street.

'What're we doing?' Ruckman asked, picking at Dobby's shirt sleeve. 'What'd you hear? I thought we were waiting for that dumb-arsed kid. He didn't come in, did he? Where're we going now?'

'You ask too many questions. Don't worry about the kid. We'll take care of him later. Right now, I want to find that red-headed newspaper reporter. We're going to become her shadows for a while.'

Ruckman frowned down at the pavement. None of this made any sense to him.

Gabbi had heard what the woman at the bar had said. It didn't make any sense to him either. But that wasn't important. What was important was watching those two big men get up and walk out. For a while, he was safe. Now he had to think about what to do. Getting out of town would be the first thing. Hitch a ride back to the village. Nodding, he started to step out of the back room but stopped. Better to wait until that bartender wasn't watching.

'Gold and diamonds, you say?' Harry said, disbelief in his words. 'Somewhere around here? Or maybe out on the reef.'

'No, not here,' Samantha said, sipping at her beer. Funny, she hadn't had but one glass and her head was feeling a bit tiddly. She'd never been a drinker. One of the guys she'd dated back at Uni had called her a cheap drunk. That hadn't made her happy, being called cheap anything. But it was true and that's why she rarely drank much. Oh, well, she'd be on the train soon. She could sleep it off.

'Not here?' asked Harry, leaning closer, trying to judge just how drunk she was. For Christ's sake, she'd only put away a couple glasses. Couldn't let her get away without telling him all she had heard. 'Where, if not here?'

Samantha held the beer glass up to the light, liking the colour of the brown liquid against the light. 'Huh? Oh, I don't know. Uh, somewhere over west of here, she said. In the gulf. Some river. Hmm, I can't remember. Nelson River? Something like that.'

Gabbi, leaning against the partially open door perked up. Did she say the Nelson River? Maybe she meant the Norman River. That was the river his village was on. His field was just down the river from the village. Was that where the other white woman was going? Maybe he could get a ride with her.

'What time is it?' Samantha asked, looking bleary-eyed at her mobile. 'Oh, god. I gotta go. I got a train to catch. What do I owe you?'

Harry wasn't paying any attention but looked up at her question. 'Huh? Oh, nothing. Let me buy you the beer.'

'Yeah? You wanna shout me the drinks? Well, I guess we're some kind of friends. I mean, we did get arrested together, didn't we?'

Harry smiled. 'Think nothing of it. Now, you'd better hurry. Don't want to miss your train.'

'Yeah, thanks. Take care of yourself.' She waved as she went out into the late afternoon sunshine.

Harry stood for a moment, thinking about what she'd said. Holding up the note he'd been given, he smiled thinly. He'd have to be careful when the red-headed journalist came in. Maybe there was more he could learn.

Gabbi waited and when the big bartender had his back to the room, he quickly scooted out the door.

Gold and diamonds, Harry said to himself, not seeing the young man go scudding by. *Maybe*, he thought, *making eye contact with himself in the mirror, just maybe she knew something worthwhile*. This could be what he needed. Ever since the cops raided that damn sailboat, he'd felt he was in danger. He remembered back in the jungle what had happened to a couple men who'd lied to the wrong man. These people weren't someone to screw with. The big men down in Brisbane in charge of this end of the operation wouldn't take the loss easily. Someone would have to pay. He didn't want it to be him.

Looking around, he saw that Dobby and his asinine fool of a partner had left. Well, good. Maybe they were just in Cairns for the reasons they talked about, but maybe not. He wasn't sure how things worked in this godforsaken country. Somehow, having them around made him feel more uncomfortable. Paranoid? Well, yeah. But with good reason. Men had a habit of going missing when things didn't go right with these people.

But gold and diamonds. Now if that was the real deal, maybe it'd be what he needed to get away from it all. To make his break. Yeah, gold and diamonds. He smiled at his reflection.

Chapter Fifty-One

Inspector Lambert would never have known about the so-called "treasure" if it hadn't been for the Queensland police officer, Senior Sargent Louis Crabb. A man at the very end of his career with the Queensland Police, Sargent Crabb hadn't been happy about the request to let the three whites off on that cock-fighting charge. It didn't seem fair, and Crabb knew himself to be a fair man. A policeman with a strong sense of the law. He'd listened to the federal officer and, with the assurance that bigger things were in store for one of the three, he'd withdrawn the charge.

Well, to be honest, Crabb had been in the police long enough to know better than to go head-to-head with a member of the media. But dammit, he'd come away from that raid feeling like a gut-shot fox. He'd been trying to catch ol' Rooster Jackson for, well, a long time. And what happens? The raid not only gets Farmer Jackson but a couple dozen others. And to make it even better, a big bloke and a couple sheilas were taken in. That alone would be worth a handshake from the do-gooders over at the RSPCA. But he let that federal drug squad fella talk him out of it.

Crabb still wasn't feeling good about it. This late in the day, it didn't help to see Dobby and Ruckman coming down the street, yammering at each other. Those two were known to be drug dealers. Like Farmer Jackson, though, there was never enough to put them away. Seeing them walking along like honest men was more than Louis Crabb could take.

'Okay, then gentlemen,' he said, coming up behind them and grabbing hold of the upper arms of the two men. 'I think it's time for us to have a little talk. Down at the watchhouse, if you don't mind. Come along with you.'

Holding tight to their arms, Crabb hurried them along the street and up the three steps to the Cairns court house.

'Wait a minute,' Dobby yelled, holding back before the policeman could kick open the big door. 'What're you hassling us for? All we were doing was walking down the street, minding our own business.'

Crabb snorted. 'I'll be the judge of that,' he growled. 'We'll have our little talk and just see what that business turns out to be.'

Dobby didn't like the idea of a background check. He didn't think there was any paper out against him, but he wasn't sure. The big men down in Brisbane hadn't wasted any time getting him and Ruckman out of town, but you never knew.

'It ain't fair,' he said, pulling his arm free. 'Look, it won't do any of us good to get collected up. Maybe, just maybe, we did hear something. Yeah, something that might interest the law. How about we talk about it. And not down in any interview room. Maybe we got something to trade.'

Pulling the two men up the steps had taken some of the fire out of Officer Crabb's anger. He didn't have anything to hang on these men and taking them any further could end up being embarrassing. So maybe he'd let them trade for their freedom.

Thinking about it a little later, he knew he'd been lucky, he'd almost let his frustration get him in trouble, something he couldn't afford this close to the end of what, so far, had been a career to be proud of. Better to go out with a clean record of arrests. Well, one good thing, those two fools would know he'd be keeping an eye on them. They'd mind their manners. At least for a while. Anyhow, maybe what he'd been told would be of interest to that federal drug cop. Couldn't do any harm and who knew, maybe there'd be something in it for him.

There was, but whatever it was would have to wait until morning. Mrs Crabb didn't like him to be late for his supper.

Chapter Fifty-Two

After leaving the pub, Gabbi walked down towards the dive school. Seeing the red-haired woman standing by a car talking to a man, he stopped and waited. He didn't know if this was the woman's new partner or not. He'd wait.

When the man went into the school's main building, Gabbi hurried across the street. When he asked her if it was true, she was going to drive across to the Norman River, he was surprised to see her expression. Maybe he'd made a mistake.

Mel was shocked. 'How'd you hear that?' she asked, feeling a little panicky.

'The other woman, with all the cameras, I heard her talking to the bartender at the hotel pub. She said you were driving over to Norman River. That is my home and I would like a ride, if you are going there.'

Melissa wondered how Samantha had learned of her plans. She hadn't told anyone except JC and that only a little while ago. Shaking her head, she looked crossly at the young man. 'What did the other woman say, exactly?'

Gabbi was afraid he'd made a mistake. 'She said you had a new partner and were going to drive over to the Gulf. She was going to take a train back to Brisbane and you were going to drive. That's all I heard.'

'And that's where you live?'

'Yes. The village on the river, Karumba. I have a small farm downstream from the village. I go to school here, but now I must go back to my village.'

Mel thought about it for a moment. 'Tell me about that river. How far is it from your village out to the gulf?'

'You are going down the river to the salt water? I can help you. I have a tinnie and you can use it. It isn't far.'

Before Mel could decide, JC came out, carrying an armload of equipment. 'JC, this young man is looking for a ride over to Karumba. He lives near there and says he has a tinnie we can use to get out to the mouth of the river. What do you think?'

'What's a tinnie?'

'You know, a small aluminium boat. I had thought we could rent one from someone in the village, but if he's willing to swap, it'd be better. He could go along to show us the way.'

JC smiled. 'Sounds good to me. Let me get the rest of our gear and we can get started.'

Gabbi watched as the air tanks, fins and weight belts were stowed in the car's boot. The tanks took up most of the space and JC had to adjust the rolled-up tent, sleeping bags and other camping gear already packed away. 'Gawd, you'd think we're going away for a month. You sure we'll only be gone a few days?'

Mel nodded and chuckled. 'Yeah. If it takes longer than that, it'll mean we aren't able to find what we're looking for. Anyway, I only rented that stuff for a few days.'

Finally, satisfied that everything was stowed, he carefully closed the boot lid, he turned to the woman. 'Okay. That's about everything I can think of we'll need.'

'It would be better,' said Gabbi, 'to get an early start in the morning. Leaving now would mean driving all night. Better to drive during daylight.'

JC quickly agreed, saying the young man's suggestion made sense. Somehow, he didn't like the idea of driving at night. But all night? How frigging far was this drive going to be, anyway? They decided to get an early start in the morning.

Chapter Fifty-Three

JC wasn't happy. Getting up and on the road before the sun was really up made him grouchy. The quick breakfast they'd had wasn't to his liking. Now, with the early morning sun shining in his rear-view mirror, he was about to call it off. Except Melissa had rented the car and he'd paid for the rental on the scuba gear. And then there was the promise of treasure. He liked that, even if he wasn't totally convinced they'd be able to find the wreckage. Wreckage that'd been lost in the ocean for seventy years? C'mon, give me a break. But thinking of Melissa in her wetsuit made it all more worthwhile.

The highway out of town was the same Mel had taken out to that chicken farmer's place. Now, not entirely awake, she frowned at the memory. That certainly hadn't turned out so good. Sitting by the passenger's side and watching the world go by, she wondered what had happened to that old man. Whatever it was, probably served him right. But what about his chooks? Not her worry. Glancing back over her shoulder, she saw that Gabbi was wide awake and calmly sitting with his hands in his lap, looking out the window. She wondered what he was thinking.

'Somehow,' said JC after twenty miles or so of silence and having decided to make an attempt at being civil, 'I didn't expect the highway to be this good.'

'Yeah,' said Gabbi from the backseat, 'it is pretty good. Gets narrower soon, though.'

'And this will take us the rest of the day?'

'Yes. Karumba is on the other side of Cape York Peninsula. We'll be there before night. It is a good place, Karumba. My people have been there for many generations. The river takes the fishermen out into the salt water. It is a pretty good life, there.'

'Your people. What's the name of your tribe?'

'On the east side, north of Cairns, it is the Kuku Yalanji people. All through this land, going across are the Kunjen and on the Gulf coast is the land of the Kokoberra. These people have lived here for a very long time. In a book at school, I read how the oldest occupation of people in Australia was here. About 8,000 years ago, there was a land bridge between Australia and New Guinea. Then it was one big continent. Scientists call it Sahul. My mother's stories tell of how people lived in the ancient or story time. The stories are about how they lived before.'

'Before?'

'Yes. Before now.' Turning his head towards the side window, Gabbi nodded but didn't say anything else.

Looking out as the residential neighbourhoods changed into rural farmland, JC thought about what life must have been like in the ancient times. Hard. Maybe, like in the times before European settlers arrived in the

US, the people here had been hunter/gatherers. Things had certainly changed in the last couple hundred years. Looking at the fenced fields of some kind of farm produce, he nodded. Now, the people living here were farmers. And back on the coast, fishermen. Where the tourists come, waiters, bartenders and dive instructors. Thinking about that reminded him of Harry. And the federal drug cop. Wonder what he's going to say about this little trip? Well, maybe it wouldn't take long. A couple days of diving to show Melissa that her grandfather's airplane had really disappeared. Then what? Return to Cairns, go back to work at the dive shop? Or maybe that inspector would give up and hand him his passport so he could get back to his life. Back to delivering boats. Is that what he was going to do the rest of his days – deliver boats along the California coast?

That line of thinking was beginning to make him feel depressed. Before he could tell himself to get over it, a huge truck came barrelling towards them causing a blast of air to shake the car. Caught daydreaming, JC was surprised when the long vehicle took so long to go by.

'My god,' he said, glancing into the rear view mirror to watch the back of the last trailer disappear. 'That must have been a quarter mile long.'

'A road-train,' said Gabbi. 'They carry shipments to the larger communities. No trains out here. Huge trucks pulling three trailers can be as long as fifty metres.'

'He was really travelling. Wouldn't want to hit a kangaroo.'

'They have a heavy set of bars on the front, called a bull-bar. And thick steel mesh to protect the wind screen. Hitting a kangaroo wouldn't stop a road train at full speed.'

'Guess it's best to stay awake.'

Slowly, the landscape changed. Large fenced pasturages, many with herds of what JC thought were probably dairy cows, gave way to brown grass-covered open range. The low-lying hills in the distance disappeared as the land flattened. Soon the only sign of someone living near was as narrow dirt tracks going off, disappearing into the scrub brush. Once, a long time ago, he'd driven across Nevada. This reminded him of that country, flat and empty as far as you could see, without a sign of human habitation. Then, as now, the colours changed from green acreages planted in some agricultural products to dry, brown grasses broken only by scatterings of short scrub trees.

For the next couple hours, while Melissa fell asleep with her head against the closed window, pillowed by her folded jacket, JC focused on staying awake.

'Old story told by my mother,' said Gabbi, leaning forward so he wouldn't disturb the sleeping woman, 'had to do with one woman advising another woman to be careful on a long trip, and to keep the driver awake.'

The one woman said, 'You get too tired, you wanna camp on the road, you know. Don't travel, the man driving might go to sleep, he must be knocked up too, you know. Camp on the road. I'll give you a stick. You give him a poke in the ribs, keep him awake.'

JC waited a bit for more. The youngster had finished, sat back and went on looking out the window. 'Is that all?' asked JC. 'Is there a hidden message in that story?'

'Wondered if you want me to get a stick, give you a poke in the ribs to keep you awake?'

JC shook his head. 'No, I'm good. Sitting here thinking, trying to figure out what the hell I'm doing here.'

Gabbi didn't respond.

The two lanes of pavement, complete with a painted centreline and fog lines on either side, suddenly ended. Without warning, JC found himself driving on a single lane of older-looking asphalt. Suddenly, the sound of tyres meeting the road changed too, becoming louder. The pavement looked more like packed dirt or clay than asphalt. Narrow, without a sign of painted lines and nowhere except into the bush to pull off on to escape oncoming traffic.

'Hey, Gabbi,' JC asked, yelling above the increase in road noise, 'is that the end of civilisation?'

'Mt Garnett, turn off. We're about halfway to Karumba.'

'Half way? Single-lane from here on? What about road trains? Where would we go if one came barrelling by?'

'Not much traffic now. You'll see any long trucks in plenty time to pull over. Nobody is ever smashed. Lotsa warning.' Somehow, that didn't make JC feel any better. Glancing over he saw that Melissa had slept through it all.

JC smiled thinly, wondering how she was going to handle it when they didn't find a WWII airplane in whatever water they were headed for.

Chapter Fifty-Four

Harry had had a bad night. Earlier, after he'd been relieved at the pub, he'd gone looking for the two druggies, Dobby and Ruckman. Maybe it was time to have a real talk with those two, find out what the hell they were really up to. The problem was, he didn't know where they hung out. Walking around town, checking out the other pubs and restaurants was the best he could do. The pair wasn't anywhere to be found. He didn't know enough about them, or even who would know where they might be. What a waste of time. Giving up, he bought a six-pack of beer and went up to his hotel room.

Lying back across his bed, he thought about the so-called treasure. Standing behind the bar, he'd heard enough bullshit stories. So what was there about this one that was different? What did that cheap drunk say that made him think what she was saying was worthwhile? Well, look at it from another angle, what did he have to lose? That damn drug cop was holding his passport, so he couldn't leave the country. And if he could grab a plane, where would he go? Where would he be safe? Sooner or later, he'd have to find a way to get out of trouble with the big boys in the syndicate. But right now, going back to the big city wasn't a smart move. He was sure he was still being blamed for losing that shipment of coke.

Dammit, he'd been hired to watch over it but somehow the federal cops had learned of it and what could he do?

Harry had worked for the syndicate long enough to know how things went. Someone had to pay for that shipment not reaching the streets. No, up here in this godforsaken part of the world was probably the safest. Going anywhere now was not healthy. But what if the Graves woman really had something? Gold or diamonds that drunk chick had said. A treasure. What the hell, he didn't have anything to lose, did he? All he really had was a lot of time. Spinning his wheels behind the bar, listening to drunk foreigners joke around. There had to be more than that.

Not believing he'd ever get to sleep, he was surprised when he came awake with the sun beating against his eyelids. Groaning, he slowly swung his feet off the bed. Sitting with his head held in his hands, he tried to figure out what to do next. Coffee was the first thing and it was while sitting at a table on the street, watching people and cars go by, nursing a second long black that he saw something to think about. What was JC doing driving someone's car? And what was the kid from the pub doing in the back seat of a car going past? Sipping the strong espresso he thought about what that could mean.

It didn't take much to help him make the decision. Later, when it came time to open the pub, he had to listen to the manager complaining about Gabbi quitting. 'Dammit, I don't need this. Why can't these damn fools be satisfied?'

Harry didn't ask what'd happened. He didn't care what problems the other man had. He had his own, didn't he?

Not getting a response from Harry didn't stop the man from going on with his complaint. 'It's that damn fool, Gabbi. Tells me last night he's heading back to visit his village. Can you believe it? Last night. Too late for me to find someone to replace him. He just came in saying he'd got a ride with someone and was leaving.'

That got Harry's interest. 'He quit you, huh? Said he was going where?'

'Ah, I don't know. I guess I should have expected it, he's done it before. Goes home for a while then comes back. He's a good worker so I always hire him back. I think he comes from some aboriginal village over on the gulf, near some river. Hell, I can't remember. So yeah, the thing is, any sweeping to get done, you and the other bartender'll have to do it.'

Harry's smile was cold. 'Nope. Sweeping isn't in my job description. Guess you can pay me what you owe me and I'll be on my way.'

'What the hell am I supposed to do for a bartender now? Huh? Okay, so forget the sweeping. I'll do it myself.'

Harry shook his head. 'Nope,' he said again, 'I'm gone.'

While the manager figured what was owed and then went about getting the money from the till, Harry waited, trying to think where he'd get a car so he could take a drive. His talk with Dobby would have to wait. Yeah, maybe the kid was simply going home, but seeing JC drive out of town made him think maybe it had something to do about the treasure. So, let's see where they go. Get a car and make a parade out of it. A parade towards a treasure. Sure.

Chapter Fifty-Five

It was about the same time of morning when Sargent Crabb was having coffee with the federal officer. 'All I heard,' said Sargent Crabb, 'was that someone was talking about a treasure and I thought you'd like to know. No information on what that treasure would be, but the people involved are your friends, the big bartender and those two women I wanted to charge for being at a place of illegal betting.'

Lambert hadn't thought much when Crabb had invited him to an early cup. Now, though, he had the inspector's full attention. 'Bridges and the two women? What were they getting involved in?'

'I don't know. What I heard was simply that one of the women, the one with the cameras, was telling the bartender about something the other woman was doing. It has to do with this treasure. According to my sources, she was drinking beer and starting to sound like she'd about reached her limit.'

'Well, maybe I should have a talk with her.'

'Won't do you any good. She got on last night's five o'clock train south. The Sunliner.' Checking his pocket watch, he nodded. 'You'll have to go to Brisbane to do any talking with that one.'

Lambert frowned. 'Okay, but there's still the other one, uh, Graves, Melissa Graves.'

'I understand her new partner is that other fellow, the bartender's mate, the new instructor over at Cairn's Scuba Dive School. Possibly that's where she is.'

Mel Graves wasn't at the dive school. She had been the day before, he learned when he went in to talk with Rob Jacobson.

'Yeah, she was here. She had just gotten her diving certificate and already all fired up to go for a dive. I think she either sweet-talked that fella you sent to me or maybe she hired him. I don't know which. Was me, I'd bet she sweet-talked him. Of course, it could be something else. But whatever it is, he came late yesterday and rented some dive equipment. Said he'd want it for a couple days. Oh, and you know that young aboriginal kid that sweeps out the pub? Don't remember his name.'

Lambert nodded but didn't say anything.

'Well, he was standing off there and when McCoin came in to top up a couple tanks, I saw him go talk to the woman. The kid, I mean. I don't know what that was all about.'

'Wait a minute, you're confusing me. You say McCoin rented some scuba gear? And then the kid from the pub talked to Melissa Graves and then they all drove off?' Jacobson nodded. 'Well, what would they be up to?'

'Well, I'd say to go diving. Least ways – that's about all a person can do with a pair of tanks and wetsuits. That McCoin fella, he turned out to be a good instructor. The students all gave him high marks. I hope he comes back soon.'

Lambert shook his head. 'Come back from where?'

'Oh, they didn't say. McCoin said he'd be gone for a few days and wanted to rent the dive equipment. According to the chart, there really won't be another load of tourists until the end of the week. Man, did you see the body on that red-haired woman? I wouldn't hesitate if she wanted me to take her for a dive.'

Lambert ignored that. 'So they left here with equipment to go diving but didn't say where,' he mused almost to himself.

'Yep. That's about all I know. All I can tell you.'

The next stop for the inspector was the Crown Hotel to have a talk with Harry Bridges.

'He ain't here,' the pub manager said. 'Finished his shift yesterday and then comes in this morning to say he was quitting. Leaving me shorthanded. No reason for it, but then who knows what that kind of bloke is thinking about. Now, you asked me to hire him and I did, as a favour. Okay, so he did a good job. A bit surly with the customers, but, well, I don't think he was stealing from the till. Anyhow, I can't put up with someone I can't count on to be here when he's supposed to be. You know what I mean?'

'He didn't say where he was going?'

'Nope, just that he'd be gone. Like I said, a bit surly.'

'How about that young man you hired to sweep up around here? Is he still working for you?'

'Nope. He's quit yesterday too. He told me he was leaving and I paid him. He said something about going home. He'd do that every so often – catch a ride home. I think he comes from one of those villages over to the west somewhere. Comes here, does his work, goes to school and doesn't say much. A good worker.'

Lambert stood in the early morning sunshine, thinking. One of the women leaves town on the train. The other talks McCoin into going somewhere with her. Bridges walks out of his job. Smiling, Lambert nodded. Yep. Looks like his patience is going to finally pay off. Now all he has to do is go find out where Harry and McCoin are going and he'll know what they're up to.

Punching the air and laughing out loud, he went looking for his new best friend, Senior Sargent Louis Crabb.

Crabb wasn't having any of it. 'Wait a minute,' he said when Lambert explained what he'd learned. 'What has this man done you want him followed? Does this have to do with that story I gave you? About some treasure?' Lambert nodded. 'Is there something you know about that you're not telling me?'

'No. Look, I had arranged it so Bridges and McCoin came up here to Cairns,' said Lambert, trying to explain. 'I can't prove it but I know one of them is working for a big time drug syndicate. Before I was sent up to the Brisbane office, I worked for the AFP's Serious and Organised Crime Unit in Sydney. Well, it was while I was in Brisbane that we busted a luxury yacht that came in from overseas. A yacht carrying millions of dollars' worth of cocaine. Those two Americans were on that yacht, but I couldn't prove they even knew about the drugs. Damn it, they had to be involved. At least one of them. I'm sure of it. So anyway, I talked them into bringing another boat up here. That kept them in this country and some place I could watch them. When I saw those other two, Ruckman and Dobby, I knew I was right. Those two have a long history with the drug scene in Sydney. What they're doing up here, I don't know, but it can't be good. Now, from what you told me, and having Bridges and McCoin going somewhere, this might be what I've been waiting for. This is what's happening. They are up to something and I want to catch them at it.'

Crabb was still for a long moment, thinking. 'You mentioned Dobby and Ruckman. They're a part of this? I've been watching them since they first hit town. We've got a small drug problem up here, but those two don't deal with the small druggies. And you're talking about the bartender and the other bloke. You think they're up to something. But you don't know what?'

'No. All along, I was sure McCoin wasn't part of anything shady, but now I don't know. He and that woman reporter are up to something. And Bridges is somehow involved. You see why the need to find where they went?'

Thinking about how it'd look if he were part of a major drug bust made the Queensland police officer smile. Crabb liked it. 'And the young abo is with them? I know him. I know where he's going. Let me get some petrol for my car.'

Maybe he could catch Dobby and his mate later. If this member of the Australian Federal Police, part of the Serious and Organised Crime Unit made an arrest, Crabb wanted part of it.

Chapter Fifty-Six

JC had had enough of driving. 'Good thing I didn't know how far it was,' he snarled, directing his comment at the woman, 'I'd never have agreed to this.' Glancing over at the red-haired woman, he tried to quell his anger. He'd sailed a boat halfway across the Pacific Ocean and enjoyed every nautical mile. But driving along this narrow, single-lane piece of shit road was too mucking-fuch. 'What was it you said? "Just a few hours" drive?' How many is a few in Australia? Sounds a lot like your other famous one, heaps. How the hell many is a heap?'

'Don't take on so much,' said Melissa disgustedly. 'This isn't hard work and you don't have to put up with a bunch of tourists. Tourists,' she explained, repeating a popular complaint, 'simply good people who go somewhere and become arseholes.'

'And journalists? People who do what, sneak around in order to dig the dirt on other people?'

'Boy, you do get cranky when you miss your afternoon nap. C'mon, lighten up. We'll get into Karumba, get a room, have a shower and a couple glasses of wine and we'll all feel better.' Turning partially around she looked at the young man in the back seat. 'There is a hotel and pub in this town we're going to, isn't there?'

Gabbi smiled and nodded. 'Yes. A very good hotel, but no pub. Karumba is a dry town. There is no alcohol sold in any of the stores.'

'Ah, gawd,' JC groaned, 'we brought food for a couple days, sleeping bags and our dive equipment. But did we bring a bottle or two of wine? Why would we? A stop at one of the bottle shops and stock up. As easy as that. Except there aren't any bottle shops. We're going into a dry town. Figures.'

'No, sir,' said Gabbi, 'it is against the law to bring alcohol into this region. The village voted it dry a long time ago. Too many of the young men and women were getting drunk and doing bad things.' He settled back, again watching out the side window. Then, leaning forward, he asked, 'you are going camping and have dive equipment. Maybe I can help you find a good place. Tell me, what are you planning?'

Mel smiled. 'It's no secret now. We are thinking of spending a couple days at the mouth of the river. We want to dive along the edge of the Gulf.'

'Ah, you are looking for the big airplane. That is the only thing that would interest white fella divers.'

Mel glanced at JC. 'Well, yes. Do you know about the airplane?'

'Not for sure. For a long time, the fishermen from my village have stayed away from a certain place. It's marked and all our fishermen know. They stay away from it. Too many nets have been lost there. Since before my father's time. Nobody knows what takes the nets and hooks, but it could be a plane. Or maybe just a boat that sank. Or a rocky place. I don't know. The old stories say it is a white fella's airplane.'

'Will you show us where that is? It would save us a lot of time, searching for it. I'll pay you.'

'No. No need to pay me. Someone will rent you a tinnie. Tomorrow morning, we will go down the river to the mouth. I will show you where the float is. My farm is on Jacky-Jacky Creek, a short way before where the river flows into the salt water. I'll take you and then come back to my place. That would be good.'

Mel giggled and hit JC's shoulder with a playful tap. 'See, old grouch, things are looking up. We won't have to spend much time searching. Maybe we can be back in Cairns in time for your next set of dive lessons.'

JC liked hearing her giggle. He'd let his temper show and he didn't like that. Now he felt a little better about it.

'Hey, Gabbi,' he asked over his shoulder as he drove over a narrow one-lane bridge, 'is that the Norman River?' This wasn't the first such bridge they'd crossed. Narrow one-lane with only a low square log on either side as a barrier. A sign just before the span warns motorists to watch for oncoming traffic. Anyone coming in that direction, according to the sign, had the right of way. Not a bridge that would ever get approval in California.

Gabbi leaned closer to the window, looking down. 'No. The Norman is still about fifty kilometres. That's Blackbull Creek.'

Harry got to the Blackbull Creek Bridge about an hour later. He'd checked a map at the Cairns Tourist

Bureau and found the Norman River, a blue snake-track flowing into the Gulf of Carpentaria. The map didn't give any indication of how far it was across the Cape York Peninsula. He felt like he'd been driving forever. Should have brought more beer, he complained to himself. Who would have thought that a six-pack wasn't going to be enough? Spotting a weathered sign, he smiled. Karumba 52 km. Another hour then he'd have a cold one.

He'd have to be careful, though, and not let the reporter woman or good old JC see him. His luck, there'd only be one pub or hotel in the damn town. Have to take it easy and scope things out. Gold and diamonds. It'd damn well better be one or the other at the end of this road trip.

The shocks in the Holden Inspector Lambert and Senior Sargent Crabb were travelling in were a bit past their use-by-date. Lambert didn't feel he should say anything; after all, it was the state policeman's private vehicle. But it had been a long day. Not knowing where this parade would end or where Bridges and McCoin were made it difficult. For the first two or three hours, the inspector had sat with his eyes focused on the road ahead. They figured Bridges was somewhere behind McCoin and the Graves woman, but they didn't want to run up on the back end of Harry's car.

Not knowing where this could end, the two policemen realised they'd have to use caution.

Chapter Fifty-Seven

At an intersection, a few kilometres before coming into Karumba, the single-lane pavement became the more familiar two-lanes, complete with painted centrelines. The transition happened and JC didn't notice it. Shaking his head he realised he'd been dozing at the wheel.

'You all right?' Mel asked, the first words spoken in the car in a long time.

'Yeah. Just tired. Tired of this whole damn thing. Hey, Gabbi, is this your hometown?'

Gabbi smiled. 'Yep, sure is. Not much to look at, after living in Cairns, but it's for damn sure home.'

'And there's a hotel somewhere ahead?'

'Just ahead there. The highway turns towards the river and you'll be on Yappar Street. That runs along the river. The hotel is on the left there.'

The white lines ended at Yappar Street. JC stopped and looking both left and right, saw the town's main drag was unpaved. In one direction, a huge metal building ran for a couple hundred yards. Attached to the roof was a sign identifying it as belonging to the Decathlon Zinc Mine. In the other direction, the sign at another long, low, single-story building read Supermarket. The sign on another similar building further along simply said hotel.

'There,' Gabbi said, reaching a hand across the back of the seats and pointing, 'next to the grocery store is a cafe.' Opening a car door he went on. 'My aunty Joord, she lives behind the store. I'll stay there tonight and run you out to the gulf in the morning. You can get breakfast at the café.' Getting out, and without another word, he walked away.

The hotel wasn't as bad as expected, at least as far as JC was concerned. His room was just that – a room containing a single bed, a three-drawer dresser and a closet covered by a worn, almost colourless curtain. The spread on the bed had only slightly more colour. The bathroom, the clerk checking them in explained, was at the end of the hall. Dropping his backpack on the bed, JC stretched and started undressing. He'd slept in worse. Without a doubt, he'd hear what Melissa thought about it in the morning.

It was the sound of squawking birds that woke him up early the next day. Lying back, he listened and thought about things. Well, here he was, somewhere he'd never been and likely would never be again. Thinking back, he remembered having looked forward to the sail down to Australia. To a new part of the world. And here he was.

Groaning almost silently, he decided to get the bathroom first.

Showered and wearing one of his favourite T-shirts, the one with the Rolling Stones 1969 American Tour logo on the front, he felt a little better. He thought about knocking on the woman's door then decided not to. He didn't feel like hearing her complain this early. Let her make her own way up and out. Going over to the café for a cup of coffee sounded better.

She was already there. 'Well, you finally decided to get up, huh?' said Mel, sitting at a small table on the porch, holding a small dainty tea cup. Sitting across from her was a large brown woman. 'I was about to come roust you out. This is Gabbi's Aunt Joord.'

Joord's smile was as huge as the woman herself, a smile showing only a few of the teeth she'd once had. JC nodded at the introduction. Before he could speak Melissa continued talking. 'Hurry up and order your breakfast. Gabbi's down, getting things ready. Aunt Joord owns the café and has a few boats to rent and we're going to rent one. Gabbi says he'll take us down the river to the gulf.'

Was taking orders from her part of what he'd agreed to? JC wondered. It was too early in the day to start an argument, he decided. At least not until he had a cup of coffee. Not speaking, he went on through the screen door, coming back out a few minutes later carrying a steaming cup of coffee.

Pulling a chair over to the table, he glanced towards the big woman. 'Gabbi's aunt,' he said, then smiled a little to soften his words. 'Good morning. Your nephew is being a real help to us.'

Aunt Joord didn't speak but continued smiling while looking directly at the man.

'We've been talking,' Mel said, 'remember Gabbi saying he thought he might know where there's a place where fishermen lose their nets? Aunt Joord says she doesn't know about that, only having heard men complaining about one place just a bit off the mouth of the river. Do you think that's where it'll be?'

JC sipped his coffee and shook his head. 'Hey, you're the one who knows all about it. Didn't you say your grandfather wrote about it in a letter?'

'Yes, but he didn't say exactly where he landed. Only that it was on the flats near the mouth of the river. Guess that's where we can start looking, though.'

Talk stopped when JC's meal was brought out and he was just finishing when Gabbi came around the corner of the building.

'All right, then. I'll help you carry your tanks and stuff down to the boat when you're ready.'

'Gabbi,' said Aunt Joord, speaking for the first time, 'be careful going down the river. There's been a big, salty move into the mangrove flats. And the white fellas came over two or three days ago looking for you. Probably wanted to buy some of your crop.'

'Yeah, I'll stop by later. They only buy enough for themselves, you know. I got to talk with them. Things are changing over in Cairns. Maybe I won't be going back there for a while. Anyway,' he said, looking at JC, 'whenever you're ready.'

Chapter Fifty-Eight

It was just dusk when Harry reached what he thought was likely where the Graves woman and his old partner, JC, were heading. Looking ahead, he saw the night sky was a little lighter, like maybe there were street lights. He slowed, thinking about it. Not knowing how big this Karumba was, or where anything like a hotel would be, or even if there was one, didn't help. If that's where Graves and JC were going he'd have to be careful. Wouldn't want to run into them before he learned more about what was happening. It wouldn't be a good thing. No, better not to go barrelling into town now.

Before the other one got too drunk to make sense, she'd said she thought the treasure was near some river. That didn't help until he saw that dumb kid hired to sweep up go by in the back seat of a car being driven by good old JC. Wasn't the kid from a place like that?

Stopped at a junction – actually the end of the highway he'd been following. Looking in both directions he saw a big sign advertised the Star Supermarket and Cafe. That seemed likely. Karumba's supermarket. Was that the kid's village? Well, that's where he was. Had to be. Not many buildings – really, not much of anything. But there was a river over there, just behind what buildings there were. Didn't look like there was any place other than here. Whatever "here" was. A damn fool move: coming here, a million miles away from anything, chasing someone claiming to have a treasure map. Someone who might have turned off at any one of the side roads in the last hundred miles or so. Okay, he said to himself, you stepped into it, so make the best you can of it. But do it soon; it's getting dark.

Turning back away from the little business area, he drove back a half-mile or so. Spotting a corner of a street going off to the right, he made his decision and turned off the highway. So tonight he'd sleep in the car. Wouldn't be the first time he slept rough.

Pulling far enough off the highway and then off the street, he angled around behind a screening of scrub trees. Far enough, any passing motorist wouldn't see him parked, turning the car so the sun would wake him up. Yeah, he'd be more able to keep out of JC's or the woman's sight in the morning. He'd go on in early, have breakfast and scope things out. Things would either work out or they wouldn't, he told himself, so there's no reason to worry. He should have no trouble falling asleep.

Lambert and Crabb's trip ended at a place called Normanton, about seventy kilometres out of Karumba. For some time, the heat gauge on the Holden's dash had been rising. Crabb was driving and noticed it but didn't say anything until he had to. That was as they came to Normanton. Not much more than a fork in the highway, according to the official sign off to the right, was Burketown. Ahead was Karumba. Someone using the sign for target practice had shot out the mileage. If anyone needed to know they could ask at either the little petrol station in front of a small grocery store. Across the highway, a rustic-looking string of individual shacks sat in the silence. The sign over the first shack identified it as a motel. A huge semi-truck with four equally huge trailers was resting just beyond the motel.

'Uh, Inspector,' he said, slowing down and pulling off the highway. 'We got a little problem.'

Lambert had been dozing, coming abruptly awake with a snort at times before going back to sleep. Now he was wide awake. 'What? What problem?'

'Overheating. Maybe just a radiator hose or something. There's a bowser in front of the store. They'll likely sell hoses.'

'Overheating,' said Lambert, like he would say shit if he had stepped in a pile. 'You ever had this vehicle serviced? For Christ's sake, how long's it been since someone lifted the hood and looked to see if the engine was still there?'

Crabb hadn't liked the idea of driving across the peninsula in the first place. Somehow, when the federal policeman talked about how necessary it was to keep on top of that bartender, it had sounded as if it was his duty, becoming the big man's offsider. Same thing when talked into not charging those three fruit loops when he had the chance. After spending the day in his car burning up his petrol, now he has to take the man's digs. Mentally counting the months until retirement, he didn't say anything.

'Nope, ain't no leaks in the hoses.' Neither policeman felt secure about the old man who came out to look under the hood. Lambert, standing to one side could see instantly where the radiator water was going; a slowly diminishing series of drip was falling, hitting something hot and turning instantly into steam.

'Nope,' the old man said, ducking his head under the raised hood and pointing towards the engine's front. 'It's your water pump. Happens with these older Holdens. Something about the impeller shaft I read somewhere.'

'Can you fix it?' asked Crabb, knowing the end of his day wasn't going to improve.

The old man chuckled. 'Nope,' he said once again, 'gotta be replaced.'

Lambert had just about enough of the man. 'Okay, then,' he said quickly, 'do you have replacements in your store?'

'Gotta order one from Cairns. Closest place. Could make a phone call and have one come out on the next road-train.'

'How long will that take?'

'Well, today's what, Monday. You're in luck. The next delivery'll be tomorrow. Get the new pump and put it in, you'll be back on the road first thing Wednesday. You're heading for Karumba? Not much there. Nothing that won't wait another day or two, I reckon.'

Not much, Lambert growled silently, just his only link to a possible drug deal. And without that, his opportunity to get ordered back to the real world. Not much at all.

Chapter Fifty-Nine

Harry wasn't having much better luck. His day started out when the sun flashed against his closed eyelids. Dammit, he groused. How could anyone live in this godforsaken country? He'd never felt sunshine so heavy. Already, it felt like a weight was beating him down.

He hadn't slept much, not being able to find comfort in the front seat. Moving the seat back as far as it'd go, he'd tried to stretch out. As flat as he could make it, his knees pushed hard up against the dash board. Sleep just wouldn't come. It didn't take long before the muscles in his neck stiffened, soon becoming pain.

Getting into the back seat and leaving one of the rear doors open, he was finally able to stretch out, his feet sticking out in the night air. *Finally*, he thought, taking a deep breath and relaxing his muscles. He almost dozed off. It was a mosquito buzzing around his right ear that next ruined his night. Slapping at it, damn thing, only hurt him and at most scared off the tiny flying pest. It wasn't long before the buzzing returned.

Morning couldn't come soon enough. He bitched, turning onto one side and curling his six-foot length into a tight ball after closing the door.

Starting the day off being pissed at the world wasn't good. Driving back into town, he slowed at the big intersection, stopping to look things over. Carefully studying all the vehicles he could see, he didn't spot any that wasn't dusty. He hadn't been paying much attention and couldn't remember what kind, or even what colour, the car he'd seen that kid riding in. Even if it was one of those parked on the street, he wouldn't know it. The café sign down the street made his decision for him. He had missed dinner the night before and here he was starting out the day without coffee. The hell with them. He had to have his coffee.

Ordering his coffee, he asked the clerk about the nearest liquor store.

'No bottle shops here,' the woman said, not looking up from her espresso machine. 'Not legal here. No alcohol allowed. The people voted on that a long time back.'

Placing the large, steaming mug on the counter, and still not looking up at the big white man, she asked if he wanted to order breakfast. Harry, now madder than ever, stood for a long moment, trying to decide what to do. No beer. Damn fool place. Should just turn around and go back to Cairns. Stupid, coming all the way over here anyhow. And for what? Because a stupid young drunk broad overheard something about a treasure map? Treasure? Well, shit.

Shaking his head slowly, he took a deep breath and shrugged. Okay, so he could do without beer for a day or two. Nodding, he picked up a menu.

The two heavy women sitting at an outside table didn't appear to notice him when he came out. Whatever their morning conversation was about, they went right on, ignoring the white fella sitting at the other end of the porch.

'Oh, youself, youself went there?' said one woman, the older of the two by the looks of it.

'Yeah,' answered the younger one. Harry wasn't sure what made him think she was younger, they both were big, ballooning women, both wearing faded, shapeless dresses. Not looking directly at them, he saw how both women's mouths were almost toothless. The hair of one, the oldest, he thought, was a thin mass of white curls. Hair thin enough he could easily see patches of brown skin under it. They were certainly ugly women, he thought. Probably sisters, both ugly, fat old women.

Back in Cairns, he had noticed groups of aboriginal men and women on the streets, but hadn't really paid much attention. Without thinking about it, he'd just naturally ignored them, just as he would any homeless person on a street in San Diego. Yeah, it's what people just naturally do – look the other way. Somehow that thought didn't make him feel good.

Sipping his coffee he looked away, studying the building next door, but still listening to them talk.

'Didn't you go with Tom out there?' said the older one.

'No, he went fishin' with Mick,' the other said after a bit.

'Tom did?'

'Yeah.'

'Where they went?'

The woman from inside came out carrying Harry's second cup of coffee and his breakfast. He hadn't known exactly what to order. The menu wasn't very long. Something about the place made him pass on the omelette and a bowl of cereal certainly didn't impress him. He'd learned that Australians didn't understand eggs over easy. That's what he really wanted: sausage, three or four eggs over easy, biscuits with gravy and toast with jam. Pork link sausage. That and a couple cups of coffee and he'd have a real American breakfast. He settled for something called the Fisherman's Breakfast. He'd had it, or something like it, before when it was called simply the Big Breakfast. It was that: a couple eggs, fried hard, sitting on a slice of toasted bread; a few slices of fatty bacon; at least one large sausage sitting in a helping of brown beans; hash brown potatoes and roasted tomato slices. The coffee was espresso. There was, to his disgust, too much milk in the coffee.

The two women went on talking, paying no attention to anything except each other.

'I dunno-somewhere.'

'Oh.'

Harry cut up the sausage and listened. Not because he was interested but because they were talking loud enough that the whole damn town could hear.

'Catch any fish, Tom?'

'No, I didn' get there.'

'Eh?'

'I didn' get there.'

'You didn' go there?'

'No.'

'Oh, I thought you went with Mick and Anne.'

Harry, finishing the last of the soggy fried tomato slice, looked up when nothing more was said. Both women were sitting, staring off down the street. Looking at them, he wondered if they knew that kid who swept the floor at the pub. Thinking about it, he nodded. Yeah. These people probably all knew each other.

'Say,' he said, pushing away from the table and getting up, 'do you know that young guy, uh, Gabbi something? He's from around here. We worked together over in Cairns.'

The older woman looked up. 'Yas, I do know Gabbi. Why you want him?'

Harry tried for his friendliest smile. 'No, I don't want him. Just thinking about him, is all. Seems I heard he had a farm of some kind around here.'

The old woman nodded. 'Down the river, there.' Abrupt, not wanting to tell this white fella too much.

Good, now we're getting somewhere, Harry thought. 'Uh, yeah. Tell me, is there a place I can rent a skiff for a day or two?'

'What skiff. You mean a tinnie? Go down the river with?' Aunt Joord decided not to have anything to do with this white fella.

'Yeah, a tinnie.'

'No.' The answer was abrupt. 'Mebbe over at the airport, them white fella they have a tinnie. I dunno.'

'The airport, huh?' He remembered seeing a sign back a ways saying something about a transport facility.

'Uh, yeah. Okay,' he said, looking first at one, then the other and nodding. 'I'll go ask over there. Thanks.'

Damn fool women, he said silently as he walked back to get in his car. I should have asked about JC and the Graves woman, but likely those two had gone over to the 'white fellas' place. Hard to get anything from these small town people. Too busy taking care of each other and bugger outsiders. Well, he'd not have to deal with them again. No reason to even come back to this dump of a town.

Harry figured he had seen all he ever wanted of Karumba.

Chapter Sixty

Gabbi didn't say much as they motored down the river. Mel, sitting in front next to the young man, was taking it all in. He had loaded the white fella's scuba gear and camping equipment in a second boat, a hard-bottomed inflatable, which they were now towing.

JC, sitting behind Gabbi and Melissa, had time to take in his surroundings. All along the far bank, a dozen or so boats, houseboats and fishing boats were anchored. On the town side, the backs of buildings, a few jetties, fences and houses lined the bank. Leaving the village's businesses behind, scrawny trees and brushes covered the river bank. Looking closely, he noticed a few houses set back from the water and scattered among the growth, most needed paint. The river itself was a chalky, washed-out brown colour. JC couldn't tell if it was even flowing. Possibly they were close enough to the ocean that this was more of a gulf than a river.

'How far is it to the river mouth?' he asked, leaning forward to talk over the sound of the outboard.

'Few kilometres. Won't take long.'

A sweeping curve in the river and all signs of the village were gone. Gabbi kept the boats running at a steady speed, not kicking up much of a wake.

'What's that over there?' Mel asked, leaning forward and pointing across the river.

'Mangrove flats.'

To JC, it looked like a huge hair brush, the thick, short, black sticks reminding him of the bristles. The flats, hugging the shore, spread out twenty or thirty feet from the shore.

'Is that what those sticks are, mangrove bushes?'

Gabbi slowed the boat a little. 'No. The mangrove seeds float in and sink. They set down roots. As they grow, those spikes come up and soon they will become bushes and small trees. The mangroves catch more sand and unless a storm washes them out, in time becomes part of the shoreline.'

'Good fishing in there?'

'Naw. It's shallow. Good for a crab pot, but not good now. Aunty says fishermen have seen signs of a salty around here. He probably makes his nest close there.'

'Yes, I heard her warn you about that. What's a salty?'

'Saltwater crocodile. Very aggressive and dangerous. Always good to stay on this side of the river,' he explained and pushed the throttle forward. 'Jacky-Jacky Creek is there' – he pointed – 'my father made his farm there. He's dead now, so I raise the smoke. Open water is just around the next bend.'

Looking ahead on the near side, JC saw a string of buildings.

'What's that?' he asked, pointing towards the near side.

'White fellas airport. Been there a long time. Used by a couple regional air service companies for refuelling and maintenance.'

The river bank along there was so low that JC could see the large doors of two large hangers. A handful of buildings marched in a straight line between the hangers and the river bank. The river curved away from the airport.

The river, flowing around a couple wider, sweeping corners, soon broadened out. *Coming out of the confines of the river*, JC smiled. It felt good to see the open ocean again.

Gabbi turned to the left, following the shore but staying a ways off. 'Very shallow along there,' he said, pointing. 'There' – he pointed – 'where the trees are, is a good place for your camp.'

'And the place your fishermen lose their gear, where is that exactly?'

'There.' He pointed ahead and out to sea. JC saw a large, faded orange float bobbing in the swell. 'Someone a long time ago put a marker out. All fishermen in this area known to stay away. That is where.'

Beaching his skiff, it didn't take them long to unload the second skiff and tie its bow line to a tree branch. Once free of that boat, Gabbi waved and without another word, took off, back towards the river mouth.

JC and Mel watched him go, then started carrying their equipment farther from the water.

'Let's set up the tent,' said JC, 'and get things a little squared away. There'll be enough time this afternoon to do a dive out by that marker.'

A quick dive would, he was sure, be enough to show the woman how impossible her search was. Being out here, camping with the red-haired woman was, as far as he was concerned, treasure enough.

Chapter Sixty-One

Harry paid for his breakfast, stopped by the supermarket for a couple bottles of water and a bag of flavoured chips, before leaving town. Yeah, he smirked, some town. No alcohol. And crisps. Not potato chips, but crisps.

The turnoff to the airport was the same way he'd gone down and spent the night before. The side street was again a single-lane of pavement. A short way along and he noticed brown water through the trees off to the left. Must be the river. The pavement ended at a small parking lot directly in front of a small, single-story house. Harry figured that would be the office. Other than the sign out at the highway, he hadn't seen anything that explained what an airport was doing way the hell out here.

Standing beside his car and looking around, he took his time, expecting someone to come out and ask him what he wanted. Nothing moved anywhere. Disgruntled, he stepped up on the narrow porch and, opening the door, stepped inside. Except for a desk, a couple chairs and filing cabinets, the room was empty. A stack of papers, forms of some sort, a large glass ashtray overfilled with cigarette butts and an old big box computer covered the top of the desk. The odour of stale cigarette smoke made the air feel thick and heavy.

Shaking his head, he went back out, closing the door. Maybe over in one of the hangers, he thought, and headed in that direction.

'Help you?' someone called out as he stepped out of the bright sunlight and into the shadowy darkness of the large building.

'Uh, yeah. I was told over in town you might have a skiff to rent,' Harry said.

As his eyes adjusted he saw three men, two leaning against the white painted side of an airplane, the third one hunkered down facing them. Slowly, the one man stood up, turning to face the newcomer.

'Huh, I'll take care of this,' he said over his shoulders to the others. Stepping quickly towards Harry, he smiled. 'Let's go out into the sunshine. A skiff, you're after? Must be a Yank. We call them tinnies down here.' Harry felt he was being herded out of the hanger but didn't complain.

'Yeah, I got an old aluminium tinnie that ain't being used right now. Bet you want to go on down the river, don't ya?'

'Uh huh. Keep it for a day or two. What'll it cost me?'

'Well, let's see. You know, we had a plane come in a few days ago. From down south. Get those every so often. Not a regular route, but we serve some of the outback stations. What you'd call a ranch.' Not stopping, he continued talking as he walked. 'Uh huh. Some of these cattle stations are damn big and a long way from anywhere. We get a lot of private planes coming in from places like that. This one carried a fellow I used to know when I was working down in Brisbane. Now we get to talking. He was telling me about a couple of Americans who came sailing into the big city with a large shipment of drugs on board.'

Harry stopped walking. 'What are you talking about?'

'You see?' – the man stopped, turned to face Harry, and still smiling, nodded – 'my mate, he was telling me about one of those two Americans. Described him. Got it right on the money, I'd say. Taller than me, say two metres? Uh huh. Dark hair tied back in a ponytail. A mean look to him. A Yank, he said. Now that pretty much describes you, doesn't it? Don't get many Yanks out here, so when I hear you speak and I get a good look at ya, I say to myself, Wilson, this here's that bloke old Whitey was talking about. I wonder what you're doing out here. And looking for a boat. Care to tell me?'

Harry didn't like this at all. 'I don't know what you're talking about.'

Wilson chuckled. 'Of course, you don't. See, one of the things we do here is supply fuel for a couple small companies, mining companies for the most part. Do some maintenance and repairs as their aircraft needs it. Got planes coming in from all over the place. Some even from Bali or some other of those foreign places over east of here. Now once in a while, when a plane leaves after taking on a full load of fuel, a suitcase gets left behind. Later, another plane comes in and that suitcase gets picked up. No paperwork, no customs, no records. Hell, I don't know for sure what's in the suitcases. Not my job to know. I just get paid to make sure the suitcase gets on the right plane. Course, when my old mate, Whitey, comes by, whom I know has been dealing with drugs as long as I've known him, well, it doesn't take a genius to know what's in their suitcases, now, does it?'

'So what's that got to do with me?'

'The rumour I hear is that a Yank let a shipment slip away. That Yank has, for some reason, left Brisbane. Whitey was laughing when he told me. Said the Yank is over in Cairns. Guess there's someone over there keeping an eye on the fellow. Then one morning, I look up and here you are, a Yank with a ponytail. Wanting to rent a boat. It makes me wonder why. You know?'

Harry didn't know what to do. Was he being threatened? Damn, wasn't there anywhere he could go to get away from the syndicate? Looking off down the runway towards the river, he shook his head. 'This has nothing to do with any of your drug buddies. Yeah, I've been over in Cairns. There's a federal cop holding my passport. I get it back and I'm gone. But right now, I've got some personal business to take care of. Now, you have a boat I can rent for a few days or not.'

Wilson nodded. 'I watch things around here. Yesterday, I saw that aborigine kid go down the river. He's got a marijuana patch over on the other side there. Comes over here once in a while and we buy our smoke from him. So yesterday I see him going by and I wave to let him know he should be coming over soon to sell us some of his product. Only he didn't see me. Had a couple of people in his tinnie. And he was towing a second one. Doesn't make any sense to me. But now, here you are, wanting my boat. Okay. Makes me wonder, though, what's in it for me?'

Chapter Sixty-Two

According to the man, Wilson, the mouth of the river was only another kilometre or so. Around the next few wide bends in the river. Actually, as the crow flies, the gulf waters was only a few hundred metres away, but to go on the river, salt water was twice as far. That information, along with the skiff and gas for its outboard, cost Harry nearly all the cash he had in his wallet. That made it a sure thing, whatever JC and that woman were after was going to be his.

The sun hitting his back felt like a smouldering weight as he aimed the front of the boat down the river. He'd filled a couple water bottles at a tap and wrapped the packages of cookies he'd bought at the village store in a blanket he'd found in the car's trunk. Not knowing where he was going or how long he'd be there, those meagre supplies would have to do. If it looked like it was going to take more than a day or so, he'd have to make a run back to the village. Not knowing what he was getting himself into pissed him off. But he was too deep into it to turn back and that pissed him off even more.

Motoring along, keeping the boat pointed in the right direction, Harry watched the other bank, trying to see where that kid had his dope farm. All he could see, though, was brush and some kind of low, straggly tree.

Finally coming to where the river fanned out and seeing nothing but open water ahead, Harry nudged his boat tight against the nearby bank. Holding onto the limb of a tree that hung out over the water, he searched for any sign of JC's boat.

The trees along the other side of the river followed the shore line, curving around, disappearing in the distance. Movement in those trees, a couple hundred yards along, caught his eye. It was the woman – the damn reporter. Harry watched as she stood for a long time, staring out towards open water.

'Must be looking for JC,' he said softly. Was this where the so-called treasure was?

He'd have to move. It wouldn't be good to be hanging around if some idiot fishing boat came by. Turning his boat back, Harry went across the river, then screened by the brush and trees, slowly edged along, stopping when he thought he was near enough to where the woman had been standing.

Waves from the gulf pushed against him as he climbed over the side of the boat. Pulling it up as far as he could into the brush, he tied the boat's rope to a scrubby little tree. Carefully, taking his time and moving as quietly as he could, he made his way through the brush stopping when he saw the woman.

They had set their tent up a few yards from the shore. Harry wondered if old JC was getting lucky with the red-haired woman. Harry smiled, remembering how she looked in her tight jeans when they were at the cock-fight. Yeah, I certainly wouldn't mind a little of that myself.

Moving back a bit, he cleared the twigs away from a small patch of sand and got comfortable. He was just going to have to wait and watch. If there was any treasure to be found, he wanted to be ready. Whatever it was, it was going to be his. The news that even this far away from Brisbane, the big men running the drug scene knew where he was bothered him. That treasure had better be enough to get him a long, long way from them and this frigging country.

Chapter Sixty-Three

It was the smell of food cooking that changed his mind. He had watched as JC came out of the water. For a time, he and the Graves woman had stood talking. When they walked back towards their tent, Harry watched, wondering what their sleeping arrangement was going to be. Damn it, he thought, rolling over to rest his neck, I know what kind of sleep I'd get if I was there and old JC was out here in the scrub.

He watched as JC dug a pit and then gathered wood for a fire. Melissa, using some kind of camp stove, was heating a pan. Whatever dinner they were having, the smell reminded Harry that he'd missed having any lunch.

Okay, he said to himself, what's to stop me from going back to town and having dinner? They won't be doing any diving tonight and for sure, I'm going to have to have something to eat.

Slowly backing out of his hidey-hole and keeping the trees between him and the campers, he dragged the skiff back into deeper water. He thought he was far enough away that the sound of his outboard wouldn't be heard. Looking out at the river mouth, he saw a fishing boat coming in. Even if JC did hear his motor, maybe he'd think it was the fishing boat. And keeping a short distance behind that boat was probably a good idea.

Maybe he'd stay in town tonight, too. He could come back out and watch things in the morning. Might as well be comfortable. Nothing was going to happen tonight. Nothing he could be part of, anyway.

Chapter Sixty-Four

Melissa and JC got a good night's sleep, each in their own sleeping bag, after an early evening of talking around the camp fire. A swag, Melissa called it. JC had wondered how he'd handle spending the next day or two and, more importantly, nights with Melissa. One scenario he'd come up with while driving halfway across the continent – or at least it felt like that – had him comforting her when her grandfather's plane wasn't found. He'd liked that one a lot.

But the next morning's dive blew that dream away. The plane was the cause of fishermen's complaints. Long strands of ripped, knotted fish nets streamed out, moving in time to silent music. Seaweed intertwined in the netting was swaying away, moved by the ocean currents, streamers pointing towards deeper water. When he spotted it, JC's first thought was that it was nothing more than a huge rocky outcropping.

'Look,' JC said earlier as they were pulling on their wetsuits, 'I'll go out and see what I can find. I'd feel a lot better if you'd hang around up here,' he said, then shaking his head before she could argue.

'C'mon, think about it. A couple days ago, you didn't know anything about scuba diving. Do you really think you're ready to dive into who-knows-what? This isn't something to screw around with. Remember that safety lecture I gave back at the dive school? One of the basic rules, never dive alone. Okay, so you're up here, swimming around near the surface. You're my dive buddy. I'll go see what's there and we can talk about what to do about it. If there is anything there.'

Mel didn't like that. 'I seem to remember you telling us how little you know about diving wrecks, too,' she said forcefully. 'Didn't you say most of your experience came from diving in harbours, looking at the bottom of boats? So now you're the expert?'

'All true. But for damn sure, even if that's the extent of it, I've had more time under water than you have. So, I'll go down. You stay near the surface. Then we'll talk.'

Mel was silent, thinking. Finally, with an abrupt nod, she pulled her face mask on. Following JC, she swam slowly, then after he disappeared, she simply floated, using her hands to stay in about the same place. It didn't take long before she was tired and decided to give it up. She could watch for him on the beach just as well.

JC had followed the marker buoy's anchor line down and there it was in about fifty feet of water, a dark cigar-shape. At first, it was no more than a long shadow, a darker mass in the thin sunlight. Maybe, he thought it was simply a rock outcropping. A fishing gear-stealing pile of rocks. Swimming down, the outcrop slowly became an airplane.

At the start of his dive, slowly working his fins, he was astounded at what he was seeing. Diving in a boat-filled harbour was one thing; this was fairy land. Fish, small schools, not paying any attention to him, flashed as they swam here and there. Streamers of seaweed, growing like thin trees, huge leaves branching off, all waving slowly back and forth as if slow dancing to the music of a silent orchestra. This, he realised, was why people dove on the reef.

A large, mottle-coloured fish, its mouth opening and closing as if swallowing gulps of water, swam by him. That fish, hooked and landed, would be something to brag about. Watching the big fish slide silently past made him think of sharks. Quickly, feeling his blood pressure surge, he spun around, expecting to see a grey monster coming for him. Nothing. Slowly, chiding himself for his panic attack, he forced his breathing to settle. He smiled into his face mask, thinking about the lecture he'd given to the group at dive school about the dangers of getting too excited when underwater. He'd warned them of one aspect of diving that could lead to trouble. Gaining control, he turned back to the weed-discoloured nylon anchor rope. Using it, he pulled himself downward, stopping when he neared the sandy ocean bed, seeing how close he was to the darker shape.

Excited, he let go of the anchor rope and slowly swam the length of the crusted grey body. It was as close as he'd ever been to the exterior of such a large airplane. Being so close, he was surprised to see how huge it really was. Careful not to disturb the sandy bottom, JC slowly swam along the length, coming up on the edge of a wing. With the first thrill of discovery fading, his breathing calmed, he took a moment to study what he was seeing.

Reaching a handout, he rubbed against the plane. Rough and discoloured by marine growth, it felt like coarse sandpaper. Looking closely, barely discernible under the layer of seashells encrusting the entire surface, he could see the lines of rivets where sections of aluminium had been joined. All around him, fish swam, darting in and out of windows empty of any sign of glass. Taking his time and swimming slowly along the length of the plane, he saw the aircraft was on a slight incline, the tail disappearing into slightly deeper, darker water.

Swimming back along one side, heading towards the front of the hulk, he passed by an opening. A large square door. Back peddling, he stopped, thinking about going into the dark interior and not liking it. As he watched, a crab came scuttling out, swimming sideways before disappearing into the depths. Not stopping to inspect the interior, he swam up to follow along the top, dodging a series of slender rods, probably antennas of some sort. Next was another, smaller square opening, a hole into the interior, its cover now missing. Looking down he saw he was looking into the plane's cockpit. In the weak sunlight, he could barely make out the half-circular yokes, one on each side, with banks of shell-encrusted throttles in between. The pilot and co-pilot seats were masses of weed-covered springs and bent rods. Quick movement as another crab scurried out from underneath the remains of the instrument panel, raising a cloud of sand before ducking out of sight.

The windows in front and both sides of the cockpit were missing. Pulling himself forward, JC swam down over the nose of the plane. The sea bottom was far below, almost out of sight in the gloom. The nose of the plane rested on a jumble of rocky shapes.

At some time in the aircraft's watery journey, the metal had come into contact with something. Jagged-edged holes were all that was left of the once-rounded nose cone.

Swimming back along the other side, he found the other wing. Tiny fish swam in and out of a series of holes. Bullet holes, damage from when the plane had been attacked. He'd seen enough.

Taking one last look at the length of the aircraft, JC slowly rose to the surface. Time to think about what had to come next. Going inside the plane wasn't going to be fun. Or safe.

Looking towards the surface, he looked for Mel's black wet-suited body but didn't see it. Concerned, he pushed away, rushing towards sunshine. What could have happened? He'd told her to stay on the surface, not to dive deep. Fear filled his chest as he visualised her getting into trouble.

Reaching the surface, his head came out of the water. Looking quickly around, he spotted her on the beach, waving to him. Calming down, he used his hands to stop. He took a moment to think. Diving wrecks in any water was dangerous. He didn't need to read any of the dive brochures to see that. But as soon as she was told he'd found the airplane that's what she'd want to do. The problem would be to keep Melissa from rushing things. Slowly using his flippers, the strain on his leg muscles, he knew that there was something else to think about. The amount of air they had and his physical condition. Diving took muscles he rarely ever had to use. Breathing calmly, he frowned into his face mask. He'd much rather be sailing than where he was, in deep water. That would have to come later. Right now, somehow, he'd have to convince her to let him dive into the wreck himself. She'd have to stand aside and wait. That wasn't going to be easy.

Chapter Sixty-Five

JC had called it; once he told Melissa what he'd found she was ready right then to head back out. She wanted to see the aircraft for herself.

'Not now,' he said as seriously as he could. 'Think about it. What you want is down there in about fifty feet of water. Our air supply is not going to allow many more dives. If you go flying around, what'll you find? Nothing but a barnacle-covered airplane. It's certain you won't be going inside; hell, I don't even want to do that. Now, common sense says if there is going to be anyone going inside, it'll have to be me. There'll be a limit to how many dives I can make if I have to search for something. Unless we run out of air and have to go back into that little village, which puts a limit on things. Plus,' he continued, holding up a hand to stop her from interrupting, 'it's doubtful there's a dive shop closer than Cairns.'

Mel sat silently for a moment, thinking. 'Okay,' she said finally, 'I don't like it but you're right. Tell me again what it looks like. Damn, I wish we had a camera.'

Once again, he took his time and described what he'd seen.

Coming out of the water, he'd told her about the aircraft as he stripped off his wetsuit. Sitting now in swimming trunks, with his back against a large piece of driftwood, he felt his body relaxing. Feeling his calf muscles twitch, he was sure it wouldn't be long before he stiffened up.

Sitting side by side, looking out over the water and sharing a packet of Anzac biscuits and a bottle of water, JC thought about how to make her see things the way they really were.

'That's a big airplane,' he said, holding up a biscuit, trying to determine exactly what he was trying to eat. 'We don't have a camera and we didn't bring any lights. Searching through the entire plane, especially after all these years of it being in the water, is going to take time. Do you have any clue to what exactly I'll be looking for?' Putting the biscuit aside, he shuddered. 'Is that the only cookies you packed? What the...' and stopped. 'Uh, not to be a complainer, but do you actually like those?'

'Yes, they are Anzac biscuits, not your "cookies". You're in Australia and that is good Australian food. And to answer your question, yes. According to my grandfather's letter, you won't have to search the entire plane. He wrote that when he'd been given the box, he'd stuck it out of the way, shoving it under the pilot's seat.'

'Oh, wonderful. The only way to get to that will be to swim half the length of the plane. Wonderful. So it's under the seat. If it's still there. What is it, anyway? Can't be too big, if it goes under the seat.'

Mel frowned. 'He mentioned it was about the size of a cigar box. He wrote that it was wrapped in canvas. At the time, someone handed it to him; he didn't know what it was, but later, well, he was accused of stealing it. He wrote that was when he found out it was so valuable.'

'They accused him of keeping it? What was in the box that was so important?'

'Grandfather had applied for a bank loan to use to buy some property. The bankers apparently got all upset and that's when they questioned what had really happened to the box. He had told them when he and his passengers had been rescued, that he'd landed in the best, flattest place he could find. Sometime in the night, the plane had floated or been washed away. He hadn't thought about the cigar box and as far as he knew, it was still on the plane. That's what you're looking for – a canvas-covered cigar box.'

'It's doubtful the canvas is still there. So I'll have to swim into the cockpit and feel around for a cigar box. As I remember, you never did say exactly what was in the box. Thinking about it, a box that size, it wouldn't be gold or art. A box like that wouldn't hold enough gold to make it so valuable. So it has to be diamonds. Is that it? Diamonds?'

Silence. Glancing at the woman, he saw she didn't look happy. 'Oh, well,' she said, 'yes. Grandfather had been involved with flying civilians out of parts of Indonesia that the Japanese military was invading. Civilians and some military big shots. The box he'd been given, he learned much later, had held diamonds belonging to a very wealthy Dutch family. For some reason, the Dutch family didn't want to leave their home and business but wanted to keep their diamonds out of the hands of the invaders.'

'And so that's what's down there. A box filled with Dutch diamonds.'

'Grandfather said in one letter he'd been told the value was about 500,000 guilders. I Googled the value of guilders at that time. They'd be worth close to $20 million today.'

She'd said the words twenty million so calmly that he almost didn't hear them. Twenty million? And he'd asked for fifty per cent of whatever the so-called treasure was? JC was speechless. Twenty million? Half his? Ten million dollars? What would he do for ten million? Hell, what wouldn't he do? Dive into a sixty- or seventy-year-old wreck? You damn betcha.

Chapter Sixty-Six

Mentioning huge amounts of money, just the words themselves put a halt to conversation. The rest of the day went by fast, neither of them talking much, both thinking about millions of dollars' worth of diamonds and what that would mean. Even when his legs started to cramp and all he could do was get up and walk up and down the beach, it was never far from his mind. With that much money, would he go back to delivering boats? Hell no, with money, he'd be able to buy his own sailboat and go wherever he wanted. And what kind of boat would that be? A whole new line of thoughts filled his mind.

Once, a few years ago, he'd got into a conversation with a couple people. It'd been during a quiet time when they were taking a sailboat some place for someone. The game of what would you do if you won the lottery came up when someone mentioned the millions of dollars in the next Powerball lottery. That one in the eleven-state game was worth more than a hundred million. So the question they played with was, what would you do with it, if you won?

One of the negatives of sailing long distances was boredom. Set the sails, watch the weather, all the time keeping an eye on the compass. Every day, hours could be spent planning the evening meal. A lot of thought could be given for that. For some, a great deal of time for sailing was spent thinking. Other times, it might be reading novels or learning to play the harmonica. Playing games of 'what if' was a biggie. What if I won… and now it looks as if JC has won. All he had to do was dive into the wreck and find the box. That's all.

Melissa was also deep in thought. Later in the evening, JC quietly went for a walk, returning with a big armload of dry drift wood. Rebuilding the fire pit, he took his time lighting a fire. Memories of his days as a Boy Scout weren't enough to replace thoughts of diamonds. Meanwhile, Mel busied herself by starting the single-burner propane campfire and, using the heavy cast iron skillet she'd bought, started cooking supper.

Without asking JC what he liked and didn't like, while he'd been arranging the dive equipment, she had gone grocery shopping. Loading up on freeze-dried meals, the kind made popular by campers and back-packers, she was able to load enough for the two of them for a few days without breaking the bank. The heaviest part was the bottles of water needed to prepare the food. The cast iron skillet was perfect for the food preparation.

Stirring the packaged meal into boiling water, she let her mind wander. What would JC do, now that he knew about the diamonds and their value? He'd bargained for half, but would he be satisfied with that, or would he get greedy? How would she protect herself if he tried to pull a fast one? He could go down, find the box, come back and say it wasn't there, then come back later for it. She couldn't very well dive with him, could she? No. He'd pointed out they only had so much air. Anyway, what could she do if he did steal it from her? People get killed every day for a lot less than twenty million!

Thinking about that, she remembered reading about the man who, while on a diving holiday with his bride, let her die. That man was an American too, wasn't he? Yes. On their honeymoon. Somewhere on the reef. Millions' worth of diamonds was incentive enough for a lot of things to happen. Thinking, she stopped stirring.

'Hey,' JC called, 'you're going to let our dinner burn.' He laughed as she jumped, and quickly took the skillet off the fire. 'I'll bet you're thinking of how you're going to spend ten million dollars.'

Melissa felt herself blushing. 'Well, it is something to think about, isn't it?' Spooning half the meal, a beef stew, on to a plate, she handed it to him.

JC shook his head, breaking open a package of plastic forks and handing her one. 'I'd wait until I had it in my hand before spending any of it. A lot of things can go wrong. Hell, we haven't even found the box yet. All we've got so far is a good day's dive and a rust-bucket of a World War II airplane. Isn't there a saying about that, something about counting chickens?'

Once they started talking, things seemed to get back to normal. The rest of the evening went comfortably for the two. Later, after Mel brought out a bottle of red, they sat back and enjoyed the campfire.

'Too bad I couldn't find unbreakable wine glasses,' she said, lifting the same cup she'd used for tea earlier.

'Somehow wine out of a plastic mug just doesn't taste the same.'

JC shook his head. 'Well, there's been a lot of time out on a sailboat in the middle of the ocean when a coffee cup was the closest thing to a wine glass we had. This red tastes just fine. I'm glad you thought of it. Fact is, your effort in the food department is very appreciated.' He lifted his cup in a salute.

Setting back, watching the fire, they once again fell silent. Finally, after the bottle was emptied and the fire had burned down, Melissa broke the silence.

'You know, I think it's time for me to retire,' saying the last word in the voice of a fancy, high-toned lady.

'Can't argue with that. Seeing as how the wine's all gone.'

Neither of them made a move to get up. 'JC,' said Mel after a bit, 'you know, we're awfully close to becoming partners.'

'Counting chickens again?'

'No, just being realistic. I mean, even if we don't find the diamonds, well, we are partners in the search, aren't we?' JC nodded and waited.

'Okay then,' she said, looking him directly in the eye. 'I don't see why we don't put our two swags together and see what happens.'

The smile slowly coming to JC's face was answer enough.

Chapter Sixty-Seven

Harry felt sure he was going to vomit up his breakfast. The eggs, cooked rock hard, or the greasy sausage – even the soggy, limp toast wasn't the problem. It was the two old crones sitting at the other end of the café porch. Chattering away at each other, their almost toothless mouths flapping, words coming out lubricated by what looked to him to be gallons of spit.

After having spent one near-sleepless night in the back seat of the car, having a bed to stretch out on was great; he'd slept like a log. Waking up to the chattering of birds, he took his time in the bathroom at the end of the hall, showering and shaving. No reason to hurry. What treasure JC and that woman were hoping to find wouldn't be something in plain view. According to the story, the gold or diamonds or whatever it was, had gone down on a plane somewhere in the ocean. *Okay*, he thought, stopping with half his chin still covered with shaving cream. She was a journalist, wasn't she? Maybe while working on a story somewhere she heard something. Something that told her where the plane had gone down. Yeah, maybe she knew something.

Wiping his face, he thought about it. Still, finding an airplane under water wouldn't be easy. And if it'd been down there for a long time, hell, it'd be covered with seaweed, wouldn't it? Yeah, so even if JC knew what he was doing, it'd take some time. Time enough for a good breakfast and even another cup of coffee. He'd have to tell them not to put in so much milk, though.

Motoring back down the river to the edge of the ocean, he once again eased the skiff up into the brush, out of sight. The tide was a little farther out than it had been when he had crept up on the camp before. Where he'd had to wade through the shallows, this time he was slogging through black mud, making a mess of his shoes. Circling around so, he came in behind the camp, he found himself on a low, brush-covered sand hill, looking down on the tent. Pushing the sand around a little, making a depression for his hips, he got comfortable. Another day of watching and waiting.

Crawling out of the tent, JC, naked as the day he was born, stood up and stretched. He felt great.

'Hey,' Melissa called from inside the nylon shelter, 'you trying to scare the fish? Standing out there, bare-assed nekkid?'

JC laughed with a deep, throaty sound. 'Nekkid? Yeah. Standing here in the sun nekkid as a jay bird feels good.'

'What's a jay bird?' the woman asked, lifting the tent flap and coming to stand beside him. Unlike JC, she had pulled on the bottom of her bikini and was tying the top.

'Just a saying, naked as a jay bird. And I'll have you know, I ain't nekked, I'm nude.'

'Nope' – she laughed – 'women not wearing clothes are nude, men letting everything hang out are naked.

That's the way it is.' Slapping him playfully on his bare butt, she went over to the cook stove. 'I suppose you want some breakfast before making your first dive?'

'Uh huh,' he said, still standing, facing the ocean, enjoying the heat of the sun on his skin. Until she said something about diving he'd been thinking of their night on top of the sleeping bags. That memory evaporated, replaced with the memory of the darkness inside the plane's cockpit.

'Sure wish I'd thought about bringing a light,' he said, grabbing his swimming trunks from where he'd hung them on a tree limb. 'I have to tell you, I'm not all that excited about going inside that wreck.'

Making cups of instant coffee and handing one to JC, Mel looked pensively out towards the faded-coloured buoy. 'Think of it this way: diamonds. A cigar box full of diamonds. And if that's not enough to make you keen about it, then think about this; the sooner that search is done, the sooner we can leave. Personally,' she said, letting her voice drop a little, 'I wouldn't mind another night here. Just you and me in paradise, our own little private paradise.'

JC put cup down on the driftwood log and leaned over to hug her.

'Now don't go getting too frisky' – she laughed – 'you do the diving and I'll find something to entertain myself with here.'

Sitting in shallow water, JC put on his swim fins. He wasn't looking forward to this dive. But what could he do? Dive, spend some time swimming around looking at fish then come up and tell her there was nothing like a cigar box anywhere?

'I looked everywhere I could reach,' he could say. 'It's dark in there, you know?'

And she'd say something like, 'Crap. So there goes our twenty million dollars.'

Yeah. Twenty million dollars. Sitting down there. And never getting found because I'm too chicken-shit to make a dive. C'mon, jack-off, stop thinking about her wonderfully smooth body and think about making a dive.

Spitting into his face mask, he chuckled, remembering that when starting the first dive lesson, he'd directed the students to spit in their dive masks. Melissa, of course, it'd be Melissa; had asked why? He didn't know her name then. Certainly, he'd noticed her. Hell, any red-blooded man would notice her shapely body all tightly wrapped in a black rubber wetsuit.

'Why?'

He smiled at the memory. Thankfully, one of the first questions to be asked was one he could answer.

'To prevent the mask from fogging up, you should spit into your dive mask and rub it around with a finger.'

'Uh huh. But why?'

He'd thought she was being a smart-ass but then realised she wanted to know how spitting could prevent fogging.

In all the dives he'd ever made, in harbours all along the west coast, he'd just naturally spit in the mask just before jumping in the water. It was simply part of the procedure he'd been taught.

'You know,' he had to say, 'I don't know. Not a good way for me to start the lesson, I'll admit, but a darn good question anyhow. Tell you what? Let's go on with the lesson and during our break, I'll find the answer. That good enough?'

It was and he did.

'Hey,' called Mel, 'you going to sleep sitting there?'

'No,' he yelled back over his shoulder. 'I was thinking about when you asked why we spit in our face mask. Remember?'

'Of course, I do. You never did come back with an answer, either. Now, are we going to reminisce or are you going diving for treasure?'

'Gonna dive, masta', gonna dive.'

'But why do you spit in the mask? How does that work? Did you ever find out?'

'I said I would and I did. And I'm sure I explained it to the class. You must have missed it.' She shook her head.'

'Okay, so tell me.'

'Has to do with the fact that the spit gets between the water molecules and stops them from clumping together. That cuts down on the surface tension of the water, preventing bigger water droplets. When you dive, the temperature difference between one side of the mask and the other causes any water drops inside to fog up. So, spitting prevents fogging. Every diver knows that.'

'Uh huh. But as I recall, you didn't. Okay, stop fooling around and go find our treasure.'

Chapter Sixty-Eight

It was another great day for a dive. The water temperature was only slightly cooler than the outside air. The wave action was, as it had been the day before, gentle. Under the cloud-free blue sky, visibility in the shallows was crystal clear. Swimming out to the buoy, he floated a minute, looking down and now, knowing where to look, he could make out the dark mass of the aircraft. Down there, somewhere, was a cigar box. Treasure. With a flip of his fins, he headed down.

Thinking how he could get to like scuba diving, he quickly reached the plane. Swimming along the side, he stopped at the square open door. Shafts of sunlight streamed down, illuminating ever-moving areas. The soft, dappled light only made the inside of the plane darker. Carefully, with one hand on the lip of the door, he slowly pulled himself in, stopping to let his eyes adjust, taking a long look around.

Fish darted here and there, none seeming to be frightened of the intruder. Metal seat frames lined both sides, going off in both directions. From what he could see, there was no evidence of any of the material or padding that once must have covered the seats.

Fully inside, he turned towards the cockpit and kicked his fins, sending up a cloud of thin dust cutting out what little light there was. Grabbing onto the back of a seat frame, he floated still, waiting for the dust to settle. When he could make out the grey lightness ahead and moving ever so slowly, he used the metal seat frames to pull himself along.

The door into the cockpit was merely another opening. Ends of the wires hung down and waving in the slight movement of the water on one side were, he figured, where the navigation equipment had hung. There was no sign of any radio or other electronic gear. Someone at some time had been on board, salvaging things.

Moving ahead a bit, he bumped his oxygen tank against the cockpit's ceiling. Air. Holding still, he tried to judge how long he'd been down. That was something to pay attention to – his air supply. Quickly, he pulled against one of the pair of seat frames and being careful of any sharp edges, ran his hand under the seat frame. Nothing. Moving to the other side, he repeated the movement. Again nothing. No cigar box.

Where could it be? Did the person who had ripped out the radios and other gear find the box? Was he too late?

Maybe Mel had a better idea of where it could be. Thinking about his air supply, he cautiously turned and started back down towards the open door. Like a beacon, even in the gloom of water, the opening was much lighter. Pulling himself out, he could almost feel the weight of the metal structure lift. Taking a breath, he started up only to stop. How long had he been down there? How deep exactly was he? Should he be worried about decompression? Why hadn't he thought of that earlier? Boy, was he out of his element?

Standing upright, keeping in place by slowly fluttering his hands and fins, he thought about it. Not once in any of his harbour dives had the question of decompression come up. When he'd taken his lessons and certainly when he was teaching basic diving, nothing about decompression had been discussed. All he knew was enough to frighten him. Come up from too deep, too fast and the build-up of noxious particles in your bloodstream could be fatal. Better to go up to the surface slowly, stopping a couple places along the way for a bit.

But that used up air. How much did he have left? How did he ever get himself talked into this and how come he wasn't better prepared?

Chapter Sixty-Nine

Harry had watched from his hidey-hole as JC pulled on his wetsuit and then went down to the water. When Melissa went over to talk, Harry cussed. Get on with it, he yelled silently. He wasn't close enough to hear what they were saying, but the body language made it clear enough. Dammit, he said silently, I hope the hell they don't get all lovey-dovey and forget the treasure.

They didn't. After a bit, JC swam out, disappearing into the waves. That left the watching man with nothing to do but watch Melissa's body in her little bikini. He didn't mind, it was a pleasure. For a time, she swam around, then, coming out of the water, she spread out a colourful beach towel and laid down. Keeping an eye on her, he let his thoughts picture what it'd be like to jump out and grab her while old JC was out diving for treasure. Treasure. As nice as her body was, it wasn't enough to make him forget that. He didn't move.

After what seemed like hours, Melissa stood up, shading her eyes, stood looking out to where JC had disappeared to. Turning to the stove, she heated up a pot and poured the steaming liquid into a cup. Making a cup of coffee? Harry could almost taste it.

Careful not to make any noise, he slowly cut the cellophane around a package of cookies. ANZAC biscuits, the label read. Munching the hard, almost tasteless cookie and sipping from a water bottle, Harry ate his lunch. Watching and waiting. Something had better happen to make all this worthwhile. Or by God, he told himself, he couldn't be blamed for what happens.

He was still lying there, quiet and almost still when JC came out of the water. As quiet and patient as a sniper spying on the Viet Cong. Still and patient as an Indian about to attack the fort. Or as one of the natives he'd watched back in Colombia. It was out in the jungle near a town he couldn't remember the name of. He and a couple others had been hired to guard the lab. The funny thing was, there was nothing threatening the place. Hell, it was just a couple shacks in a clearing in the middle of trees, vines and bushes. Jungle, you know? Miles from anyone or anything. At any moment, he expected to see Tarzan come swinging out of a tree. But that didn't happen. All there was to watch was when some near-naked natives came up the trail, each lugging their long blowgun. He'd been amazed, watching them walking along, staring up into the tall trees. Then, having seen something, they came to a halt to stand as still as a statue with the blowgun held up, pointing into the sky. Harry had looked upwards but couldn't see a thing. Then, poof, and a little monkey come falling from somewhere way up there. One of the native hunters had been successful. It all happened in front of him without their knowing he was there, hidden and silent. Now that was watching and waiting.

Natives could do it or starve. He wondered if the kind of native people they had here were patient.

His day dreaming came to a halt when JC came out of the water. Squinting his eyes, Harry checked to see if he was carrying anything. Watching as the diver swung the tank off his back, it was clear, he was empty-handed. Damn.

Relaxing, he watched. After stripping off his wetsuit, JC drank water, then sat down in his favourite place, on the sand, with his back to a big piece of driftwood. Melissa, with her own bottle of water, sat down facing him.

Thinking about it, Harry nodded. It wasn't likely there'd be any more diving today. Maybe there was a limit to how long someone could safely be underwater. He didn't know. But it didn't look like anything was going to happen. No reason then for him to hang around. He could go back into town, have a couple glasses of beer, get a good meal and another night's sleep. Yeah. And come back out tomorrow morning.

And damn it, something had better happen soon.

'It's too dark in the cockpit,' JC explained to Mel. 'All I could do was feel around under what's left of the seats – just the steel frames and seat springs – no sign of cushions, leather or whatever covered the seats.'

'And you found nothing.' She wasn't asking, just making a statement.

'Just sand. Someone had pulled all the radio gear out. The only sign of what had once been there were broken wires hanging, all covered with seaweed. You think maybe that thief had found the box and took it too?'

Mel thought about it for a moment and then shook her head. 'No, not likely. Look, if anyone from the village had found a treasure like that, don't you think everybody'd know about it? In a village like that? It'd be damn near impossible to find a box full of diamonds and be able to keep it to yourself. No. I'll bet if you could get them to talk, they'd tell you who stole the radios and stuff.' She waited until JC nodded his agreement. 'So,' she went on, 'what's your plan now?'

'Well, as I see it, we've got two problems. First, the amount of air. The school fills their tanks to just under three thousand psi or pounds per square inch. That's what we started with. According to the gauge on my tank, I'm down to about 700 psi. That's getting close to the danger point. If there's any more diving to do, it'll have to be with your tank.'

'So that means what? One more dive is all we've got air for?'

'Yeah,' he said, sipping water. 'I figure the plane is at about fifty feet, that's something like fifteen or sixteen metres. I've made two dives and spent some time swimming around. Say more than half an hour or forty-five minutes total. I don't know exactly. That's one of the things I should have kept track of. Anyway, less than an hour to be safe. I'd say that was about the limit – thirty- or forty-minutes max. Okay, so your tank still has enough air for that much more time under water. But, face it, there aren't that many more places to look. Oh, and there's another problem to think about. Decompression.'

'What's that?'

'It has to do with the amount of oxygen getting into my bloodstream when I'm diving. Breathing air from the tank. Along with not having any light, I didn't pick up a dive table. Boy, there's a whole lot I screwed up by not planning.'

'Well, don't beat yourself up over it. As I recall, you weren't too happy about diving into a wreck anyhow. Okay, so not having a, what was it, a dive table? Will that stop you? Huh, what is a dive table anyhow?'

'Now that I can answer with some knowledge. Read it in one of the school's information brochures. It's like this: water has weight, so when a diver is under, the air he's breathing is entering his bloodstream with some measurable density. The deeper you go, the denser the air is. That means the air is compressed and if, when you come back up it isn't given time to decompress, it will mess up your system. Can lead to something called the bends. Can cause unconsciousness. Can do really bad things. Okay, so the dive table is simply a complex chart to tell how long to take little breaks when coming up from various depths. Like I said, I'm guessing I've been diving to close to fifty feet. Without a dive table, I have no way of knowing how much time I have to give to decompress.'

'Wow. So how much danger were you in with the dives you've made?'

'Don't know. The first time I didn't think about it and like a fool, simply came up. No damage, but the second time I thought about it and stopped a couple times for a minute or two. Somehow, I don't think I'm going deep enough to get into trouble, but I don't know. And then there's the length of time I'm down there. I seem to recall that being a factor. I just don't know enough about it.'

Mel crawled around until her back was against the log, sitting next to JC. For a time, they sat, not talking, just watching the ocean. 'So,' she said after a while, 'what's the plan? Give up on it? Say the box is gone and go home? I don't know if it's worth the danger.'

'Well, I agree. However, if we call it quits now, there'd be no reason to stay out here another night. We could boat back into the village and have a restaurant meal.' Mel frowned, but nodded. 'But,' he went on, smiling, 'that would also mean not sharing our sleeping bags again. So I'm going to vote on staying tonight, diving once more tomorrow before hanging it up.'

Mel leaned her head over onto his shoulder. 'It's up to you, but that sounds good. But do we have to wait until night? Couldn't we sort of take an afternoon nap?'

Chapter Seventy

Melissa didn't bother getting dressed and was naked while heating water for breakfast. Pulling the top of his wetsuit on, JC stopped to watch her.

'Wonderful,' he said softly. 'Uh, look, uh, Melissa, do we have enough food to stay here for another few days? Man, I could get used to this.'

Glancing over a bare shoulder, she smiled. 'Fraid not. But I do agree, it'd be yummy spending a few days out here, all alone with you. Tell you what, find the box of diamonds and we'll find a private beach where we can be the only people around.'

'Find your box of diamonds and we could buy a whole damn island.'

'Are you going to wait until after breakfast before making your dive?'

'No. I was thinking about that. When I was down there before, it was around the middle of the day. The sunlight was strong. Probably the strongest it'll get throughout the day. I think I'll wait a couple hours before I try it again. Might not make any difference but then again, it might. Probably won't matter.'

JC thought long and hard about making the dive. Watching the woman as she poured boiling water first into the two coffee cups and then into the freeze-dried packages, he felt himself growing hard. It had been a long time since he enjoyed the pleasures of a naked woman. Nude woman, he corrected himself.

Over the years, he'd had what he considered to be his share of women, but Melissa was the first red-head. Typically, the few red-haired people he had met were stuck with pale skin, which meant they had to cover up when in the sun. Melissa didn't have that problem. In the morning sunshine, her body glowed with a light tan. No tan lines either.

'Stop staring,' she said, handing him his coffee. 'Didn't your mum teach you it was impolite?'

'Nope. And even if she did, I'm only a red-blooded American. Of course I'm going to stare.'

Smiling, she sat back about where she'd been the evening before, her bare back against the driftwood, and ate her breakfast. After tasting the warm mixture, she reached over to read the package.

'Yeah, the label says we're eating beef bacon, scrambled eggs and beans all in a tomato sauce. Tomato sauce, maybe, but bacon? I certainly don't taste any bacon.'

JC chuckled and kept spooning the food in, stopping only long enough to respond. 'Not as good as last night's meal,' he said, washing the last of it down with coffee. 'However, your shopping before we left Cairns was good thinking. We wouldn't have been able to stay out here without the back-packing meals. Not so great, but a lot better than any restaurant within a country mile.'

'I don't know how far a country mile is, but I doubt there's any restaurant closer than back in the village. So, are you going to dive the airplane again or sit around staring at my boobies?'

'Ah woman, nag, nag, nag. Okay, I'll go do another search and leave the clean-up duties to you.'

Bending over to kiss her lightly, he softly pressed his hand against her breast.

'Better stop that,' she warned.

Laughing, he picked up his fins and mask and headed for the water.

Enjoying the clear water, he swam leisurely out to the buoy before jack-knifing down into the depths. With his hands trailing alongside his body and pushing with his fins, he felt his leg muscles begin to loosen up.

Reaching the dark opening in the side of the crusted metal tube, he stopped, holding on to the lip. *Add a ball of string*, he thought, *to the list of things he could use*. A light and a ball of string. Having something to help guide him like a trail of breadcrumbs would save him from bumping into the edges of the seats. Not hesitating long, he swam inside. Taking his time, letting his eyes adjust to the gloom, he pulled his body along, heading towards the cockpit.

Just as before, he was half through the front cabin door opening before he was able to make out any of the cockpit interior. Now, where, if he were a little cigar box, would he be hiding? Not under the seat where Mel said her grandfather had placed it. So where would it be if someone hadn't beaten them to it?

With one hand holding tight to the metal seat frame, he twisted his body and felt along the back wall of the cockpit. There wasn't much room behind the left-hand seat and it didn't take long to discover there was not anything but sand. The area behind the other seat was more open. It was in that area the wires were hanging. The navigation station, likely. It took a little longer to search that. But again, nothing.

Where else? Not in the back, how about in the front? Moving slowly so as not to disturb the sand too much, he came up and then, hanging over the seat frames with his head down, he ran his hand lightly over and around the pedals. It was darker under what was left of the instrument panel and when his hand touched something that moved, he panicked. Jerking back, he automatically pushed himself away and slammed his air tank into the cockpit's ceiling. Stopped from going any farther, he almost choked, gulping air. Frozen in place, he watched silently as a hand-sized octopus came jetting past, heading out through one of the pane-less windows. A blacker cloud of ink floated up from where the beast had been hiding.

Taking a long minute and consciously working at slowing down his breathing, he forced his body to relax. Damn. Reaching into the dark wasn't too smart. There could have been any kind of sea monster hiding in there, waiting for a meal to poke in. Something with sharp teeth. He wasn't laughing.

For a time, he didn't move. Curled up with his back firmly against the ceiling, his legs hanging down behind the seat frames, he watched the water world through the open windows. *Well, now what? Where else… Oh, the foot-well on the other side. I wish*, he thought, *I'd brought along a stick to poke in there.*

Slipping one fin off and holding tightly to the heel strap, he bent over the left seat frame and reaching into the darkness, waved the flipper around. Nothing came swimming out. Maybe it was safe to stick his hand in. Maybe.

But it had to be done. The last place anything could be. Then get the hell out. No business being inside this wreck anyhow.

Again, only slower this time, he reached his hand in, feeling gently around the pedals, rubbing lightly across the bottom surface, prepared for something to grab him. His fingers automatically jerked away when they touched something hard. Thinking crab, he pulled back, expecting the claw to seize a finger. Nothing came after him. Slowly, he once again reached out, stopping when he touched the edge of something half buried in sand.

Not daring to think, his hand almost by itself scraped away until finding another edge. Curling around it, he gently pulled it out. A cigar-shaped box.

It had to be it. Holding the thin, square, solid shape up into what light there was, he stopped to stare at it. Sea shells encrusted nearly the entire surface, not canvas. Just a solid box with a small lump of shell in the centre of one thin side. A lock. Breathing slowly, he felt his heart pound. Time to get out of here.

Chapter Seventy-One

Mel had watched JC swim out before going into the tent to get dressed. Pulling on shorts and a T-shirt, she thought it being her last clean clothes was probably a sign they'd been out long enough.

Harry arrived back at his spy-hole just in time to watch her come out of the tent. Not seeing anything of JC, he figured the day's underwater search had probably already started. Settling in, he relaxed, burping quietly, tasting again the greasy sausage he'd had with his breakfast. Damn, he vowed, I've had about enough of this. Time for something to happen so I can get back to civilisation.

If Harry had taken a little longer over his coffee, he would have had Inspector Lambert and Senior Sargent Crabb to talk to. These two, having left Normanton early and coming up to the crossroads in Karumba, spotted the café sign and headed straight there, parking in front. Conversation was still spare and sparse between the men. Crabb was seething, blaming Lambert for being where they were, for no good reason he could see. Lambert, on the other hand, was upset because it took so long to get there. Silently sipping their coffee, it was Crabb who finally asked the question. 'Okay, so we're here. Now, what are your plans? Isn't this where you said that young dope smoker was heading?'

'Dope smoker? What's that all about?'

'Oh, hell. Yeah, I've known what he was doing for a long time. Bringing in marijuana and selling his little baggies. The story is he's got a patch somewhere around here.'

'You were aware of it and did nothing about it?'

'You've been in the big city too long. What do you think would happen if I arrested him and held him for trial? On what charge, selling a little dope? Remember, he's a Koorie, an aborigine. Take him in and I'd have half the town on my back. The half who are connected in some way, you know, family, and the rest dope smokers. Not worth it. Hell, the amount of dope he was selling was nothing. So I ask again, what're your plans?'

Lambert shook his head in disgust. Glancing up, he noticed the two women sitting at a table at the other end of the porch. Obviously aboriginals. Maybe they'd know something. Without saying anything to Crabb, he got up and walked over to the women.

'Excuse me,' he said, trying not to sound like a police officer, 'we're looking for a young man named Gabbi. Don't know his surname, but I believe he is from around here.'

The two women sat for a long moment, staring up at the police inspector. 'What do you want with Gabbi? Are you going to arrest him?'

The question stopped Lambert. 'Arrest him? No. Why would we want to do that? No, all we want is to talk

with him. What makes you think we'd want to arrest
him?'

Aunt Joord showed her near-toothless smile and
nodded. 'You're both police. Why else would you want
to know about him?'

Lambert wanted to ask how she knew they were
policemen but decided not to ask. 'No. Actually, it isn't
him we're interested in. A couple days ago, he got a ride
over from Cairns with a man and a woman. It's the man
and woman driving the car we're really interested in.'

Joord flicked a glance at her friend, then sat silently
for a long moment. Finally, deciding it would do no harm
to answer the policeman, she nodded. 'The man and
woman rented a boat. Said they'd be gone for a few days.
Something about going down a river to the ocean. Gabbi
wasn't going with them there.'

'Rented a boat? Well, where can we rent a boat?
We'd really like to talk to those two.'

'Another man wanted to rent a boat too. I'll tell you
what I told him: the only place I know is over at the
airport. Maybe they have a boat to rent. I don't.'

Crabb, carrying his coffee cup, came to stand next to
Lambert. 'What other man? Someone else asking about
that couple?'

'Yes. A big man. Little ponytail. Mean looking.
Never smiled. He has been at the hotel. Came here for
meals. Left a little while ago. He's in a boat, I think,
coming from the airport.'

'Okay,' said Lambert, 'then I guess that's where we
should go. Thank you for your help.'

Aunt Joord wasn't finished. 'Gabbi is a good boy,' she said, 'he went to school in Cairns, graduated too. He's a good boy.'

Crabb nodded. 'We're not here to cause him any trouble.'

After a moment, Joord nodded, then turned back to her friend, ignoring the two men.

'Okay,' Crabb said, getting behind the wheel of his car, 'guess that's your plan, to go see about renting a boat. I do hope we're about to the end of this cluster fuck.'

'Cluster fuck? Sargent, think about how it'll look, you being in on a major arrest. Didn't you say something about nearing retirement? Going out with a big arrest would make you look good, wouldn't it?'

'Big arrest? So far, I haven't seen that any crimes have been committed. Except for people involved in illegal cock-fights. Please, tell me again, who are we going to arrest and for what crime?'

Lambert's frown wrinkled his forehead. 'There has to be something going on. That damn Harry Bridges is up to something, coming clear over here following his old sailing mate. That's who the old crone back there was talking about – a mean-looking man. That's Bridges. He's here, but not with McCoin and the woman. So he's still up to something. It's got to be something big. That'll be your arrest.'

'Uh huh. I'll believe it when it happens.'

'Let's see if we can get a boat and go talk to McCoin.'

McCoin, he was sure, would lead him to Bridges. It had to be something big. Had to be.

Chapter Seventy-Two

Full from breakfast and with the sun warming his back, Harry caught himself nodding off. Damn, he cussed silently, snapping awake. Don't fall asleep now. Stretching, he watched Melissa pacing back and forth on the beach. She's very tense, he noted. *Another sign something's up*, he thought.

Dozing again, he jerked awake when he heard her squeal with excitement. Rubbing his eyes, he stopped when he saw she'd stopped pacing and was jumping up and down, clapping. Unable to see beyond her, Harry stood up, crouching a little, keeping himself partially hidden behind the scrub. There. Coming into the beach, JC was stoking with one hand and holding something up with the other. Harry couldn't make out what it was; too small. Too small to be much of a treasure. What the hell's going on?

'Is that it?' he heard the woman call. *Damn fool woman*, Harry thought. He can't swim and answer you. If you'll wait another minute, you'll know.

JC came out of the water, kicking his fins off and jerking the face mask off his head. 'I found it,' he said, words coming loud and fast. 'Somehow it'd slid down and got jammed behind the pedals, under the instruments.'

Melissa grabbed it and turning it over and over gave it a shake. 'It's all rusted shut. How'll we open it?'

Harry didn't hear JC's answer. Thinking he wouldn't have a better chance of taking it, whatever it was, away from them, he bound out, running across the sand. Neither were aware they were under attack until the bigger man rammed his shoulder into JC's back. Reaching out, he grabbed at the hard, thin box the woman was holding.

JC, pushed forward, slammed into Melissa, knocking her back. Her hands automatically tightened on the box, jerking it away from Harry's grasp.

Falling to his knees, JC came up, catching Harry off balance, slamming him away. 'Damn!' Harry yelled, coming back, grabbing JC's shoulders and swinging him aside.

Harry turned back, grabbing to catch Melissa. 'Give me that damn thing,' he ordered. Getting a handful of shirts, he jerked her around. JC came up, throwing an arm around the man's neck.

'What the hell…' was all he had time to say. Harry quickly bent over, throwing JC over his body, slamming him on his back into the sand, his head striking the driftwood log.

'You damn fool,' Harry snarled, reached out and picked up the heavy skillet, swung it around and caught JC full in the forehead. 'Now…' turning, he saw Melissa, carrying the box, running down the beach. 'Come back here,' he ordered, taking off after her.

The tide had been out when JC and Mel had beached their rented boat. Now, with the tide at its highest point, the boat was floating free. Tugging at the bow line tied in a slip knot to a low mangrove tree and without slowing down, Mel tossed the box into the boat, pushing it out into deeper water. Jumping in, she grabbed the starter rope. Just as Harry's fingers grabbed the rubber side of the boat, the engine caught and almost instantly the boat shot away. Harry's hand slipped away and he fell face-first into the boat's wash.

'Shit,' he sputtered, coming to his feet and watching the woman's boat skim across, heading for the river mouth. 'Well, stupid,' he growled, 'don't just stand there. Get after her.'

Chapter Seventy-Three

Full out, her boat's wake streaming out behind her, Mel had barely entered the first large river bend when Harry got away. Cursing Wilson for not having a bigger, more powerful outboard, he reached the river mouth in time to see her make the sweeping bend and disappear. The wide, brown, slow-moving river curved to the right. Harry laughed out loud. 'Dumb broad,' he growled happily. Cutting across the inside of the bend, his cold, humourless smile grew when she came into view again. He had gained on her.

Staying on this side of the river and leaning as far forward in the boat as he could and still reaching the tiller to keep it running flat, he focused on her boat.

The next bend flowed to the left, giving her the shortest distance. All the distance he'd gained on the first turn, he lost on the second. No longer smiling, he tried to remember how many of the sweeping river bends there were before reaching town. Dammit, he'd been over it enough times, he should have been paying attention. Watching her, he tried to remember but couldn't. What to do? Stay on this side and if the river curved left again, he'd be too far behind to catch up. Go over and if the next bend went right, the same thing. And what happens if there are more than one more?

More important, he asked himself, still keeping all his attention on the boat receding into the distance, what will I do if she gets to town before me? What'll she do then? Get in her car, wherever she left it, and head for Cairns. Okay. Wouldn't it be better to get her somewhere on the highway? Wasn't all that much traffic. He could outdrive her. Run her off the road and the box and the treasure it held were his. Yeah.

Either way, he decided, his smile back in place, it was his. Sooner or later.

Chapter Seventy-Four

Gabbi had gone across to the airport, delivering a few baggies of his air-dried product. He'd chosen the best bud and even added a few more than usual. If he wasn't going into Cairns any more, this was his best market. That was a problem he'd have to give some thought to. Until he'd started going to school in Cairns, the nearest high school, he'd only grown enough marijuana for his own use and for a few customers in the village. There wasn't that many dope smokers and even if he added in his own use, it didn't take many plants to satisfy everyone.

Things had picked up when one of the men at the airport approached him in town one morning. 'Say, understand, you grow a good smoke,' the man had said, smiling and being friendly. Gabbi had seen the men around town a few times. He knew where they worked and that the airport had something to do with the mine. Back when his pa had been alive, the village hadn't been much. Then the mine opened up and a lot of new people came to town – white fellas. That was all right; they brought a lot of business to Aunt Joord's cafe and the hotel was filled much of the time.

The first thing the mine people did was build a huge metal building down at the east end of town, between the street and the river. Barges were coming up the river, bringing more people and more new little businesses opened up. The village grew prosperous.

The airport came next. For a while, only the planes and helicopters belonging to the mining company used it. Then planes carrying both freight and passengers between small towns in the outback started making it a refuelling stop. Soon, owners of the outlying cattle and sheep stations started having their aircraft serviced there and buying their fuel there. With the increase in business, a minimum of two and sometimes as many as four men worked there.

Gabbi didn't know any of their names but he had started selling them baggies of smoke every so often. It was enough. His pa had warned him not to get greedy, not to sell too much. He followed that rule until going over to Cairns for school. Boarding in that much bigger town opened up a new market and before long, he was selling all he could grow. During school breaks, he'd come back to work his patch and stock up on more dried plants. Things were good. Until that is, those two hard men threatened him. Now he had more plants drying than he'd be able to sell. At least for a while.

At the airport, talking to the two men who were his usual customers, he'd made sure he smiled a lot and laughed at their jokes. After all, they always paid without complaining. *Customer service*, he thought as he pointed the bow of his tinnie across the river towards the mouth of Jacky-Jacky Creek.

Hearing the roar of an outboard, he cut his engine and turned to look down the river. Fast, as fast as he'd ever seen one of Aunt Joord's boats go, the boat rented to the couple he'd ridden over with came barrelling by. It was on the river's far side, but close enough he could see it was the red-haired woman driving. 'I wonder what happened,' he asked, talking out loud as people who live alone often do. 'And wonder where the man is. She's in a panic. I wonder if something happened to the man.'

Before he could decide on an answer, a second boat came screaming by. This time the boat was on this side of the river; close enough, Gabbi could see it was the bartender fella who was running it.

After both boats powered on up the river, he sat down thinking about what that could mean. 'Probably nothing good,' he said to himself. 'I think I'd better go out and see if something happened to the man. Maybe the woman is going for help. But maybe not. Why would the bartender man be chasing her?'

Not coming up with an answer, he turned his boat around and, glancing back to see the two disappear at the beginning of the nearest bend, turned the throttle and headed down the river.

The other thing his pa had told him was not to mess with white fellas. Nothing but trouble would come from that, the older man said. Gabbi had believed him, but like the rule of not getting greedy, he couldn't see how to ignore this. Not when he was the only one who knew where the white fella was. And not when the nearest help was in the village.

Chapter Seventy-Five

Crabb and Inspector Lambert still had little to say to each other. Following the old woman's suggestion, the Queensland state police officer had driven back along the highway to the turnoff to the airport. Coming onto the facility, he parked in front of the little building that was adjacent to the larger hanger.

Getting out, Lambert stretched and studied his surroundings, first the office building and then the paved landing strip. Crabb, after a quick glance around, went up the steps and, not waiting for the other man, through the door.

'Well,' said the man seated behind a desk, 'you almost caught me napping. Happens right after morning smoko when there's nothing going on. What can I do for you?'

The man, Crabb saw, was younger – not many years out of his teens. Forms and other pieces of paper covered almost the entire desk. A microphone on its stand sat on one corner. On a low shelf behind the seated man sat a large gunmetal grey-coloured radio receiver. A pair of earphones hung from a hook on the shelf.

'I'm, uh, we'd like to rent a tinnie. A woman over at the cafe in town said you might have one.'

'What's going on? You're the second person,' he stopped when Lambert came in, 'uh, persons to want a boat today. We get pretty regular visitors coming in by plane but it's rare to have anyone interested in river travel. This is an airport, you know, not a boat hire business.' While he was talking, he was studying the two men. 'Wait a minute, you guys are police, aren't you? You're here in answer to my call.'

'Uh,' Crabb started to ask but hesitated long enough for the young man to go on.

'You know, I didn't think anyone was paying attention. But here you are. I'm Chris O'Hare,' he said, standing up and holding out a hand, first to Crabb and then to Lambert.

Lambert glanced at Crabb and shook his head.

'Uh yeah,' Crabb said, pulling his identity card from a pocket, 'Senior Sargent Crabb. Queensland Police Force.'

'Wow. I expected someone from the federal police, but I'll take what I get.'

'Mr O'Hare, why,' asked Lambert, 'someone from the federal police?'

'Well, it was a federal officer who asked me to call the next time it happened.'

Lambert frowned. 'What federal officer?'

Digging through the papers on his desk, O'Hare found a business card and handed it to Lambert. The name on the card didn't make him happy. Dwayne Edwards, Deputy Commissioner, Australian Federal Police Serious and Organised Crime Unit.

'Mr O'Hare,' said Crabb, taking the card from Lambert and reading it, 'you called this, Officer Edwards? And now here we are. So tell us, what'd you call the federal police about?'

'Drugs. It's that damn Wilson. Look, me'n Turner, we like our job. Not hard and since the planes from the outlying stations started coming in, the pay has gotten pretty good. So when one of the regional air taxi services started using us for refuelling and even doing some of their maintenance, well, we couldn't ask for anything better.'

'But,' said Lambert, cutting in, 'but this Wilson is not part of things?'

'Yeah. He's got something to do with one of the regionals. It's never been made clear, just that he'd be here and would help out once in a while. Yeah, sure. Once in a while. Well, at first he did help when we needed him, but that didn't last long. I noticed how his helping out slowed down. The first I saw what he was doing was one day when I was fuelling a private plane that belongs to a big sheep station down near Mt Isa. Turner. He was finishing up replacing a fuel pump on one of the mines aircraft. It's one of two they have, both Falcon 900C's. They're 2004 models but still a great aircraft. Well' − noticing the look the two officers were giving him, he hurried up − 'Wilson was helping me with the refuelling but about then one of the regional freight service planes came in. Bam. Just like that, he took off. Left me to finish up. That's okay, I'd rather do it myself. Know it's done right, you know?'

'But it ticked you off?' asked Crabb gently.

'Yeah. I mentioned it to Turner and he said he'd noticed it happened whenever that company's plane came in. Wilson would rush to fuel and take care of things. That's all right. The Hawkers don't come in all that often.'

'The Hawkers?'

'Yeah. A little company. Out of Darwin, I think. Flies freight mostly, from Singapore and Jakarta, I think. Well, that's when I got interested. I mean, was he hired just to service that company's planes? I watched the next time it happened and saw how when the plane landed, while he fuelled it, the crew would go over to the little refreshment stand we have for coffee. Sort of a lounge, you know, with a couple sofas, chairs and tables and things. It's for the pilots. Give them a chance to stretch their legs and have a cup of tea. Anyway, I saw how their plane always pulled up at a certain spot. That position put the side door on the other side, close to the big hanger. Well, when he was finished with the plane, Wilson would go get the crew and they'd take off. But it seemed to me when he went in towards the lounge, he was pulling a suitcase.'

'A suitcase?'

'Yeah, you know, one of those wheeled cases people could put up in the overhead when they travel. Okay, so I watched and saw where he put it. In behind cases of my equipment, out of sight. Later, when we were sitting around not doing much, having a smoko, I said something about taking a leak. Only I dug out the little suitcase and unzipped it. Bags of pills. The thing was filled with bags of little white pills.'

'Drugs,' Lambert said decisively. 'We've known for a long time that there are a lot of drugs coming in from Asia. Just can't ever catch anyone at it.'

'Well, that's what I thought too. And I didn't like him using our maintenance facility for that, so I called the Federal Police. That's when that Federal officer came out. There hadn't been any Hawker flights, so there wasn't anything to show him. But he gave me his card and told me to call him the next time it happened. So I did. And here you are.'

'There's been a delivery?' asked Crabb. Lambert noticed the excitement in his voice.

'Yep. Yesterday afternoon.'

'And the suitcase is still there?'

'Uh huh.'

Crabb looked at Lambert. 'Man, I think this is it, don't you?'

Lambert nodded, but was thinking about something else. This couldn't have anything to do with JC and Bridges. This was something bigger. If it had someone from the AFP's OSCU people involved, it would have been a lot bigger.

'You know,' he said, pulling Crabb aside, 'this could be just the thing. For you. For your gold-star retirement.'

'But it's a Federal Police he called.'

'And they aren't here, but you are.'

Crabb studied Lambert's face. 'Yeah. Okay, so how do we do it?'

'You take Wilson. I'll back you up. It'll be your deal all the way.'

Crabb nodded. 'I appreciate it. Maybe you're not so bad a guy after all.' Turning back to O'Hare, he smiled. 'Where will this Wilson guy be right now?'

Chapter Seventy-Six

A lot of things were happening on the river. Harry, focusing all his attention on the woman's boat ahead of him, didn't see Gabbi's skiff moving into the creek. The next sweeping bend in the river was to the right. He was laughing when he saw her stay near the far river bank. Angling across the inside corner would put him right in behind her boat. He may not be able to catch her, but he'd be right on her tail when they reached the village. She couldn't get away.

Glancing ahead, he nodded. Cutting across the inside of the wide bend was the answer. Obviously, this broad had never played billiards. The way to win was to play the angles. Keeping the throttle cranked as high as it'd go, he was already thinking of what he'd do when he caught her. Whether on the river or later, somewhere on the highway, she was his. First the treasure box and then...

At full throttle when the skiff ran into an unseen sand bank, the sudden stop nearly pitched him into the water. 'Damn,' he swore. A sand bar. He'd been focusing on the woman and hadn't noticed the black-spikey, grass-covered shallows. Don't panic, he told himself. Get out and push the boat off the sand. It doesn't matter. She can't get away.

The water was only about knee deep. Planting his feet firmly in the sand and lifting the boat's bow, he gave a big shove. The boat slid easily back towards deeper water, leaving him standing there. The sand held his feet just long enough. He never made it to the boat.

Chapter Seventy-Seven

Before Gabbi even got to the beach, he could see there had been trouble. Jumping out of his tinnie, he rushed to the man's body. The man was breathing but was unconscious. He needed medical care. Gabbi didn't hesitate, he knew what he had to do and did it. As carefully as he could, he lifted JC into a sitting position, then pulled the wounded man forward over his shoulder. Carrying the limp body to the water, he gently lowered the bigger man into the boat. Before shoving away from the shore, he placed a faded orange life preserver under JC's head.

As fast as the tinnie would go, he was nearly past the airport when he spotted a helicopter coming towards the landing strip. It was the familiar yellow-and-blue CareFlight chopper. Everybody knew about that Flying Doctor's medical rescue service. How'd they know? That was the medical help this man needed.

Chapter Seventy-Eight

JC fought, coming into the bright light. He tried to bring a hand up to shade his eyes. His hand wouldn't move. Something was holding his arm down. Voices, garbled and rumbling, sounded somewhere. Trying to make out what was happening, he felt the darkness flow over him.

Silence – the deepest, emptiest silence. He couldn't hear himself breathe. He couldn't feel his heart beat. Slowly, soft, blurry light filled his vision. No noise, no light, no breathing. He was back in the sunken airplane. Only it was night. Everything was shadowy. The only light was weak and fuzzy, as if seen through a silk screen, a long way away. His muscles wouldn't move but he felt himself floating towards the faint, misty haze. Swimming but without motion, no weight of air tanks on his back. His nose was stuffed up.

Gliding along, he tried to reach a hand out towards the metal seat frames, his hand wouldn't move. Close to the pale light. Close to the opening, he heard voices, garbled and rumbling. Slowly, the light grew brighter. He was looking up at someone's face. A woman, her lips moving, any sound she made muffled.

'He's coming awake,' the nurse said, smiling across the bed at the doctor.

JC couldn't make out the words and gave up trying as blackness flooded in.

'He's asleep,' said Doctor Cauldon, nodding. 'That's normal. He'll come in and out a few times.'

Inspector Lambert, standing at the foot of the bed, frowned. 'When do you think I'll be able to talk to him?'

'Oh, not long. He's coming out of it. Had a hell of a blow to the head, you know. Luckily, his forehead took the worst of it. Hard bone, there. Except for the nose. But that'll heal, once we take the packing out, the only sign of his being hit will be the black eyes. His heart rate is steady, blood pressure holding at 120 over 80; that's almost perfect. No reason for him not to join us right away. Now, Inspector, if you want to wait, I'll go see about another patient.'

Lambert had wanted to get this over with so he could leave. He had a plane to catch. Deciding to leave the package and go, he was clearing a place on the side table when JC woke up.

'Muphmm,' he said, sticking his tongue out and licking his lips.

'Dry mouth?' said Lambert. Taking up a water bottle, he pointed the plastic straw at the patient's mouth. 'Welcome back.'

JC lay back, keeping his gaze on the policeman. 'What…?'

'Don't try. Relax. I'll try to explain. But do try to stay awake. Okay?'

Raising his head a little, JC looked around the room, then laid his head back against a pillow. It hurt. His whole head was filled with a dull, throbbing pain.

'Look, don't go back to sleep,' Lambert said. 'I don't have all night. I've got a plane to catch. So here it is, in a nutshell. Gabbi brought you to the airfield just as the CareFlight helicopter was taking off. Crabb had called it in, he wanted to get Wilson to jail as quickly as possible and that was the only aircraft available.'

JC frowned and, keeping his eyes closed, spoke. His voice was raspy. 'What the hell are you talking about?'

Lambert held the water bottle out again and JC drank.

'Oh, yeah. I'll back up. Senior Sargent Crabb's a local cop. You probably didn't meet him. He and I followed Bridges across to Karumba. Your friend Harry was following you and the girl reporter. Anyhow, Crabb had arrested a man at the airport, a bloke named Wilson. This Wilson had been part of a drug importing deal. He had a suitcase with what turned out to be four kilos of amphetamine tablets. He didn't want to make the long drive back to Cairns, so he called for transportation and the CareFlight helicopter was in the area, on their way back to Cairns from somewhere. You with me?'

JC nodded cautiously and sipped water.

'Okay, so when that young aborigine, Gabbi, came running up from the river, yelling you were in his boat and bleeding, well, the CareFlight EMT's went to see. Your nose had been broken and you were unconscious. But apparently, all the life signs were good. The doctor here says you were just asleep. He ran you through all the machines – CT Scan and an MRI – and I don't know what else. Said you had suffered a blow to the head. I reckon it was your mate Harry who did that.'

JC nodded. 'Where did he go? And where is Melissa?'

Lambert shook his head. 'We're not exactly sure. Gabbi said he saw the Graves woman go by in the boat you'd rented, followed closely by Harry Bridges. After the CareFlight helicopter left, I drove back into town and found out the boat you and the woman had rented had been returned. Well, later, Gabbi and I went back to your campsite. We brought in all your scuba gear. Apparently, Melissa Graves drove back to Cairns. I checked. She had no more than got here before booking a flight out.'

Reaching to take the big envelope from where he'd put it, he laid in on JC's chest. 'She left this out at the front desk. It's addressed to you. Now, I'm heading back to Brisbane. My holiday is over and it's time to get back to work.'

'Where'd Harry go?'

Lambert smiled. 'Haven't seen him. When Gabbi and I went out to get your stuff, we found his tinnie caught on some mangrove growth there in the river. When we told Gabbi's aunt, she nodded and said something like Ol, Mr Salty got him. Seems there's been a big saltwater croc nesting out there. Someone'll have to do something about that, I suppose. Now, there's one more thing.' He took a little booklet from his shirt pocket and put it on top of Melissa's envelope. 'Your passport.

If I were you, as soon as you get out of here, I'd be booking a flight back to America. You've had enough fun here in paradise, I'd say.'

JC put his hand on top of the material. Looked up at Lambert. 'I thought Harry and I were supposed to hang around for some kind of hearing. You remember? Having to do with the Marsh couple.'

'Nope, that's been dealt with. Don't know how much those two settled for, there's a non-disclosure lock on it. Anyway, that's old news.'

Once again JC nodded. 'And,' he said, his voice gathering strength, 'with Harry out of the picture, you're satisfied. Didn't get what you wanted after all, did you?' It wasn't a question.

Lambert shook his head. 'No. I admit it, I wanted to arrest Bridges. That boat load of drugs you brought into Brisbane cost me a lot with my boss. Having Bridges might have gotten me out of trouble. But as it worked out, now it's at Crabb the Crime Unit's mad at. His bringing in Wilson got in the way of another undercover set-up they had going. Damn fools.

'But anyway,' he said, smiling and heading for the door, 'nothing more to keep you here. It's been interesting but not much fun. Don't bother hurrying back, Yank.'

Alone in his hospital bed, JC lay quietly for a bit, thinking about things. Thinking about Melissa. Taking up the envelope, he ripped open one end. Inside was a bundle wrapped in a colourful brochure. He recognised the brochure as one from the dive school. Within the folds of the brochure was a banded stack of Australian hundred-dollar bills. He hadn't seen the green bills before and had to read the numbers twice. He smiled. Well, the box must have held some treasure after all.

Hoping she might have written something, he opened up the brochure. It was the one listing the five best scuba reefs in the world. She had drawn a line through the first one, the Great Barrier Reef. A line was drawn under the second on the list, the Belize Barrier Reef.

Thinking about the woman, he laughed. Maybe his dive lessons had been worthwhile after all.

Epilogue

JC carefully spit into his face mask then washed it out with salt water, before swimming out onto the reef. Kicking smoothly through the water, he closed in on a group of tourist divers. Coming up on one, a red-haired woman in a lime-green wetsuit, he touched her back. Standing in waist-deep water, the two smiled at each other.

'How's it going? How's your head?' she asked, touching the side of his face gently.

'I'm good. So, what do you think? Do you agree with the brochure? Are the Belize Reefs second to the Great Barrier Reef?'

'Oh, yes. But it'd be interesting to see what the others on that list are like. By the way, isn't it time you told me what the JC stands for?'

'Hm? Well, okay,' he said hesitantly. 'James Cash. My mom thought it funny, naming me Cash with a surname of McCoin. Think we can afford to dive the remaining reefs on that list?'

Mel smiled. 'Remember I said the diamonds my grandfather had been carrying for the Dutch family were valued at half a million guilders? Well, that was in 1945. I wasn't able to get the twenty million we talked about. But got awfully close. Yes, I think the rest of that list is doable' – she hesitated, then continued, her smile growing bigger – 'or we could simply go find that private beach on our own island. Either way, let me ask you a question. You being the dive instructor and all, how long can a pregnant woman scuba dive?'

JC frowned. 'Well,' he said, hesitantly, 'I don't know. I suppose as long as she can get into a wetsuit, but…' he stopped. 'Hey, are you…?'

Melissa smiled. 'We've got a while. Time enough to go check out the rest of that list.'

The End